Books by Charles W. Bechtel

The DREW NOLAN series

> A Hole in the Water
> Hell's Cold Furies
> When the Ball Drops Foul
> Running Before Thunder
> And Then You Don't
> A Hypocrisy of Oaths

Novels

> The Odor of Orchids
> Book of Days
> The Lady from Spain

Non- Fiction

> On Second Thoughts, a collection of essays
> Writing Tips, a guide to writing better sentences

Short Story collection

> The Long and Short, collected short stories

Poetry collection

> Sound Words Seen, collected poems
> 100 Shadows

When the Ball Drops Foul

By *Charles W Bechtel*

Ruk Publications
Mesa, Arizona
2013

Revised edition

ISBN-13: 978-0615864013 (RUK Publications)
ISBN-10: 0615864015

When the Ball Drops Foul
Charles W Bechtel
RUK Publications

.

To two of the finest men and educators I have had
the fortune to befriend:

David H. Bradley
author of *South Street* and
The Chaneysville Incident,

and

Norman 'Butch' Ingram
of the singing group *Ingram*.

The only measure of a successful life is to have earned
the friendship, if not the admiration, of those you admire.

When the Ball Drops Foul

Over and over again you are called to the realm of adventure, you are called to new horizons. Each time, there is the same problem: do I dare? And then if you do dare, the dangers are there, and the help also, and the fulfillment or the fiasco. There's always the possibility of a fiasco.

- Joseph Campbell
The Hero with a Thousand Faces

One

'**They hanged Willa Maes!**' Those four words torched the crowd watching the pickup baseball game like a hot match on a string of firecrackers, each alarmed face turning to pass them on to the next. Wherever those words touched down, the crowd exploded with weeping, wailing, fat arms dropping around rubbery necks, loud injunctions begging Jesus for salvation. I heard a few phrases that I'm sure got said with the hope that Jesus wasn't listening.

When those words and sentiments reached our lawn chairs, June and I — a pair of marshmallows in a sea of black eye peas — could do little more than turn to the other and gawp. You know, eyes wide, mouth popping goldfish style.

We had no idea who Willa Maes was, why he got hanged or by whom, what it might mean, but we sure as Hell knew exactly how much it meant to everyone else there at the church picnic. Pandemonium barely covers what ensued.

At the far end, from the direction where those four words had seeded fury, more than a dozen men — a few young, most not — and a pair of big women split for the field where everyone had parked their cars. Engines fired, rocks and sand flamed into the palmetto bushes, and tires seared the blacktop. Big cars, five, snap, gone. A shroud of Florida dust the only tell they'd ever been there.

June later said it was my imagination, but I smelled a new uneasiness about us being at the game. We were more than just strangers, faces never before seen at the ball field, and certain never to be seen again. They didn't know us before that day, we didn't know them, and all of us were pretty sure that knowing each other better wasn't in the cards.

We were there because Wiley had brought us. It wasn't exactly a place we'd have sought on our own, but once there we felt welcome to enjoy our time. That ended with the brushfire of bad news.

A real separation between those around us, like what happens when a drop of dish soap falls into greasy water. Saw it, felt it.

We'd been segregated.

We were not just strangers at a ball game, we had become the Opposite, the Different, the Not Them. Until those four words dropped into the crowd, our singular, separated selves had been tolerated, kind of like a dog an old maiden aunt had brought to dinner.

Well, that was over.

As none of Wiley's friends had known us when we'd first sat down, they'd offered up those polite, non-informational questions about who we knew. *Wiley, that big guy over there.* Nod nod. Where we were from? *Key Largo, Philly, New York.* Were we married? Uneasy sidelong looks at the other, *No.* Eventually they had left us in a pool of quiet to enjoy wordlessly the bats smacking horsehide, the smell of vinegared collards, smoky pork and beans, barbecue and slaw. A few had even offered us some of what came out of their coolers and cardboard boxes.

But those four words, *They killed Willa Maes,* once they passed over our heads, pressed a kind of wordless disquiet on our neighbors, spread a sudden hush over the crowd, turned things cold.

Those nearest averted their eyes from ours, turned their heads to a distant direction. What had been a smooth, dull discomfort in being strangers among so many people so familiar with each other had turned into a jerky, fractured awareness a lot like one gets when flopping about in a boat with a broken tiller, storm a-comin'.

I searched for Wiley. He had gone off to chug beers with what might have been distant cousins. His big shape had been easy to spot hanging over what had been a laughing lot, now no more. Uncle Wiley was Sasquatch at Little League practice. When the words reached him, he got way taller than Sasquatch. He went pure sequoia.

Stood up best I could, the lawn chair flipping over behind me. I waved. Maybe just standing up would have been enough, but like I said, jerky, fractured. Seemed as if everyone but Wiley turned to watch me slap the air over my head, but I finally got his attention. Our eyes locked, he returned my head wag.

I felt gratitude about Wiley reaching earshot, but any comfort that might have come from a friendly face dissolved when I heard the big man say, 'Y'all oughta get youselfs back on the *Discourse*. I'll be long in some while.'

His hand chopped toward where the cars were parked, which left no argument. Then all we had was his back. He turned and cut through the crowd like a refrigerator on wheels that had broken loose. June had risen immediately, gave me a face that hollered, *Well? You stupid or something? Let's go.*

We weren't the only ones walking fast and stiffly to a car, but it sure felt like it. I don't think I gave a gnat's fart for how or when our friend Wiley would make it back to the *Sweet Discourse*. All I knew was that we no longer had his association linking us to a crowd swelling into a mob. We were out of there and in our rental car, away from of the field and down the county road leading to the Gulf coast.

When events change suddenly, a person doesn't take the time to run a string of logically-ordered thoughts through his head, working in dedicated fashion toward some cogent opinion or deduction. From the first absorption of the four words, my thinking bounced around like a dinghy in a hurricane. Who is, who *was*, Willa Maes? Who were 'they' who hanged him? *Hanged?* What's someone got to do to get hanged these days? And who hangs people anyway?

The only question I had any answer for was why the afternoon crackled. Lightning had hit, and a storm was soon to follow.

Discombobulated and discordant, fractured and careening, all my thoughts whipped around the armature of those four words like debris in a tornado. It wasn't until we were halfway back to the marina that either June or I put any of the bits into a coherent sentence. June got there first, but with exactly the words I planned to use.

What the Hell?

That said it all, for both of us, until we had parked, scurried down the dock, scooted up the finger dock to the *Sweet Discourse*, climbed aboard, dashed into the main cabin to crack two beers and put our feet up. I found myself holding an opened bag of humidity-staled corn chips, munching like a stoned madman.

'Think it's happening again?' she asked. I took a long time saying anything, which was pretty much the answer to her question. June had referred to my predilection for landing in the piss whenever someone dead popped up nearby.

Yeah, it was happening again.

People getting dead in proximity to my whereabouts had an unnerving continuity. First time was two decades ago when I stumbled onto the body of a murdered policeman. That event turned me from a pen-totin', not very eager newspaper stringer into a surprisingly not much happier gun-wielding policeman. But once dead people became my business, business picked up.

Drive-bys, domestics, holdups gone terribly wrong, mob hits... then one day I almost became one of those corpses. Coming so close to that condition said, *Quit the business, Nolan.*

I did.

Or so I thought. The business, however, seemed to have no end. I'd bought me a boat capable of charter fishing, and moved to quiet Key Largo at the southern end of Florida where all I wanted was to slip into a life of flip-flops, bottled beer and the bikini-clad. I wanted guaranteed distance from any more mortal coils being shed, especially my own mortal coil.

Didn't happen quite so completely.

Oh, there'd been a peaceful spell, a dull lull, until June re-entered my life. She'd been an old girlfriend with whom I'd reconnected at a high school reunion. After adequately being seduced into a two week laze-about around the Caribbean, which went sexily well, I managed to sink a marlin hook into a shrink-wrapped corpse floating over the waves.

Not that I placed the blame on her. Her re-appearance in my life and the appearance of that dead floater were purely coincidental, but that started what was beginning to look like a pattern of me getting involved where I shouldna oughta be lookin'.

Which is all, and exactly, what she meant by *Think it's happening again.*

Had we just felt another twitch of metaphorical fishhook snagging another mystery-shrouded dead body of yet another person we didn't and wouldn't ever know?

Damn straight.

We had no idea that I could wind up back in the piss, back in Largo when Wiley'd come hat in hand to ask us please consider attending his kind-of adopted nephew's post-boot camp coming home party. What he needed was a ride. I didn't mind, and June loves a vacation.

He never mentioned the sandlot baseball game. That came as just an extra thing to do.

I'd met his 'nephew' before the boy had entered high school, one of those basically decent boys destined for trouble and a hard life, but of an age that's prone to asking questions when all that his adopted uncle wanted him to do was shut up and go to sleep. What kid can fall sleep on his first overnighter out on the wide waters of the Caribbean? He had fish, his fish, not only already in the live well but in his belly. Doesn't get any better.

I have a theory, which I got from my father, and he probably, from his: Take a kid fishing, he never gets into the kind of trouble that swallows kids, and lives, whole. My generosity then was civic duty. My acquiescing — our, for by then June had a say in my affairs — to Wiley's request that we all ride to the kid's picnic party in my boat, the *Sweet Discourse,* was payment for friendship happily and readily paid. I'd do anything for Wiley, especially since he rarely asked for anything. As for June, some days I thought she might toss me over for the big guy.

Besides, June had just finished up one Hell of a tax season, and she needed a boat ride, bad.

It had been a nice Saturday afternoon picnic beside a seemingly popular Southern Baptist church, which had an incongruous but necessary ball field carved into the Florida sands in the back. We were strangers to everyone except the soldier boy, his mother, and of course Uncle Wiley. But being the captain of a charter boat taught me how to fake jollity and good cheer, and June, well, everybody loves June.

Although it's a rare event for me to be a representative for the smallest minority in a crowd, I had never before felt constrained by that condition. Not until the word *hanged* whipped through the crowd like a hot foul ball.

Actually, it was not the word *hanged* that separated the crowd from the two of us, but rather the first one. *They.*

We were *They,* instantly lumped with the lynch mob by race, color and historical affinity for cruel social practices. Coupling the word *They* with *Hanged,* our dance card got jerked, and really fast. Didn't anybody say so, just felt so.

June, of course, New York liberal lawyer and all that, said I was being uncharacteristically small-minded, but it's what I felt. June scowled as I confessed it, an affront to her illuminated mind, and her expectation that I had a like one. Hey, at least she had used *uncharacteristically* small-minded.

Around an hour before dark I got Wiley's call. He was not planning to return with us right off, but he was coming back to the boat, would make it soon after sunset, and that we should expect company.

'I got somethin' t'show you, and you got to tell me you seein' what I think I sees. If it's what I be seein', you say so straight out. It's a favor, Cap'n.'

Ask though I might for better detail, Wiley doesn't say more than he has to say. I knew I'd have to wait before my curiosity got any satiation. What could he possibly have for me to see? No idea. So I informed June, who asked me no questions — not a surprise, as whatever Wiley wanted, June would provide, even if he didn't ask her to lift even a finger. She set about doing what a woman expecting unexpected company does. She made snacks.

The sun had gone well down, which I on the flying bridge had watched drag behind it a new moon night. I was fairly sure the snacks June had prepared were getting a bit leaden in the humid evening, the corn chips she allowed me for dinner having the same crunch as did a cereal box. I'd been scrounging for crumbs at the bottom of the bag when I spotted headlights to three cars bouncing into the marina's lot. Being May, the snowbirds who kept watercraft at the Gulf were pretty much all gone, so headlights entering any Florida marina would be few. Not unusual, but not easily ignored. Therefore headlights from three cars in obvious tandem got my attention quick.

'Honey, I think you didn't make enough snacks.'

She hadn't, but the several men and women following Wiley to the *Sweet Discourse* hadn't come for a neighborly late-night nosh.

Three sets of high beams slicing through a marina lot may be rare, but a dozen African Americans, even as superbly well-dressed as were Wiley's friends, climbing out of the cars was a positive unknown — especially on the Gulf Coast of Florida. Even on the moonless night I sensed more than a few semi-nautically inclined heads swivel toward their direction, jaws dropping and eyes bulging. And, truth be told, privates shrinking.

I loved it.

But again, Wiley's friends hadn't come to unsettle the white boatey folks, nor to provide anti-social entertainment for me.

My fifty-foot custom-built Hernandez the *Sweet Discourse* out of New Jersey has a commodious deck that lights well, so entertaining was not usually difficult. But this was a big party.

Permission to come aboard was certainly — but carefully — granted, though only three of them, plus Wiley, had accepted. Those who preferred to not come aboard gathered uneasily on the floating dock at the stern, eyes darting about, taking in the luxury and impracticality of a half-million-dollar boat. If we hadn't been a *them* before, we surely had become a *them* because of the *Discourse*.

I realized from the paucity of introductions that those three were the only people I was supposed to stay mindful of. The foremost was a man who introduced himself as Pastor Something or Other, a man used to being a spokesman in such crowds, but who had a touch of reserve because of the proximity to the other man among them, an old one-armed gentleman whose name I later learned was Coleman Davis. At that introduction, though, the Reverend only called the man Mr. Davis, which Wiley later said was all anybody ever called him, and never nothing less.

The third, a woman who never said a word the whole while she was on my boat, was the mother of the hanged Willa Maes. She periodically heaved great soppy sighs while twisting the Hell out of a white handkerchief. Whenever one of her blubbery bubbles broke, sounds aft of the stern rose from the dark sea of faces like a following wave.

Coleman Davis had that crinkled, weathered look of an old and hard-worked man, but his bound onto the deck was vigorous. What remained of his right arm was a stub that protruded from his wide white sleeve looked like the working end of a walnut baseball bat.

Once the padre's voice tailed off from his introductions, Davis said 'Mr. Nolan, Wiley said we should come here for confirmation.'

I looked at my friend and ship mate, with the *What the Hell* look I usually gave whenever someone got me involved in what shouldn't have been my business. Wiley motioned to someone in the crowd, and a white shoebox got handed out of the dark. He handed it over, and I opened it. 'That's what they hanged Willa Maes with. You look, Cap'n.'

I had looked, but I knew he meant more than for me to merely glance down.

In the box was a fair length of rope, but not just any rope. I understood immediately why Wiley had wanted *me* to see it, and why he wanted them to get my confirmation. I'd handled miles of such rope, but that which had dragged a kicking and gagging Willa Maes into death felt — okay, I'll say it — spiritually different.

What I fingered was common — though old-fashioned — cotton line that boat owners used for holding onto their boat anchor. Even without my lights, I would have been able to tell that it was gray from continual dips into salt water and subsequent re-exposures to a hot tropical sun. It had that unmistakable smell of salt water and estuarial mud. It also released a faint odor of diesel.

One end had obviously been sliced recently, the cut too clean, no fray, probably made by whoever had cut Willa down. Whatever knot had been used to choke him had either been a victim of that panicked slice, hastily though nervously untied and tossed or taken away. Wiley said he had had no chance to see it, therefore ensuring that I would never have a chance to see it either. It would have spoken volumes.

There was, however, rope talking plenty, enough to kick my conjecturing nature into high gear.

What I had been handed was half-inch cotton weave — old but still strong, tensile enough to haul and keep aloft a one-hundred sixty pound thrashing body. Most telling was the end opposite the cut, the end that had been anchored to a live oak.

Think of rope, when properly employed, as a machine. It has working parts.

In most cases there's a fixed end, the hold-down, tied in some fashion to an anchoring point. That fixed place could just be your hand, a wooden hitching post or an iron bollard down in the harbor. Could even be a live oak hanging tree.

The other, the grip end, one fixes to an object needing to be either moved or kept immovable. In the case of a hanging, it was the end that both moved the frantic and panicking body into the air, then held on until all went still.

Think of a rope run up a mast to raise a sail. The hold down will eventually get tied to some kind of fixed stationary point, usually a cleat at the mast bottom. The other end, the grip, passes through or over a pulley — to make the work easier — and then gets tied or fixed to a moveable load, which would be either the sail itself or a spar that the sail has been lashed onto.

When the machine is 'put into gear,' the grip end holding the sail or spar is moved by hauling on the length of rope until the sail reaches where it is wanted. Then the hold down is affixed by an appropriate knot to the immovable anchoring point, a cleat, a belaying pin, a bollard or a bit.

The important thing to note is that whatever the ends of rope get tied to determine what knot will be used.

It's very important to know the right knot, and knowing knots is what separates watermen from day sailors and land lubbers.

I'll get to that in a moment. First the rope itself.

Almost all rope these days is made of twisted nylon or polyester fiber. Cotton is still used, but rarely for anchoring, or where the line goes in and out of the water.

That's what the smell of sea bottom and the dried-out feel of the line told me. What I held was an anchor line that hadn't held a boat in place for some time.

These days cotton anchor line like that most often winds up at the bottom of storage areas called gunk holes, stowed away because cotton is no longer the best rope to use for anchoring. The reason it was still around is because old salts can't toss away any length of rope, no matter how rotted or worn out. They consider doing so violates some maritime law, such a heinous thing that would incur the wrath of sea gods, not the least among them Davey Jones of the locker fame. Rope saves lives, and no one tosses away a savior. Sure, weird. But if watermen weren't weird, there'd be no boats.

Like all things plastic, polyester and nylon has replaced all things old and made of natural hemp fiber. Thank you, Mr. Dupont. The fact that what I held was cotton meant that whoever owned it didn't need it, didn't toss it, and wouldn't miss it either if someone else took it. The easy thing to recognize was that a waterman had owned it, and that whoever took it had to know a waterman.

And he had to know the waterman wouldn't miss it, which meant the waterman also knew who had taken it.

More importantly, the one who took it for the purpose of lynching a black boy in the south had to know that if anyone did miss it, that person could and would probably guess who it was that had taken it, and therefore could consequently point a finger at the murderer. So whoever lifted the rope had to know the rope wouldn't be missed, or recognized, at least for a while.

Of course the murderer and the waterman could have been one and the same, but experienced watermen aren't known for lynching, not on land anyway. Snatching an old line from a gunk hole would have been a smart move, but not a waterman's smart move. So if not a waterman, someone who knew some waterman well enough. That pointed to a harbor rat, a fellow who works boats and marinas but doesn't own one himself. And if there's one thing I knew about harbor rats, they haven't the same disposition as men who own boats. There are exceptions, men like Wiley, who lived among boats all their lives but never had two nickels to rub together. But for the most part they are drifters, scabrous vermin who'll steal from a boat quick as taking a free offer of beer.

Or they were related.

I had to put any decision about exactly who had lifted the rope aside. There was more to the rope to consider.

Since I didn't have either the grip-end or tie-down knots, I inspected what I did have in the end opposite where the rope had been cut.

All rope unravels when not prepared properly. To keep ends in usable shape, unfrayed and neat, watermen seal them off in one of three ways. They are either burned, as polyester melts into a nasty but effective blob of brown-black. They may be taped, if done in haste or by an idiot. Or they are whipped, if the owner is a waterman who knows his stuff.

With polyester rope, weekenders and watermen alike will often use fire to fuse the end. Maybe thereafter a cautious weekender will wrap it with tape, if somebody has directed them to the kind of tape that won't float off as soon as the line hits water. Can't count the number of times I've seen landlubbers use duct tape around a cut line.

But what I held was cotton, and a cotton cut-end must be whipped properly and firmly with waxed thread, or it will fray out to a rat's nest of string and wadding. We use good, heavy-gauged thread, cotton or silk, waxed to prevent water rot. The thread gets wrapped in several tight turns around the end and tied off.

How you begin a whip is even more important than how you end one, and there is a trick to doing it that's been taught mouth-to-hand for centuries. No one becomes a salt without learning, and no one becomes an old salt without mastering a whip with hidden ends.

That anchor line had a hidden whipped end, and one done beautifully.

A finishing like that almost points a finger at its maker, serving as a kind of signature like surgeon's knots reputedly do. Problem we had at that moment was that the rope had been found where no sailor wants to tie off, in the woods and on a live oak.

By the way, the end of a rope that gets tied to a bit to hold fast is known as the bitter end — ironically in this case.

I had to ask Wiley if he had seen where the rope had been tied to the tree. He had.

'That's the point, Cap'n. A clove with a double half hitch.'

Meant nothing to all those gathered around, but meant a deal to Wiley, and to me. What that knot said, which had led Wiley to seek confirmation from me, was that whoever tied a clove and double half hitch hold-down on that hanging tree wasn't the same person who had whipped the bitter end. I still held onto the idea that, in all likelihood, they did know each other.

The old hand who'd whipped the end would never have used a half-hitch on top of the clove hitch, because he'd know there'd be no need for the extra knot. The clove would have held as tight as necessary. An amateur or youngling, insecure from not knowing what knot he could trust, would have added the extra knot, fearing one would not do as a hold-down.

The thief, which he was before he became a murderer, probably was a grandson or nephew to the waterman. And most likely the waterman wasn't a snowbird. Transients don't just go off and hang a local black kid. A murder like that takes real hate, long developed hate. And to use that method in those historically disturbed lands like the Gulf Coast of Florida meant the kind of hate that runs through generations.

As I turned the fibrous rope in my fingers, Wiley asked the question. 'Wa'n't no suicide, was it Cap'n?'

'No, Wiles, don't believe so. Who thinks it was?'

'Nobody here does, but that's what they sayin' it was. Sayin' Willa killed hisself.'

There was that *They* again. But this time I didn't feel myself among them.

Live in the rural parts of Florida — Hell, even the Keys — and you get to understand exactly who *They* were, every time.

'Wiley, what happened after we left the game?'

It was the Reverend, who had been listening to me but not as intently as had the one-armed man Davis, who filled me in. I could tell that everyone who had gathered more tightly at the stern of the *Sweet Discourse* bent forward to listen, although I was pretty sure only June and I were the ones newly come to the confirming opinions I was sharing.

If the congregation wasn't so solemn and upset with what the Reverend had to say, the accompanying *Uhh huhs, Oh Jesuses* and repeated head nods would have seemed comically out of place, like a church service in a parking lot. But there was no comedy there, none at all.

He said that after the first five cars pulled out, several others — including one carrying Wiley — also headed off to where reports had said Willa Maes had been hanged. By the time Wiley got there, the boy had been cut down, carried to a sandy hill and left to rest uncovered until the county ambulance had come screaming up to carry him away.

Wiley spotted the rope left tied and dangling in a live oak. My mate's trained eye saw what all the others would have never seen, that neat clove hitch and a double half secured the bitter end to a low branch, and he'd jumped immediately to the same conclusion I had just reached. And I am pretty sure he jumped to it faster and in a more direct line. He had a different culture raising an antenna at the hanging than mine.

His wise hands, made even smarter by an unofficial but already spoken verdict by the local officials who'd pronounced it a suicide, knew what had to have really happened. But since what he knew and what they said differed, he felt no compunction about pulling the lynching rope down. He untied it quickly, hid it under a bush until he could fetch it later. It was Davis who had driven Wiley out to get it, which they did before calling me with the warning about me getting company.

Wiley had given Coleman Davis his reading there at the lynching ground, who only said, 'Just one man's opinion. Ain't gonna do us much,' to which Wiley responded that he could get another one just like his.

After I'd held the rope a few more minutes, done my sniff again, raised it higher under the light and said my say about there being no need for a second knot, Wiley took it from me. He then tied the bitter end in a clove hitch around a vertical stile to my chrome-plated ladder rising up to the flying bridge.

Then he pulled on it, hard.

I heard a few gasps and one *Lord Jesus* come from my guests.

I had to say it, though I'd been guilty of the same wrong in the past, 'You should have left it there, though. Evidence.'

'They don't gonna want evidence, Cap'n. They's already p'nounced suicide. Now we know it wa'din't. But they's some gonna keep on sayin' that's what it was.'

They again. Made the hairs on my neck rise. I frowned at the suggested division, though I appeared to aim my displeasure at the rope. 'Wiles, what else that knot set tell you?'

He pointed to the clove hitch. 'This here knot's a Boy Scout knot. And this here's one too.' He added the unnecessary half-hitch. 'But together they's boat knots. But, Cap'n, Willa Maes din't know boats. He's 'fraid a water.'

I felt my lips purse, and knew June's were doing the same.

Wiley went on, 'And he didn't learn no boat knots at Boy Scouts neither. He never tied thems. And you know you don't do no clove with a double half-hitch accidental.'

He had a point, a big one, and it was the distinction that made sure I'd be back in the piss again. June hadn't pick up on it right off, but the more I eyed the bitter end tied to the gangway stile, the more aware she became that the rope would soon be tying us up in knots as well.

I began to explain to the group, though more to her, exactly what the configuration of knots said about the impossibility of suicide.

A clove and the half-hitch are two of the five most basic waterman's knots, which is what Wiley meant calling them Boy Scout knots. Boy Scouts might learn *how* to tie them, but they don't learn *when* to tie them. Anybody owning a boat learns all five quickly, or pays for their ignorance soon enough with a hole in the hull, or worse.

Wiley's deduction said most people, especially Willa Maes who had not been a Boy Scout, would tie off that holding end with a mess of crappy ties, what educated knot makers call 'Grannies.' Even more likely, 'Boy Scouts' would have wrapped a whole lot of rope several times around that live oak branch. Someone who understood knots and had used them correctly would understand implicitly that a clove hitch alone would have held fine, would not have slipped.

People overdo most knot-tying, when they don't know better. With the double half hitch thrown on top of the clove, the hangman knew enough how to tie a knot, but not enough to trust one.

That meant someone knew enough about boats, knots and load-securing to choose the clove hitch, but then they took a further step, an uncertain, unconfident step by adding a double half-hitch. That didn't point to a waterman, but to a novice. And not a seasoned wharf rat, but rather a grandson or nephew of an old salt, as I was more seriously suspecting.

'So, whaddya think, Cap'n?'

'Could be stolen off anybody's boat.' Can't say how desperately I wanted the lead to go nowhere, or at least to go somewhere I couldn't follow.

Wiley gave me the eyeball he used when he suspected me of shortcutting. 'Don't think so. Come off a particular boat.'

'Yeah,' I said, 'it did.'

That's when June got it, fully and confirmed. She didn't put her hands on her hips and give me the hairy eyeball, but she may as well have. I earned it, or was about to. 'You aren't going to let this drop, are you?'

Funny thing about many things we commonly say. *Letting it drop* is a phrase that waterman use about rope. So is *following the lead*.

All we two boys could do was shake our heads at the other.

We're back in the piss, old friend.

Two

June put her hands up palms forward, shook her head and barked, 'Goodnight, you all. Been a long day.' A few eyes followed where she disappeared inside, but mine didn't. Neither did Wiley's. 'Sorry, Cap'n.'

'S'okay.'

Wiley's company, seeing June leave, began *en masse* to shuffle, thinking hers was the message that our meeting should come to an end. They may have come for confirmation, but I sensed my word, my verdict, was nothing without the right person hearing it.

I looked into the face of the one-armed Coleman Davis for my own confirmation. His countenance was one carved from Honduran mahogany by an artist who had discovered that character is best made evident by hacking scars and deep lines wherever there was a flat plane to hold them. His was an implacable countenance, though at the moment rigid with suppressed expression. It told me that more was needed. I urged them not to worry, stay.

I put on my professorial voice and manner. 'Problem I have is the rope's perfectly long enough for what it was used for, but not long enough for what it was made for. This here is anchor rode, rope that goes out to your anchor. Usually a hundred feet or more. This isn't a hundred feet by a long shot. Somebody had to cut it to length, at least approximate, to the work. Please excuse me calling the hanging that, but I'm trying to be clear. Whoever killed Willa Maes saw what he wanted to do to him in terms of work that lay ahead. That meant somebody had to plan what they were going to do. In my experience, suicides, people who kill themselves unexpectedly don't do it with much of a plan. Some do, but they are the one's who've wanted to commit suicide for a long time. Was Willa Maes one who might want to kill himself?'

The racket that caused might have awakened the next marina down the coast as well.

The wretched woman cried out, not exactly a scream but something like one coming from somebody getting strangled. Most in the crowd shook their heads collectively, and began talking not exactly to say anything, just to make some noise. The reverend maintained his passive Reverend's composure. Davis just looked darker, which I took for angrier. Though he didn't say it out loud, his face had *Fuck no* all over it.

I thought I'd just landed my confirmation on their collective chin.

One of the big men standing on a dock box, voice scary, head high over his crowd, said, 'Willa got no reason to kill hisself.'

I had to smooth those upset waters. 'I think you're right. You see this?' I held up the whipped end, 'Somebody who knows what he's doing finished this end off, and he did it ages ago. Whoever owned this rope wasn't the one who used it, I would bet my boat on it. More important, the length of this makes me think somebody tied it off first, tossed the rest over a strong branch, to figure out how much they'd need. Then it was cut to length, maybe a bit extra. Then they untied it, hid it or took it away, somehow got Willa to the tree, and only then did they... well.'

Blank wet eyes all around.

'You didn't find the forty missing feet to this, did you?' More blank but stupefied into silence eyes looked at me. I went on. 'Somebody tied off that rope for sure who knew something about knots, boater's knots, got everything ready for a hanging. I'd bet the other half of this rope is back in the hole it had been taken from. We find that, we get one step closer to finding who killed Willa Maes.'

I couldn't believe my own mouth.

I was in that *We*.

To deflect any of them from realizing what I'd just implied, I continued on the vein I'd already opened. 'Once that rope was readied for the hanging, they walked away. A suicide doesn't walk away.' I gave them a moment to let my suggestion sink in. 'Besides that, a suicide climbs up on something, puts the rope around his neck with maybe two, three turns, then makes a knot without much care how somebody will see it, and then he kicks away whatever supports him. But he doesn't kick the support so far away it can't be found. You find something to stand on like that?'

Again, blank, heads shaken side to side.

'Suicides, the sad ones, not the sick ones, go about things alone, lonely, not caring about how neat his knots are. His thoughts are not on clove hitches and double half hitches.'

I held back with my final pronunciation, but Wiley knew my mind. He just said it, like he would say the day was Tuesday. 'Willa Maes din't die without company.'

Had to nod, as did several in the sad, silent crowd gathered at the back of my boat.

One-armed dark mahogany-face Davis again put the words on everyone's mind into everyone's ear. 'Killed, then.'

I nodded. Confirmation surely taken. I said to him, 'Figure more than one person, two at least, and young, young as he was. Everything I know about rope and suicides says Willa Maes was murdered, but unless the cops got pictures of this rope, you all destroyed the key evidence.'

The wretched woman with the Reverend and Davis finally made like she was going to say something. She started, though, with *Mmmm hmmm, O yayya.* To which a few of those dockside came back with the same *O yayya.* Then in that slow, rumbling manner of back woods natives of the Florida pinewoods, a language used by people habituated to speaking to themselves, she began say-singing a hymn I'd never heard before.

Davis said directly to me, as the voices joined, 'Cops won't want evidence no more, not from nobody. Sure as Willa lays dead, they'll never gonna take evidence from us.'

The woman closed her eyes, and where she found more tears to rain down her smooth cheeks I don't know, but like water spilling from an overfilled cup, down they came.

'Thank you, Mist' Captain. Wiley said you'd tell it to me straight. We come for certainty my Willa didn't do what ever'one us knew he wouldn't never do. You gave us that, and I am putting my thanks for you in prayers tonight. Come on, y'all, we go now.'

At first, while she just kept looking at me, nobody moved. Then all of a sudden they all moved. I noticed it was a toss of Coleman Davis's head that launched them into the conclusion of my night's events.

Wiley stood beside me as they climbed off. He made no move that said he'd be going with them, but I knew that was his plan.

I put my hand on his arm. 'They want to know who killed him?'

'They know, Cap'n. Not in the partic'lar, but they know't in gen'ral. Ain't nothing they can do but bury their boy, and pray now. Funeral's here are done quick, an' I'm goin'.'

'You want me, June and me, to come along?'

'Don't think that's a good idee. You two keep on your vacation trip. I'll work things out.'

'Don't you want to know the particular?'

'Part a me does, most a me don't. Goin' after it ain't my business, 'less they asks it. They asks, I let you know.'

One ritual that the long length of our friendship had never eroded was that we always shook hands when we parted. Always. Except then. I put my hand out reflexively, but he just patted my forearm, worked up a feeble smile, and walked away.

I let June sleep alone for a while. Spring evenings along the west coast of Florida don't get cool, and the Gulf side humidity had turned the air into the sauna I despise. Living on an island that's almost constantly swept by breezes makes me unfit for tolerating that kind of humidity, and the hot, sweltering city nights in the hot humid Philadelphia of my youth were far enough behind in years to dis-acclimate me. Still, I wasn't ready to drop into a coma in our air-conditioned cabin. I did go into the salon to pull three longnecks from the fridge box, but went back out to settle myself out on the foredeck.

The *Sweet Discourse* had been tied up stern-in to the dock, which I had planned to use for mindless gazing from the bow onto lilting water, those slippery reflections of lights from other boats and distant stars providing distraction from any picture show in the mind's eye. Loneliness never feels so good as when you can feel lonely on a boat.

But that night the main feature was a boy dancing for the Devil at the end of a rope, a loneliness that can never have any good about it. Couple the diesel-tinged smells of the marina with what I had sniffed from the hanging rope, my sense-memories were locked. I could not let slip what had recently transpired go into faded memory. The feel of that old cotton anchor rode lay in my fingers, and the dark faces hung in the air.

Sorry, June, but no, I wasn't about to let this drop.

I sipped the beer and put my head back against the rising slope of the cabin's outer wall. My thumbnail scratched at the label. I watched the movie.

The rope told me that whoever killed Willa Maes, who wanted him dead, could not have acted alone. Somebody had to hold Willa Maes aloft enough for the knot maker to do his biz. That meant there had to be at least two who wanted Willa dead. And if two, why not three? Or even four?

I rolled back to scenes before the struggle to get him aloft. How had they caught him? Why had they chased him? What had he done?

Who would have hated Willa Maes that much? Who wanted a public lynching to send what message about how much Maes had been hated?

Whoever they were, they didn't just want Willa Maes dead, they wanted him found. People who kill people in Florida have a wooded western coastline edging the Gulf with thousands of places to hide the dead. Every one of the possible thousand places insures that the dead would never be found. The Glades were not far off, less than a hundred mile drive south, full of gators who love to eat whatever they can chomp down on. The history of its dark waters is rife with man-fed gator stories.

Then there were — surrounding that marina, and into which the church and her ballfield had been cut — unlimited, untrammeled pinewoods filled, and filling rapidly these days, with wild boars. Back when I worked Philly there'd been a murder of a New Jersey housewife whose only remaining bit that they found was her skull. The pig-farmer husband had shoved it into the rafters of his barn. His hogs had eaten the rest of her, bones and all. Only reason the skull was left? Too big to chomp down.

Some work with a big hammer might have let him get away with the killing, but several people suspected he wanted somebody to find that skull, just so they'd know he'd gone and done what he always said he might.

His expressed reason, though, was creepier: *Just liked having her looking down at me.*

Willa Maes had been found hanging just inside a scrubby woods rimming a public park where kids not already signed up for Babe Ruth and Little League played baseball.

Where Willa Maes was found was where somebody had meant for Willa Maes to be found.

The end of the boy had been something that somebody fiercely desired displayed, but could not effect that without help, support. The murderer had not only planned the death of Willa Maes, he had convinced others to join him, then kept them all together during his mad act despite the horrors of what they were to do.

That young man had been brought to more than just death. He was brought, and carefully, to his execution by a team under the direction of a leader who had something to say.

It felt apparent to me that whoever wanted Willa Maes lynched hadn't performed from sudden rage. He did want it done because of rage, a long simmering rage. He, and maybe they, had killed him with hearts full of smoldering hatred. A long-standing, crackling hatred that finally had gotten blown by something into a life-consuming fire.

That they lynched him meant they wanted to shout about their hate to whomever was there to hear it. And I suppose it was to the crowd of African Americans assembled at kid's ballgame, and who'd just left my boat.

People the killers thought of as *them.*

Three

Falling asleep on a foredeck, how many times has that happened? But then wide awake. Smoking anger hovered over me in the familiar outline of loveliness standing between my blinking eyes and the winking lights here and there beyond the marina. I smiled, June didn't.

'I thought you went off with Wiley and left me here by myself.'

'I wouldn't do that.'

'Right. Suddenly there's a dead guy and I'm supposed to think you're going to act normal?'

Now we don't fight, haven't since she came back into my arms one hot Philly night nearly a year ago. *What the Hell?*

So, I asked her. 'What the Hell stole your bait?'

'I, oh, it's just that, shit Andrew. Just because.' Was this one of those things I was supposed to get used to? She pointed at the bottles, 'Give me one of those,' then she sat down beside me. I twisted off the cap and snapped it into the harbor.

She said, 'I never have sympathy for suicides. One lousy reason to live trumps any good reason to kill yourself. Pisses me off, is all.'

'Wasn't a suicide.'

June took a long swig and stared into the nothingness that had put me to sleep. I was glad she wasn't pissed at me.

'Well,' she finally said, 'that's worse.'

'Worse?'

'Of course. Then he was murdered. That means three things. A boy died for nothing, and somebody out there's a murderer.'

She didn't drop her last speculation, so I had to ask. 'The third?'

She took another swig. 'Third is you're not going to walk away from it, and there goes yet another fine vacation of mine.'

'I could fire up the engines right now and head out, you want me to.'

'Right.'

I stood up and without another word went forward to untie the forward lines from the cleats.

'What about Wiley?'

I tossed the port dock line onto the pylon cleat, though badly. 'He said just go, so let's go.' An end snapped at the water. *Screw it,* I thought, but set about doing a better job with the starboard line. When I turned around, I saw that June had started the label scratch-off game. 'Yes?'

'What about the car?'

'I'll call and extend time on it. No big deal.'

'Sit down, Drew.'

I did, and willingly. Stay or go, no never mind to me. Of course, staying meant I'd have to retie those forward dock lines. But instead I sat, knowing that right in front of me was another one of those instances about which either *Honey, I've been thinkin'* or *Honey, we need to talk* was about to get said. First one was fine, the latter tended to freeze my blood. Luck was with me that night.

June asked me, 'So what you mean, not suicide?'

'It's complicated, but too much evidence to the contrary.' I tried to remember how much she heard before she went off and left me alone with the company. And just because she heard it didn't always mean she listened. 'The rope Wiley...'

'You got everything from a knot?'

'Not everything. But mostly, enough. What I saw of the rope, and what Wiley said about Willa Maes. What a name, huh? Bet there's a story there.'

'Don't change the subject,' she said. I was afraid to look, certain there was a fresh-plowed field of wrinkles on her forehead that said she was still an inch from being even more pissed off, and sure as shootin' she'd aim it at innocent me. What was she mad at?

One thing I learned about people long ago was that usually they get pissed off at whatever they are *not* angry about. Pissed is a symptom, the cause harder to discern. Time, as they say, would tell. Just really hoped it wasn't me.

We discussed all over again what led me to a conclusion that Willa Maes had not committed suicide. Abruptly in the middle of my explaining whipped ends to her, she asked me, 'They going with any of this to the police?'

'Won't do them any good if they do, and all's it would do is get Wiley in trouble for tampering with evidence. Mood Florida's in right now, especially with that guy shooting that unarmed black kid wearing a hoodie, this one's going to stay a suicide.'

Scratch, scratch. *Bye bye label.* 'Don't Wiley's friends want to know?'

'I asked that. No, they don't.'

June picked up my empty to scratch off that label. I chanced a glance at her forehead. *Yep, those were thinkin' furrows.* I tend to wear them myself when there are unanswered but answerable questions. I felt she was so far down the plow line she'd not expect anything coming from the left, so I saw my chance. 'Why you get so pissed about suicide?'

It worked. Took a moment, but she started. 'I had a cousin hang himself. Stupid. Probably didn't even mean to, but like most things he did he got himself in more farther than he'd planned. Right in my aunt's basement. Stupid.'

I wished to hear it, but didn't want to say so, in case she didn't wish to say it. But she did. 'They were playing cards and he was losing. Him, his mom and dad and his girlfriend. Seems he tossed his last hand on the table and got up saying he was going downstairs to kill himself. My aunt thought he was just going down to get another beer from the fridge they kept down there. But then he didn't come back. His girlfriend went, and she was the one found him. Stupid ass.'

'How?'

'He'd tied a lamp cord over a sewage pipe and wrapped it around his neck one time too many. They think he slipped, that he was probably going to call her down to see him like that, but he slipped and the plug got caught and it knotted around his neck, too tight for him to get it undone. Stupid, stupid shit.'

I wasn't as firm in my belief that the boy had died in a stupid accident, having found more than one lonely soul shedding his mortal coil that way, but didn't say so. Her description did reinforce my suspicion, conclusions, about Willa Maes. His manner of dying was a planned event, no ifs nor buts.

What I also didn't believe was that it wasn't June's cousin who'd found the boyfriend in the basement. I stood looking a long time at June, finally concluding to let it lie.

I stood and put out my hand to help her rise. June didn't take it.

She said, 'Can we really just go?'

'Ready and willing, and able. You know me on an hour or two sleep.'

'Then let's. Yeah, let's go.'

One thing about harbor living, somebody fires up engines in the wee dark hours, you don't pop open even an eyeball at the sound. But somebody whispers at the end of your boat, your eyes go wide as dinner plates. So I wasn't concerned about waking the neighborhood when I started the lovely new engines to the *Sweet Discourse*. Taking the helm while my lovely shipmate removed the rear dock and spring lines, I got to watch her do what she'd taken to doing with such precision.

June had fallen in love with the orderliness of boat life. Ship shape isn't just a phrase, it's a way of life, required for safety. To insure it, there's a proper method to just about every task on a boat, and taking up the slack of a dock line into a neat set of loops, then tying it off into a stowable bundle, requires practice, a precision, and a grace. Done right it becomes a sort of dance, one that doesn't translate into words so you'll just have to trust me on it.

June loved the dance, and I could almost sense her purring in tune with my engines.

One of the reasons she loved the dance is she loved the *Sweet Discourse* as much as I did. Unless a captain loves every timber, cord, screw and fiber of his boat, any journey out from the harbor will be fraught with a hidden, lurking danger. But love your boat, you'll learn to love her properly, and all will be as safe as any sea voyage allows. And when the crew loves the boat, voyages out become happy ones.

When finally I dropped the shifter into forward the *Discourse* lurched under our feet. That creepy sense of having been considered a *Them* had disappeared. June and I were just *us*. We both felt it, a return of the impending possibilities for happiness. In no time she had climbed up and taken her seat beside me. I maneuvered our way through the slips and the muddy bottom bay.

I contend that happiness requires a voyage. I've heard, but not had it confirmed, that the concept of happiness is a northern European concept, that the word *happy* derives from a nautical origin. Among seafarers of the treacherous north, arriving at your destination — which usually meant either out to the fishing grounds or back home to safe harbor — was iffy.

To arrive safely at the destination for which you've set out is to reach happiness.

Happiness is not the same as joy, nor does it include serendipity. Serendipity just happens, you *find* joy, but you *get* happy. Serendipity arrives unexpected, and Joy surprises.

Happy takes work, careful maneuvering, lots of concern and effort, and a clearly identified destination.

Our destination? Away, just plain old away.

We took joy in clearing the last boundary of the marina, felt our bosoms fill as we rounded the last stand of mangrove. There we saw, even through the ink dark of a still night, a large heron lift off with thumping broad wings. Serendipity. It had been startled by the engines and lights, disturbed by our proximity.

But happiness? Impending. We hadn't specified a destination except *away*.

And away we went.

One thing about a fixed destination, though. You know when you've arrived, and you can be happy about having reached it. *Going from* has no actual destination. That's why *going to* is always better. Still, going *from* something has its merits, and June and I both felt sincerely and consistently that what rumbled landward of the rapidly disappearing marina was a world full of trouble well worth going from.

Of course every boat owner has a little Peter Pan in him, so following a star straight on 'til morning can be good enough for any of us. The reward for pushing on is Dawn, that slow putting into play of changes. There is the change in light of course, and that suggests a change from the realities of yesterday to the more pleasant possibilities of the coming day. It seeps into your muscles and bones, affects your stream of consciousness, maybe even tips your luck or spins your wheel of fortune.

To reach morning after an emotional evening and a night of no sleep, though, says *Change, Big Boy*, from somehow awake to definitely flat on your back out cold in even a hot bunk below.

I called June to prepare for dropping anchor.

'Where are we?' she asked, hair messy in that lovely I-got-a-woman-on-my-boat way that told me I really had to get that anchor dropped and both of us back in bed.

I dropped anchor all right. Let's leave it at that.

We saw the dawn, a bit of it through the starboard window, but not much else of the morning. Glad that anchor held. I was a solid four hours into unconscious when suddenly I sat bolt upright in bed.

No matter how tired a captain is on his boat, his ears remain awake. And if everybody is asleep on his boat, those ears pick up minnows farting downstream.

Sounded like a thumbnail drawn down a shirtfront, just a little *scritch*, but it was enough. I bounded from bed, snatched up a pair of modesty shorts that had enough holes in it to prevent any form of modesty, and bounded onto the deck. A quick look forward said we weren't about to go aground. Land was still a quarter mile off, the bed of the gulf sloping away from the shoreline at maybe a foot drop every hundred yards. There was plenty of water under the hull.

So I looked behind. A mat of tree trunks seemingly tied together raft-like. I had binoculars on the flying bridge, so I climbed up for a better look. I was right, not some accidental coming together of downed trees but a man-made raft of trees and rope. There was a water-stained little red cooler tied to one end, but no one aboard. Rising up from it was a snagged chunk of cypress, probably what had caused that scratching noise along my hull. Wadded in the cypress's branches was a Miami Marlins baseball shirt, the kind bought in the stadium gift shop.

I guess a log raft drifting in the Gulf of Mexico had to stir my memories, or rather recollections, of being a kid floating with his buds on tied-together telephone poles that meandered recklessly down our nearby water road, the Pennsylvanian Schuylkill River. Happy days, happy boys — and once a rogue girl who wouldn't go away — pretending we were a half dozen Huck Finns from Pennsissippi.

As I watched the clot of trees twirl in the current, it occurred to me that none of us ever played Nigger Jim, the runaway slave fleeing for his freedom in the wrong direction. I suppose the reason nobody emulated him was that we were all little white people.

Watching the raft dwindle to a pinpoint, I kept thinking about Jim. How many real men had slipped downriver, running from what chained them to the expectations and restrictions of other men? I could almost see Jim, wide eyes, attuned to dangers more perilous than running up on a mud bank. I looked across the oily water toward a grove of trees, dark and gloomy, and saw among them cottonwoods and a thick-wristed willow leaning over the bank. Then I saw a hundred of them in a hundred fields and against a hundred rivers, a hundred years of them sprouting that strange fruit of Dixie.

From one dangled an anchor rode flung over a stout limb, taut against the neck of a boy whose arms hung straight down at his side, head cocked a bit too much, toes reaching for a ground already useless.

Shit.

It was all I could say to myself.

With binoculars in one hand, elbows on my thighs, wrists fighting the weight of the eyeglasses, eyes watering from the glimmer of high noon careening off small ripples, I knew that when June's head rose into view, she'd climb up into the flying bridge just in time to hear me say those damned magical words:

Honey, I've been thinking.

Four

June, though, was way ahead of me. Way ahead, except she used that female version of blood freezing phrases. *Drew, we should talk.*

All I got to talk to was a pretty head, chin resting on the fiberglass deck, as she came no farther up the gangway onto my flying bridge. But that head was enough. Her eyes stayed fixed on mine, jaw set, brow rumpled. Plenty enough. The rest of her body would have just served as distraction anyway. The head spoke.

'Whoever killed Willa Maes, we have to bring them to justice.'

I concurred, but not heartily. 'We?' The head looked stern. *Say a different word, and quick, Drew Nolan.* I said two.

'Okay. How?'

'How? I don't know. I do tax law. You're the cop, ex-cop, but still. How many times you said the one who knows has the responsibility? Well, I know, and you know. So our responsibility. And Wiley knows, and a whole lot of people who care know. But they're the people who can't do anything, and since they can't do anything they won't do anything, and something needs to get done. And the people who don't

29

care are exactly the ones who could do something, and they're not going to. But we care. I'm a lawyer, and you were a cop. Who else is there to care who could do something? When I think, when I see that poor boy...' Her ferocity surprised me, though it shouldn't have, 'You can't let this thing that's happened just go past, like some shipwrecked ship too big for us to do anything about. And not like you haven't gotten yourself involved where the people pretty much didn't need you.'

That one, ouch.

I'd given reluctance to dive into the piss a pretty high priority since my last misadventure. But yet there we went.

Up came the anchor, on went the diesels, down went the throttles, fast away went Happy, Joy and Serendipity, for here came the piss into which we had to step.

When action is called for, though the first step remains unclear, a person's natural tendency is to dither, do whatever else, simply because that is what we know we can do. So glad I had a wheel and a throttle to occupy my hands and guide my thoughts. They gave me a sense that I had control, that I had something I knew how to do without worries.

One thing I knew was that I, we, June and I, would naturally be denied any access to any legal, official evidence. And not because we were strangers, but because we'd be kicking a dog better left asleep. Regardless that neither of us had a legal standing, denied access was most likely simply because whatever evidence there was had probably been destroyed. But access would also be refused because, when a closed society wants things hidden, things get hidden first from those on the outside.

But was I, were we, truly on the outside? We were bound to find out.

The killer? Killers were white. Not *maybe*, not *probably*, not *allegedly,* not *suspected.* Were. No if, no but, no possibly, nothing. If there's anything calculable as to what divides white from black, it's not Hate, but how Hate gets manifested. And this hate got manifested in a way that no black man would touch.

Cop experience says there were plenty of black men capable of vicious, hateful crimes on other black men, but lynching is so deeply a scarred part of African America history that's unspeakable, completely unpardonable. It's the gas chamber to a Jew, a smallpox-infested blanket to a Native American, a hydrogen bomb to an Asian. Being so heinous a white crime, not one black in two hundred million would ever perpetuate that crime on another. For any reason.

Lynching surely is where the line will always be drawn.

We were strangers to that tangle of woods and mangroves of west Florida, total strangers to the life of those inland poor, because I was white, because I was already known as a cop, though an ex cop, and because I had ridden in on a big expensive white boat.

If that was where I'd get to play, that's where I'd start the game.

When nothing physical remains for investigation, or when what remains cannot be investigated, there's only the story to which to turn. As sure as I was about the course leading us back to the marina, I was sure there were people talking about Willa Maes that held the clues to his death.

I could count on white people's natural indifference to anyone not them, which often leads them to saying out loud much more than what they thought they had thought. In thoughtless thoughts much could be picked out that could prove useful, once I had enough to assemble a clearer picture.

Willa Maes stories from the deep pinewoods a dozen miles inland would of course be revealing, but I'd never hear them. I knew the clues to his story that I would hear would come from a world closer to the shoreline, which is where the preferred properties of those indifferent people get built.

June and I had during the dark hours of the previous night motored a fair distance away from the marina, or maybe I should say we *ran* away a fair distance, so getting back meant piloting the *Sweet Discourse* along a straight and uneventful line over oily flat water under a high hot sun. June had gone back to sleep, so all I had to do was listen to the steady drone of the boat's diesels, the rhythmic *whup-whup-whup* of water against the hull, watch an occasional seagull wheel about in search of a place to drop its ass, and think.

I felt confident supposing who the killers were, or had to be, if only in the general rather than specific sense, but presupposition will kill an investigation if not reined in. I had already presumed far too much, but it was what a person does when staring at a straight line dotted over a digital watercourse on the GPS.

I started with thinking there was something else about the killers that had nothing to do with black and white. If I was part of the same *Them* as the killers, what could there be about me that maybe separated my white face from theirs?

My deductions about the relative experience, or inexperience, of who tied the knots led me to consider faces a good deal younger than mine. Would any face years older than Willa's want him dead? I didn't think so. An older man makes another man dead in the simplest, fastest, most straightforward fashion, assassinations excepted, because there are very few reasons — or ways — to kill a person slowly. Again, assassinations and political torturing aside, which had nothing to do with Maes, he would have made Willa Maes dead in a most meaningless way, goal achieved.

The killer wanted Maes more than just dead. He, or she, wanted him lynched, which was a cruel, crude, message-laden death. And they wanted him found, a message sent.

Lynching, in the modern estimation, is a Hate crime, pure and simple. But it's a mob crime, an event that's supposed to connect viscerally every witness to the hanging by a similarity of their collective hatreds. The act itself, conceivably to rectify a perceived wrong, is meant to justify that collective hate. Doesn't, ever, but we're talking about a response perverted by fear and distrust.

Men my age may still hate, but there're few who'd hate enough to plan and do something so drastic unless it was for an audience who needed a reminder of the message. Okay, men from the White Power movement, maybe, Nazis. But if they had been even those clowns, they'd have made a louder noise. And they would have picked a target who, in their warped perspective, deserved a lynching.

Why lynch a young boy who had done nothing? What message had been sent? The neo-Nazi message of *We don't like you* was known well enough not to need resending.

For Willa. there was no mob to witness the death of a poor, talented baseball-throwing black boy from the back woods, but there was a desire to have the killers' hate shouted at whoever learned about it. They knew what they were doing.

The possibility that the killers intended to send a message was not absolute nor conclusive, but I felt it pointed to a message more specific than general hatred of a race.

Before that party of locals had left my boat, I had stopped the Reverend to ask what kind of kid Willa Maes had been. Didn't say a whole lot, but the man said enough. Willa Maes played baseball, pitched, and played better than anybody around had for a lot of years.

'Not since him,' he said, nodding toward Coleman Davis. The one-armed man had just then stepped away from a knot of companions trying to comfort the weeping woman. 'Shame, there. Maes, he was going places. Can't see nothing suicidal about him at all, ever. He meant a lot to all of us, and he knew it. He was the one who was going to get out.'

I knew what that meant. So few get out, whether out of the woods or the hoods. Another curious thing I noticed when I had been a cop: the less people had, so long as they had each other the more they valued life.

Murder. Surprising to most who never give it much thought, there are not a whole lot of motives for killing another person.

There's Greed, which will induce someone to remove a person who gets in the way of getting what the greedy wants. Think drug wars over turf. Greed will also fire up somebody who wants to get his hands on what another person already has. Death often results in taking what someone has, evident in how many store clerks get off'd during robberies.

What could Willa Maes have had that a greedy person wanted? Had he stood in the way of a greedy person getting what he wanted? And what could have been wanted? Drugs? Drug money? Doubtful. Star athletes may fall into drugs, but usually not until after they start earning the big bucks. Always the possibility he sold drugs, but people who sell drugs aren't usually also working really hard and really visibly to escape the people he sold drugs to.

Gambling debts? Again, possibly. But it's a staple of bad dialogue that dead men don't repay.

Greed's not the sole province of the young. They are simply more passionate about it. Greed can run an older person to do some nasty things, no question, but usually they choose a cold and efficient crime. At least simpler. Those older who kill out of greed have no interest in sending messages. That's horse-head-under-the-sheets horse pucky out of gangster movies.

All this led me to rule out an older person, or persons, in favor of people the same age as the ball player, people he knew and brushed up against every day.

We reached the marina late afternoon on Sunday. The humidity had piled up against the shoreline as a wall between the Gulf waters and the empty slips. Even with snow birds pulling out or moving off their boats, the marina seemed especially desolate, desperate, something I'd not really noticed until our return. I knew a little something about marinas, and the number of empty boat slips under the white light of a nearly tropical sun made the place appear more empty than what was commercially healthy. Had to wonder if the joint wasn't about to go under, that in a few years all anyone would get to see there would be rotted planks, pylon stumps and the fetid smell of forgotten. Not like Florida hasn't a few of those in her history.

As for that humid wall, soon as it hit I was forced to weigh the influence of both Sunday and Hot on my plans. Realized there might not be anywhere a soul I could find who might be young as Willa Maes. Schools were closed for the day but not for the year, and most likely more than most were either trying to avoid thinking about final exams by thumbing the controls of video games in air conditioning, or, scared to death by them, had locked themselves in bedrooms to study.

In Willa Maes' backwater Gulf-side community, church would have been in session pretty much all day, sucking up even those I couldn't reach even had the weather been balmy and perfect.

Our first step taken was the ride over the watery line back to where the trouble had started. I was thinking on the next step as June tied the rear dock lines, when serendipity struck, sort of. I saw one of the only moving things in the marina carrying down to his boat a small cooler in hand, a bag of charcoal slung up on his opposite shoulder. Like magical special-effects, possible footprints emerging, my next step began to appear.

The destination? Where white people go to talk. Even better was some place they'd go to tell and hear stories. And where do people tell stories the most? Where they eat. Time had come for some misplaced Florida Yankees to go eat.

'Honey, how you feel about Denny's?'

About halfway there June saw for herself a next footprint. 'I think we should call Wiley. Ask if he wants to come. He might. But we should involve him from the get go, don't you think?'

Whether I thought so or not, June did. She had her cell out, already dialing the pocket phone I'd loaned Wiley, exclaiming that she had bars! She then generated the loveliest of smiles as she pressed the phone to her ear. I wondered if, getting reception when she had to call me, she smiled like that.

Sure, Nolan. Why not?

With me, Wiley felt free enough to speak directly what he had in mind, and he often kept things short and right to the point. With people he didn't know, or cared to know, he more often than not grunted his monosyllabic replies. With Miss June, he puddled down into a thirteen-year old girlfriend, his deep rumbly mush-mouthed self rising sometimes to a high-pitched excited squeal, if you could call a giggly gargling a squeal.

Whenever those two loaded up the microwaves overhead with their chatter I tended to walk away, so as not to witness the depths to which my massive manly shipmate would descend. That time, though, I had nowhere to go.

June started with her sing-songy *Wiley, guess who* opening, but she soon dropped down into the serious *Honey, we gotta talk* register. Obviously, June's suspicions that he had been basted too long in the solemnity of a community in despair and bereavement would allow no place for silly teen-girl talk. Somber it had to be, and became.

All I had of the conversation was her side, but Wiley's rejoinders could be figured out. For several minutes she mostly nodded, saying, *'Uh huh, I bet. I can't imagine what, you're sure a big help to her, them, I know you. Uh huh, no, we don't, change of plan, we were going to but doncha think it was best we came back? You know why, it's the way he is. We should talk. We want to talk, about who did this. I see, yeah, sure. We know that. But Wiley... Still, we... no problem, we could come get you. Sure, I'll hang on...'*

Instead of filling me in, June just stared in my direction, her eyes dancing with concern, although dancing seemed too frivolous for what they were really doing. *You sure? No bother, no need to bother him, sure. We saw a Denny's in the town here. Denny's. He knows it?*

I got the gist, and picked up my car keys.

Wiley hadn't wanted us to pick him up, had his reasons, which must have felt right and obvious to him. But I had my reasons for wanting to do exactly that. If we all were going to be poking around where we weren't wanted — possibly by both sides of the *Us* and *Them* — distance between us and Wiley's adopted community might be a good thing to maintain.

But, no. Someone had insisted on bringing him, someone who wanted in on what we had planned.

The car he arrived in was not new, but its pearl white paint made it look so. The beast had been cared for, polished, garage kept. I know the look, for I did the same thing to *Luce,* my baby 1953 Chevy Belair convertible then sleeping in a storage area back at my marina, one meant for storing a big boat.

The man driving I recognized by his having one-arm.

Coleman Davis.

In the full light of the Florida day, the man even more impressed upon us that little of his age had brought him any infirmity. I could see he had been an athlete. A man of my height, his step was springy, light on the balls of his feet, with a bit of sway that said he could go right or left as easily as anyone would lurch forward.

However, something in his scowl — and it wasn't from the sunlight — said he didn't go backward with equal ease. Ever.

Stand in his company for more than five minutes and anyone would realize that his darkened dark countenance had become permanent, natural, a frozen, penetrating stare that came from training one's attention on a fixed point, on a target that demanded complete — almost obsessive — attention. From what the Reverend had let slip about my new company, that fixed point had been a tight rectangular space between a hitter's knees and his forward shoulder, and the width of a home plate. Like Willa Maes, Coleman Davis had once been a baseball pitcher. He may have lost that pitching arm, but his habit of narrow focus had remained.

I'd seen that look on others before. The best artists to come to my father's lithography studio had had it. So did one or two nuns I'd known in my earliest school years. And it was very common among vicious thugs, those I'd had a part in catching and arresting. Not all of them, just the one's I hoped would never find out where I lived.

I'd also seen it in the one bona fide Mafia hit man whom I had the fortune, or misfortune, to meet. That one showed up in a few of my nightmares, still.

Shaking the left hand of a one-armed man always feels awkward. Kind of set the tone for the afternoon. Nothing felt normal. June was given, and gave, just a nod. She still brought forward her sweetest smile for him, though I could see Discomfort and Uncertainty had hopped on those lovely lips for the ride.

'Mr. Davis, wasn't it?' He merely looked up at me. 'We're fixing to sit for a bite, if you want...' A light at the top edge of his black eyes glittered in a way that said *You better God damn invite me. No way I'm not sitting with you on this.* I stammered out my next, 'Thanks for bringing Wiley back.'

June's bred-to-the-bone Yankee social expectations were having none of our man-chat. 'Of course you'll join us. I insist.'

Let me say this about my beauty. I've not met any man who didn't fail to melt — at least a little bit — under June Kingswood's charm. Determined as he might have been with me, Davis's responses were not so confident toward her. He looked at Wiley for quick support.

Wasn't there. Wiley looked to me for direction as well. To my first mate, I was the supreme authority, captain. Except I knew, and he knew, that I was not the *supreme* supreme authority. That was June.

Wiley had a natural deference among people of authority, and Davis had a natural authority. You didn't screw with him. But whatever Miss June wants...

Our guest's sitting down with us presented a problem about which I had concern. His presence, his especially dour and circumscribing presence, countered my intention to remain apart from the awareness and determinations of his community. I did not want to discuss the *what what* with any of them, and I really didn't want him volunteering himself into my machinations.

Because of the discomfort caused by his intrusion, conversation remained scattershot as we waited for someone to seat us. I know I kept avoiding unasked but apparent questions that the man must have had, such as why we had come back, why we were so gathered, why did Wiley trust us, who the Hell did we think we were, butting in to what wasn't our business. I was pretty sure there were four people trying their damndest to get those snakes back into the bag.

As for who the Hell we were to be butting in, I had a trump Ace. I was the guy they had come to for confirmation.

Don't remember when I said, 'Mr. Davis, you should know we've been thinking about what we talked about last night...' but I recall supposing that I should not have included June in that *we*. She shot a look that would have been rolled eyeballs had we no company. I was a better card player than that, but I felt like I was holding a Go Fish hand in a round of Texas Hold 'Em.

Stopped Davis from lifting farther a chunk of chicken fried he'd swabbed in egg yolk already half-raised to his open mouth. After an eyeball blink, he lowered his fork and closed his mouth. He stared at me, lower eyelids drooping like a Basset hound's. I could see immediately he thought I was as stupid as one of those dogs and knew I was in for a slap down.

June didn't like what she also saw coming. Bless her wise soul. She jumped conversation to another subject, yesterday's picnic in the park. Davis followed. I, however, was left hollowed out and hanging dry, full of a sense of having had my measure taken and been found wanting.

But I really wanted to get the ball rolling. Wasn't there for the hash browns.

She talked on about boats, or rather about our new Henriques, fifty feet of sleek and tuned fish-hunting wonderful, when unexpectedly Davis sent a harpoon right to the heart of what I though he'd wanted avoided. 'You're here to mess in the lynching, ain't that right, Mr. Nolan?'

Stammering. All cool lost. All I could do was dunk my head twice, *Yeppers, we sure am, you done guessed it, Mister.*

'We told you we don't want you looking in it. Why you think you got the right?'

June again, and fast as laying down a trump ace, to the rescue. 'Because it's wrong to let murderers get away with murder, Mr. Davis. I don't know why you don't want to know who did this awful thing.'

In the bit more than a year since we had become *We,* I'd discovered June had a noble streak, which had the ability to limit opposing expression that may have been anywhere near selfish. Her indignation resembled pissed off, with a huge helping of cranky. But about the lynching she was more than pissed off, she was self-righteously determined, motivated. I think Davis clearly saw that. If he didn't, he had to know she'd become a woman with a bee in her bonnet when she dropped her bomb. 'And I can't understand why you people don't want to know who the killers are.'

Found out long ago there are a few phrases that white folks utter in front of, and especially at, people of color. *You people* was one of those. I cringed, and I'm sure Wiley felt like adopting a different political affiliation, gym membership, religion and social club.

But I've also learned that there are some people truly generous towards pretty, well-meaning though blundering white women, and Davis proved to be one of them. At least to my charming pretty white Yankee woman, anyway. Not so sure I'd have been as easily let off the hook.

He said, in a quiet, direct and appealing way, 'Never said we didn't want to know who the killers were.'

'But Drew said,' she looked at me, that heart-killing look of doubt about my honesty in her eyes.

I shrugged, pleading confusion. 'Guess I was wrong.'

'What I did say,' Davis continued, 'was that we didn't want you people looking into it.'

I heard the rebuke, and knew it was meant solely for me. 'But just now — Miss Kingswood is it? I just now asked why *you* think *you* should find out.'

June set her jaw, 'I just said…'

'No, please don't misunderstand me. Why should *you* be the ones to find out?'

June, feeling the reason obvious, looked at me, then back at Davis, then for safety perhaps at Wiley, then back to Davis. 'Because we know how?' Question, about which Davis wasn't actually expected to answer. But he did.

'Y'all are living the myth.'

I could see that his statement only left June and me puzzled. Wiley had that embarrassed downcast eyes of a man whose friend farted in front of his mother-in-law's pew. People pinned by puzzlement, especially when put forward in an accusatory way, tend to get defensive, and my natural ambition to be the male defender of all women, especially of June, made me a little pissy.

'Excuse me?'

'The myth of white people. They got t'be the white messiah comin' t'rescue us poor old helpless backwoods niggers.'

There are some things barred from being said to white people, too, and the bald-faced truth is often one of them. It was fight or flight time. Though I'm sure we all stiffened, readying for the ugly that seemed surely on its way, June's lawyer sense kicked in and she defused things with the only defense we white folks have when confronting black anger. She used the *You're-right-we're-pretty-stupid* defense.

'It's just he's a cop.'

Davis grinned, 'I know that, Miss June. But let's not get stuck thinkin' we po' people need y'all. We can use ya, according to Wiley here, and we be grateful you dug out people we pretty sure we already know. Especially you come up with evidence. But us knowin' ain't gonna change nothin'.'

'You know who did it?' I blurted.

'Well, not exactly. This a damn thing done, by damned people. Just people around here'll want it t'go away, get buried, 'cause otherwise everythin'll go down the hole to an outhouse, of this, this... if it don't go down the hole, things'll go up in flames, and that fire'll consume everything, and it'll spread.'

'You want it to go away, Mr. Davis?' June the lawyer again. I saw she'd recovered admirably from the accusatory disturbance. I hadn't, but who was I to take the lead when the only place to go was punch a one-armed old man in the face?

Davis, in a carefully measured response of an amateur actor, settled his fork, wiped his lips, sat back and began tapping a hard pink fingernail against the thick porcelain plate. Neither June nor I were fooled by this effort to elevate what he had to say next to really doggone important, but the move was his, and we let him play it his way.

However, instead of saying something weighty, the son of a bitch laughed. Head back, teeth past the gums out loud, loud enough to upset the waitress watching us.

'Y'all really are white. Lady, these things been around four centuries. They don't never go away, they just go under.' A chuckle or two followed, time enough for the hot burn that his laugh had caused to drop in temperature. 'So' he said, 'what you propose?'

I wasn't sure I wanted to propose anything. Talking with Davis was giving me the feeling I'd been a tilting dummy who was supposed to take undisguised insults with a turning cheek. I can get a little sensitive that way, but June — lawyer, accountant, way smarter than her beach bum sea captain lover boy — had the skin of an NFL football.

'Drew here thinks Willa Maes was killed by at least one person who knows boats, and as the marina here's the only one for a dozen miles either way, we think, he thinks, we can pin it down by keeping our eyes and ears open there. We're already in it.'

Wiley, who'd been about as quiet as the salt shaker, which wasn't unusual, finally had something to say. Wasn't much, but it cut to the chase.

'I tole Cole 'bout you an' the knots. An' I tole him about you an' what you done, an' that's why he's here wif us. All this talkin' 'bout Messiahs and white folks ain't here ner there. Pint is, boy's dead that din't need to be, and if you thinks,' he looked at me directly, 'y'all can pint a finger ats them, then y'all should, and y'all,' he said to Davis, 'should shet it and let 'em.'

'Nuf's said that's well said, I always say.

Five

Took the heads of two men to bob okays at each other, but we *shet it* as Wiley wanted. I've already said though, when the direction is unclear people have a tendency to dither. On hindsight, all that *me black you white* garbage had been all dither. Just more of what made the lynching message begin with *Them 'n' us*.

Why June and I wanted to find the killers was immaterial, as was whether Davis and his community wanted them found. Comes a point when you just have to shet it and get your feets moving, because it's the right thing to do.

So, confrontations and negotiations over. Time'd come to gather information. I wanted to know everything about Willa Maes, but before I asked anything of Davis, who'd become my *de facto* client, I wanted to lay things out with Wiley. Just didn't want Davis there while I did it. Family, you understand.

But how to get Davis to take a hike without being a rude S.O.B.? I couldn't figure any way except to say so directly.

'Mr. Davis, I don't want you to take this the wrong way, but I think you have to go to the men's room.'

All three looked at me like I was on drugs. But I was pretty clear headed.

'Reason's this. Over there by the coffee station are three people who know something, whether they know it or not. I want them talking. I've been in a few Denny's here in Florida, and one thing I rarely see is a table in an otherwise empty restaurant in the middle of the afternoon on a Sunday at which four people, one half white the other half dark, sitting around chewing the fat. I bet the news about Willa Maes is news here as much as it was at your church, and I further bet that's what they're chewing the fat about. You get up, walk right past them nice and close, and those three are either going to keep on talking, or one of them is going to shut her trap tighter than the boss here keeps the drawer closed on the till. I think the latter, and I want to see which one hates you being here. Can you do that?'

I could see the notion didn't make him happy, but it did make him see the sense of it. Without a word he rose.

Didn't take long to spot exactly what, and who, I wanted to spot. My give-herself-away waitress was the middle height redhead-from-a-box gum chewer. Coleman Davis reached the men's door, looked back at me, and nodded before pulling open the door to the restroom.

'Wiles, I want to know everything about that boy. Who he hung with, who he dated, who he might have pissed off, how he did in school, what clothes he liked to wear, could he afford them, a ton of stuff you might think irrelevant. And I want you to make sure on the drive back that Mr. Davis understands that he's to keep his mouth completely shut about our intervention. Everything we do could lead to danger, and last thing I'd ever do was get you...'

'Don't y'worries 'bout me, Cap'n. You shoulda knowed that.'

'Let me finish. Was get you and June...' he nodded in agreement, ducking his head as if to apologize, 'in anything dangerous.'

'Like you could stop me, Andrew.' *Andrew* was one of those barriers to disagreement she had the knack of employing. We all heard it, and knew not to argue.

I filled him in on what I had been thinking, when suddenly I had a picture of that knot he'd tied around the gangway rail last night. 'Wiley, that knot you found. Did you tie it exactly the same you found it?'

He knew precisely where my mind's eye stared. Brilliance spread on his large face. 'Dang, no, Cap'n. I didn't. You's right. I tied it right hand. It was tied up left.'

Takes a trained eye to tell the difference between a knot tied by a righty from a lefty, but no question, Wiley was trained. It being a left-handed knot cut the suspect pool down to ten percent of the possibles.

'The end of this is who killed Willa Maes, and all we have so far is that somebody who knew a little something but not much about knots who is left-handed had a hand in it. With so little to go on, I plan to follow my suspicions as though they were deductions. Can't be helped. I'd prefer following the evidence where the evidence leads, but they're all gone. So glad you took that rope, though. Keep it safe and out of sight, at least for now.'

My tone had dropped to conspiratorial, and it drew the notice of those waitresses. I sat back and said out loud, 'How about those Marlins. I mean can you believe how bad these days?' Nothing loses a woman's interest quicker than two men talking baseball.

Helping distract the three was that Davis came back out of the men's. After he sat back down with us I said, 'We answer questions along the way, we'll find out who. I can only conjecture motive, and the easy one is hate. But it's deeper than that.'

Davis was about to say something about hate, but I cut him short. 'Can you think of any reason to kill him? Drugs? Gambling? Somebody maybe he pissed off?'

'You don't know who Willa Maes was,' Davis said to me, drawing his lips tight after he said it, moving his body a little closer forward towards me. Ever meet somebody you just weren't going to like? Meet Mr. Davis. 'You follow baseball?'

'I like the game, saw a few Phillies games. Why? Surely he's not related to *that* Willy Mays?'

'No, he ain't.'

Wiley broke in, 'But they give him his name, sorta, Cap'n.'

Davis took back the conversation. 'Not them, me. I give him that name. Willa Maes was my godboy.'

That surprised me. Willa Maes was at best eighteen, still in high school, and Coleman Davis looked to be pushing seventy, sixty five at the very earliest. Most people pick godparents from their flock of friends, not from old geezers in the neighborhood. 'You're his godfather?'

'I am. I was all his mama had when Willa was born. His father got killed in the Army.'

There's was something I wanted June to do, and in order for her to do it I had to lean into her and whisper in her ear. Instructions said that in three to five minutes, say out loud *What? Here? Hung himself? Oh that poor kid.*

Did the trick. I looked over and saw the out-of-a-box redhead flick an eye-slitted look to our direction.

Like I've said before, watch what they do, you'll know what they will do.

I'd had enough coffee, the plates before us all fairly wiped clean of egg, biscuit and breakfast meat — Wiley nearly picked up his plate for the last morsel — and time had come for us to go our separate ways.

Davis had said there'd be a memorial service at the same church where they played ball, but I should stay away. Couldn't help but agree. I told Wiley that he and I ought to meet up somewhere, the boat the best, maybe the evening after the service. We all but June stood. I shook the old man's hand, less awkwardly this time, and then Wiley's.

No sooner did my dark-skinned companions let the door close behind them than the red-head snatched up the coffee urn and headed our way.

Like I said, had enough coffee, but I wanted to hear what was on the red-head's mind. How one suffers for one's art.

I looked up at her. 'I just heard some dumb ass kid hung himself here yesterday. You hear about that?'

She flicked eyes at me, then passed the carafe over June's cup. 'Yeah.'

I got the feeling from watching her ever since Davis went to the men's room that our redhead wasn't exactly loquacious. The one word reply confirmed that suspicion. But I got a boat, and according to some that means I got charm. 'We're just in at the marina, on our boat, passing through on our way over to Orleans. Something like that doesn't happen every day.'

'What?'

I began to suspect her intelligence. 'Kid hanging himself in the woods.'

'Yeah.'

I felt I was earning a dental degree. June, catching on to what I was doing, joined in. 'Geez, you know the kid?'

'Yeah, sort of. Everybody knows about him.'

I said, and a bit grumpily, 'Well we don't, we're just passing through.'

'Yeah, New Orleans.' Sometimes in attempting to gain an ally in a stranger, it helps to make an enemy and let your partner gang up on you. Kind of a variation on the good cop, bad cop technique. June was right on it. 'Oh, hush, Hateful Face. Gee, honey, how come everybody knows him? He a bad kid or something.'

'Not I heard.' The waitress had her arms crossed, the half-empty urn supported in one hand. I thought it started to look a little heavy for her. 'Coffee's good. You make it?'

'We make it fresh every half hour whether we need to or not. Shame to waste coffee, but I guess that keeps people coming back. Although,' she glanced around the near empty restaurant, 'it's Sunday and early.'

I said, 'Why don't you grab a cup and join us. Not like you're swimming in customers right now.'

'Cain't do that.' She had a solid opinion of my intelligence.

June asked her, 'So, a good kid?'

'Was the baseball player took the boys to the States. I don't listen to baseball, but you can't work here and not hear least once a day somebody talking baseball, and since we gone to State, they talk baseball a lot. And a' him.'

'He was that good?' I asked.

June gave me a look that said, *Y'know, Nolan, you've had too much coffee. Go pee.* So I did.

By the time I got back, Reds had gone back into her waitress warren and June had paid the bill. She was standing outside the door when I came out.

What she learned:

46

— Reds, whose name was Ginny, had a red-headed kid also named Ginny who had a girlfriend who had a cousin who said she knew some white girl who had a thing for Willa Maes.

— June thought Box Red Waitress Ginny didn't approve of that match.

— Ginny Junior's girlfriend's cousin also had a brother who also played baseball, who had a best friend who was the white girl's boyfriend, and he found out. Said Hell to pay.

— There was a lot of planned development waiting to get put up, fancy mansion houses out in the boonies near where the *(insert unpleasant word here)* lived. There was fighting in court over it.

How June got that last bit into the conversation took an explanation longer than it took me to pee, so I'll skip it. Wasn't sure then how it had anything to do with the murder of Willa Maes, but she mentioned it nonetheless.

The last bit did prove useful later that evening, as we balanced beer bottles on our stomachs on the wide stern deck of the *Sweet Discourse*. June and I had sought privacy and coolness, to sip at the stock of longnecks that had been chilling in the fridge. Gave us something to talk about without unexpected company.

When I first got the idea that I might want to buy myself a boat, I had been lying on a hospital bed funked as all get out from being shot on the job when I wasn't on duty. One of my close friends, Jerome Pierce — a Philly cop I'd never gotten a chance to work with but from whom I'd learned just about everything in being a cop that was worth learning — had lifted his large butt off my mattress in order to leave my sorry ass in a puddle of self-imposed blackness.

Before going he'd put to me one of those Big Meaning of Life questions. *What you in it for, Drew?*

I knew he'd asked because, if I didn't have a good answer, I'd never — once the bullet hole healed — strap on the gun and badge again in exactly the best, and therefore safest, way.

Becoming a cop is much like getting married, or entering into any commitment that requires total commitment, and that's because you want to. Every cell of your body want to.

I realized that it wasn't just the cells in my blown-open shoulder that had been shot out. The commitment cells once in my brain also had gone byedie bye.

I didn't have the good answer.

Hell, I've rarely had good reasons to do anything I did. I'm among those billions of people who more often land in things rather than make things to land in. That I often landed in shit was something I blamed on Opportunity. Wrong, of course, but it was a convenient excuse for not making nice terra firma for my feetsies.

Knowing that about myself worked against June for a long time. But one day June got an unexpected offer to fly to Miami with another one of my buddies, Frank Whitcomb, a fellow known for his commitment to seduce whatever ever wore a skirt. June went without mentioning it to me.

Reason she hadn't said anything had nothing to do with deceit. It was a sudden offer, Frank does that to whomever he's standing near, friend or stranger, and June is equally impulsive. Besides, living so close to Conch Nation living does that to you.

As well, one thing I knew about Frank was he was old school, lived by the man-code, which meant that to stick his most prized part in a good friend's most prized companion was a no-no. I had about as much reason to feel jealous as I did to feel homosexual, but I did. My day of body-punching anguish about Where the Hell she was, especially after I learned with Whom the Hell she was, shoved under my nose just how badly *not* having June Kingswood in my life would feel.

I've strayed off topic, but I did so to underscore that I am not one to make commitments unless I get my nose shoved into them.

So there on the bed, without his knowing — I think — my friend Jerome Pierce, teacher extraordinaire, had shoved my nose into the rest of my life.

Truth was, I had developed the dreaded Fear of the Gun. It always approaches Those Who Get Shot in much the same way the Last Rites approach the Almost Dead. Not a whole lot a body can do about Fear moving into your psyche. The manner in which one faces the fear of the gun doesn't determine a good or bad thing. It's an *Is* or *Ain't* thing, and a person ought to pay attention to it when it takes up residence.

Great cops defeat it, bad cops ignore it.

Once Pierce had gone, I thought about happiness. My happiness. As I have said often in the past, Happiness is the destination for which you set out, and I needed a new place to head. I got to thinking about times of real joy, which is different from happy, and each one of them put me on my grandfather's boat more often tied up at a dock in Forked River over in Jersey. When that boat got untied with me aboard, as soon as we made the cut out of the inlet for wide open water, something entered my bones that entered them at no other time. A real sense that I belonged exactly there, exactly then, and exactly how.

I bought a boat that moment, my head on the pillow, my eyes staring up at the acoustical white tiles of a recovery room.

Took a lot longer to actually *own* a boat, and I couldn't have done it without a little help from my friends. Okay, a lot of help from my rich brother-in-law, who gave me the money.

I wanted a loan, but he insisted giving it just so I'd never put his wife's brother in front of a gun ever again. Sounded like a deal, I took it.

But once I did own a boat, a very handsome charter fisher that had the name *Paradise Found* already tattooed on the stern, I was Home. I was Happy.

I'd found her tied up with other charter boats, but she hadn't gone out hunting fishies for more than three years. Owner had died, widow had no idea what to do but put her up for sale. The *Paradise* didn't come with a clientele, and therefore I couldn't compete adequately with the sharks fishing for sharks off the Jersey coast. Plus she was too damn close to the very life I no longer wanted, which was in Philadelphia.

I fired up her diesels and went south, stopping for a season in a marina in Cape Fear where I met a man who said I should be in Key Largo.

That man was Wiley, and we left together. Felt bad for the skipper of the boat he'd abandoned, but Hell, Wiley and I were in love. With the *Paradise Found,* I mean.

That season I spent in Cape Fear revealed everything possible that happens living in a marina. Owning a boat got me laid, a lot, and frivolously. It also kept me mildly drunk, often. Living with boaters also turns you into a real disrespecter of propriety. I said propriety, not property. Big difference.

We became especially disrespectful about hygiene. Showers felt great for a body coming off a hot and humid afternoon on the water, and especially after a three day canyon run for game fish, but the *Paradise's* shower wasn't fit for a sardine. Marina showers are notoriously the best things about the marina, unless, of course, they also have a bar. Ours didn't have any.

My hair got long, my beard took hold, my muscles hardened and my skin browned. Some weeks I felt that a stranger couldn't tell me apart from my Seminole buddy Wiley, except he towered over me by a head and a chin. Cramming that body, or Wiley's especially, into the shower on the *Paradise* was never a preferred occupation.

It was the life. And I don't think there are nicer people than those who regularly inhabit a marina. There happens to be more people who live aboard boats than you'd image, though they are often transient and many times never seen again once they leave the dock.

Living aboard with Wiley was another thing that my Cape Fear season offered lessons in. The Queen Mary wasn't big enough for those two people to live on full time, especially as we were essentially two full-grown boys committed to that disrespect for propriety I've mentioned. We barely managed not killing each other by the time we made the Keys.

He knew a captain on Largo, Wills, who had no fear of added competition who wanted to hole up in a marina that had a bad reputation regarding *keeping* charter boats, especially once he got a look at me. That's where we went. That's where we stayed.

And that's where I rapidly made a deal with the owner of a small resort made of cabins, huts and RVs called the Hungry Pelican. I made sure Wiley got his own place to live. And on my dime.

I found a house for myself, got customers who'd had it fishing with Captain Wills, the meanest waterman since Blackbeard, and started up a pretty good living.

I've strayed off my point again, but back story has its place.

It's the friendliness inherent in marina life that I want to bring to light. It helps in explaining that unexpected company in a marina is not like unexpected company on land.

Best thing about marina neighbors is that they can pick up their houses and change the neighborhood by moving on. Whoever takes their spot brings a new dynamic to the harbors. And just about every boater soon learns that the one thing a harbor must have is Friendliness, or their marina home becomes a Hell Hole one must get out of, fast.

Not that there aren't assholes. But a marina can tolerate no more than one permanent asshole, and maybe only a temporary one. We already had Wills. So anyone coming into the harbor had to bring their A-game of neighborliness with them, and everybody already in the harbor knew that the mat was always down for whatever stranger stopped by to call in, 'Hey, Captain, okay to come aboard?'

That's what the Wilkinses did there in the marina that June and I wanted to get drunk in.

Meet Kate and Benedict Wilkins, unexpected company.

You'll never guess what they wanted to talk about.

Six

'Hey, Cap, nice boat.' We marina people accept all kinds of compliments, but we like that one the best. The man who'd said it, Benedict — *y'all call me Bennie* — Wilkins wore almost the uniform of Florida marina junkies who are over a certain age: very faded blue and tan plaid Bermudas, broken down docksiders with the untied leather tassels constantly slipping under the thoroughly worn soles, an inside-out college sweatshirt repeatedly hauled back down over an alpha-male belly, the sleeves sliced off about a hundred washings ago, and a hat.

No right thinking harbor rat would ever wear a cap that had gold braid on it, or even the crossed macramé signifying *Hey, ain't I nautical?* No, he wore a Florida Gator's ball cap. Perfect.

Kate, 'Just Kate,' Wilkins however, was obviously a housewife whose either third or fourth husband was a fellow who owned a boat. Her clamdiggers, white of course, left to the night air and one's quickly turned-away-eye those mottled matchstick shins of a sixty-something grandmother of twenty, her legs carrying more blue lines over the course of them than did a map of Connecticut. Her blouse was blue sailor suit, an ornament I am sure she felt was a concession to His Nauticalness's fetish for all things gunkholey. The thin reddish-blonde hair, which hadn't ever been at any time naturally red nor naturally blonde, looked teased and sprayed by some gal named Flo. And don't get me started on those lipsticked lips and *I Ain't No Waitress Red* fingernails.

Which meant he was hearty, and she was saccharine, and both had long become bored with the other's conversation but were already too old to do anything about it. That mutual boredom had sent them nightly to prowl for folks who'd never heard any of Bennie's stories nor Kate's mild but barbed putdowns of the storyteller.

Us, in other words.

'Thanks,' June said, 'I'm glad you like it. Care for a drink?' My sweet lass was not sufficiently enough harbor-housed or she would have recognize that she had just invited aboard our *Sweet Discourse* the Old Man and Old Lady of the Sea.

In the tales of Sinbad the Sailor, The Old Man of the Sea wraps his legs around Sinbad's neck with the firmness of iron bands, refusing ever to let go until he had satisfied himself. He never satisfied himself. Sinbad had to nearly drown himself to get free of the old man.

And so they came aboard.

I worried I'd have to drown them. Only way was leave the marina, get into deeper water, open the sea cocks and let the *Discourse* burble its way to the bottom. I was not prepared to do that. Happened to one of my boats already, and it broke my heart. Besides, Wiley would be pissed.

'Beer?'

'No, no,' said Bennie. 'Off sauce twenny four years now.'

'Anything harder?' said Kate.

Amazingly what little details reveal.

But it wasn't all that bad. Bennie was a retired developer from down in Fort Myers, one of those infectious con artists who'd raped that lovely bit of Gulf Coast real estate with uncontrolled and over-priced housing, selling mostly to suckers from the States who started the Union. Hear him tell it, he started selling before there was a Union.

'Hell, son, I sold Lincoln's daddy his log cabin. However ancient you figger I am, yer off. Yer can add twenny years an' yer still wrong. Put thutty on her an' yer closer, but yer ain't close.'

Kate, twice widowed thanks to industrial cancers, once divorced because of that bedroom community cancer, Adultery, had worked for the telephone company as a telephone operator, when there were telephone operators. She liked beer. Liked harder better, but beer we offered, so beer she liked. In fact, she liked most of a sixpack.

Bennie liked cigars, had cigars and offered me one, *fer the hospitality.* I said, 'don't mind if I do.' What he handed across was the kind that had to be smuggled onto the mainland by a sea captain buddy who had the ability to go where most people didn't want to go. I would have preferred to have seated on my stern that guy. But I had Bennie, and his cigar.

As boat dock conversations go, watermen and their women soon divide into two conversations, and I was spending so much time not listening to Bennie that I found myself drifting from our chitchat to the feminine, especially after I overheard Kate at one point mention the local, recent suicide.

'Damn fool kids think suicide'll help anything. Life's hard, supposed to be. Else why else live it?'

I interjected, stopping mid-yarn Big Boat Bennie, 'What suicide?'

But it was Bennie answered for her. 'Yer ain't heard there was a stupid nigger kid hung hisself in a tree yestiddy?'

'No. Didn't hear a thing.' I shook my head, June just looked down. I recognized that she might have been the one who'd brought the topic into the conversation, and I'd just fox-pawed on her. Kate didn't seem to have noticed, though.

'Was this boy took a rope and went inna the woods and hanged himself. A real shame, I hear. We heard a him, too, boy from back inland. Played baseball real good.' She shrugged her knobby little shoulders. 'Who knows why.'

'Sure it was a suicide?'

Kate glared at me. 'Sure it was a suicide? Of course it was a suicide. Who'd hang up a poor colored boy these days?'

Bennie, after a hundred years of matrimony and therefore probably knowing what fired his wife's cylinders, injected, 'Doesn't matter. It'll be a suicide and stay a suicide, Beautop bein' sheriff.'

June looked at Bennie. 'What's that mean?'

'Old Beau don't like niggers, don't give a bilge water barnacle what they do. Easier he gets 'em off his paperwork, faster he gets back to whate'er whore'll pour him a scotch.'

'Benedict, you watch your mouth. You see these people are educated? They deserve better. You don't call colored people that word.'

Bennie looked like he wanted off the wagon. I commiserated. Seemed he had a set of iron legs around his own neck.

'You mean to tell me that still goes on around here? Burying the truth, denying justice?'

I shot June a look that said *Keep it cool, we're here to hear, not speak.* She got the message, but not before Bennie chastised her for her birthplace. 'Yer a Yankee girl. This here's still Jackson country. Is, was, gonna be. We learn t' keep back a piece from brush fires. They've a way of leaping onto yer property y'ain't careful.'

'He don't mean exactly you, honey. But poking in one's hooter into the wrong shallows, well, you better leave that to the cranes. Took me a while learning that too, but you see it's just, after a while.'

Change of subject. Me? Agent of Change. 'So how long you and Kate been married?'

'About seven years, right honey? Right after I started that god damn Cypress Gardens mess.'

Now that sounded interesting. I remember seeing a tilted, faded sign on our way to and again back from that shattered picnic the day before. It had Homes in Cypress Gardens on it. Florida's littered with all kinds of signs like that, especially inland and on blacktopped roads one hardly has a need to turn off onto. *If you believe that, I got land for sale in Florida* became a common phrase because of those common signs.

'What happened there?'

All Ben had wanted to talk about earlier, excepting the aberrant trip onto the Willa Maes' suicide, was boats and fish until I asked that question. Having done so, I got to watch what had been a witless water rat turn into a cut-loose python that could swallow hogs, horses and little men whole back in the day. Maybe it was the slight slitting of his eyes, maybe the hiss suddenly in his sibilants, maybe it was the constrictor-like movements of his forefinger curving over his Cuban cigar, but whatever it was it made my skin tighten a little more.

'I 'da sweet deal, found a clause in an old deed practically let me have fer free one good-size chunk of good, dry land out near where them nig... black folk got their church. They thought the dirt under it was deeded to 'em, but it wasn't. Deeded to an old Indian' — yes, he pronounced it *injin* — 'tribe by some land agent feller hunnert anna haf years back.'

Wiley and I had many talks about the Seminole Wars. He may be uneducated, but he wasn't stupid, and one of the things he understood as thoroughly as he knew boats was the wretched history of the Seminoles of Florida. 'Never beat, Cap'n. Never.' That's a mark of their pride, although there had been an 'Indian Repatriation' movement that shuffled many of his ancestral cousins out of Florida and into Oklahoma and Texas, where most are today. Repatriation had been started by General Andrew Jackson, who always had been referred to by Wiley as 'that bastid Jackson.' The US eventually spent forty million trying to defeat and move out what amounted to a small town's worth of native Americans.

'I thought I had everything good on that deed, which was illegal in the government's eyes, until they came up with a nigger, well, God damn it, Kate, he was, who could claim a direct line straight back to old Abiaka himself.'

June didn't know Abiaka, but of course I did. I had gone to Wiley Seminole History school. I relayed one of my mate's proudly-repeated lessons, 'Abiaka was probably more important than Oceola, the one tourists think of as the greatest Seminole. But it was Abiaka, and Wiley says he's related. I can tell you about him later. This land deal, Ben, interesting.'

June is so smart, and she has seen me take command of what seemed idle chitchat before. It was the old cop in me, and she picked up on the fact that I wanted the old coot talking about this land. My nose said there was trouble dividing black from white, and I thought I'd found a place to put my finger on it. And June, being smart, got it. When I said I found the land deal interesting, she set up my slam.

'You would be.'

Ben's serpent-eye rolled toward me, 'Why zat, kid?'

June again. 'He loves land. He craves it. He has more worthless plots of dirt up and down...'

'They're not worthless, Hon,' I shot back, 'not by a long shot. You see, Ben, I realized a long time ago that there was pirate treasure buried all over Florida, but it wasn't treasure buried in the dirt. It was the dirt.'

'Yer got that right. I say same thing myself, don't I, Kate? So yer likin' land, huh? I got some in Florida…' he didn't even need to finish before we were all laughing. I had petted the snake, and it was about to curl up in my lap.

'Another beer, Kate?'

'I guess.'

Eleven years ago Benedict Wilkins sat in a bar waiting while he had to get a tire fixed. He'd come off the road for a refreshing soft drink, as the day was late, the sun hot, and the negotiations for a parcel of difficult land had not gone well. That bar at three was nearly empty, and the one thing a traveler can count on in a near-empty bar is a chat with the bartender, especially if you are a stranger to those parts, as Ben had been.

We tell strangers much more than we tell companions, buddies, even wives. Ben talked about the broken down development deal that earned him the flat tire, and mention of buying land prompted the barkeep to talk. The subject? His wife's brother, Sam, who was a sad case owner of about sixteen square miles of land. 'Said might be worth my while. He din't have money to do nuthin' with it, so's I says maybe you could help him out an' I'll help you out. I slipped the fella a fifty. He'd said Sam'd probably sell just to get the ex off his back.'

It was the very land the Southern Baptist church and baseball field had been built on.

'Kinda kookie, the bartender feller was white and his wife was a… black girl. A little kookie, but Florida backcountry people got a way of overlooking unusual. What the Hell, man can do whatever he wants. He wants a colored wife, that's his bed. Just ain't mine.' That Ben had a taste of land he could steal from an ignorant black scrounging a hardscrabble living out of those very woods was sugar on his serpentine tongue.

The problem for him was, the man wasn't exactly black. He was a good part Seminole, more than a quarter. And it was the ancestor who had passed on the quarter part who also passed on the deed to her favorite grandson Sam, the man Ben had to deal with. Buying Seminole land isn't like buying an undeveloped Kansas cornfield. They have their own laws, and rules.

'Took four years to work out a deal with that man, who had a son same name who'd been seventeen around the time. But didn't see the boy for years, ex wouldn't let him unless he paid support, which he didn't, probably couldn't. The boy, yer see, was in love, like young people get, with his goddam Seminole heritage. But the boy, them laws, couldn't be a Seminole.'

Kate, despite her fifth beer, chimed in fairly knowledgably. 'Back in around '57 the Seminoles created something called the Base Roll, a genealogy or record of who got to be Seminole, who got treaty rights. Seems a ton of blue-eyed hippies from Minnesota or New Jersey kept looking all over for some claim to being one of them Noble Savages, and it was gummin' up this and that.'

Back to Bennie. 'Tribe put up a blood quantum, like the niggers up in…'

'Goddam it, Benjamin. And you ain't even drinking.'

'Jeesus, folks. Sorry, all I meant was like they do up in New Orleans, I think, still do. A blood quantum, what says no one not a quarter at least of Seminole could claim it. And it hadda be documented.' Bennie looked apologetically at his wife. She had the bit-down corners of her lips that said, *I married a cultureless idjit.* 'The document that boy needed providing tribal membership to was that deed. After all the negotiation, I find out it wasn't Sam's property. It was Seminole tribal land. Time I got my hands on that land grant, kid was old enough and smart enough to get the Seminoles behind him, and sue. Tied things up right nice.'

Kate added, 'Worse, it stirred up them black people who built the church, because their properties, some of them, got built illegally on what they thought was their land.'

'Ownership a dirt in Florida ain't always clear-cut.'

She nodded at what he said, which got us to nodding.

'Ownership a the court, however, is.' Bennie's smile was pure rattlesnake.

'One good thing come out a that snafu is finding this here marina. We been coming here, what? Last five years? We live up the coast, pretty re'glar now, but most weekends, here, sometimes weeks at a time. We're reg'lars here now, and pretty much townies, we know so many people.'

'That case settle?' I asked.

'Getting' close, and we'll win. But I sunk all the money I'm gonna sink in it. It's young folks like you's gonna see the profit. I'm done. It settles, I'll get a fair chunk and some back for Kate here. But I got my boat and house. I'm satisfied.'

I bet he was. Still, that 'young folks' phrase put a notion in my head, as I am sure which was what Bennie wanted. Offered me a cover and a reason to get my snoot into local business. Who knows who I might meet?

'You think there's still chunks to be had?' I gave my best Fool and his Money Soon Parted look.

'There's some'll want a say, but sure, some pieces, sure.' *Did a Land Pirate Snake named Ben Wilkins just hiss with pleasure?*

June just rolled her eyes. She did that a lot.

Seven

But June had more she wanted done than just a roll of her eyes. What she wanted was justice for Willa Maes, and like all Yankee liberals what she wanted was a conflict-free Paradise wherever she hung her hat. To get that she felt strongly she had to bring a boy she never met the justice he deserved. She might have had a crusader's heart, but I had a southern living waterman's experience, and I was not so assured of justice ever happening. I made the mistake, after the Wilkinses had gone and we slid ourselves between sheets, of saying so.

Hit a nerve. 'Then what's the use?'

Wasn't sure I was in the best frame of mine to defend the status quo, beer for beer with unfazable Kate Wilkins, but I gave it a try. 'I just mean things change slowly where change isn't constant. You've lived in New York. Change there is not only tolerated, it's expected. Menu doesn't change one week to the next, people go find another restaurant. Here, grits and greens still made the way Mammy made them while the Marster was out back burying the family silver. Just means these people settled on the way they might not want it, but could get it, and it'll stay that way regardless of our meddling.'

'Meddling? You call it that?'

I could barely see out of the grave I was digging for myself. 'To them, sure, that's what we're doing. I feel like you do, it's the right thing. And I am not going to quit because of some back-assed ways people have, but because I do feel the way you do. I just don't know where it'll all lead, and I don't expect it'll lead where you want it to just because you want it. I don't want you to get your hopes up too high, that's all.'

'Well, my hopes are up high. And theirs should be too. I don't understand why they don't want to know who did this to one of their own.'

Wasn't until later, June almost asleep and me staring again at the holey fabric of the headliner, that I recognized that even in what she had just then said there was the *Us* and *Them*. Roots to that go way deep.

'I don't think that's the case either, Hon. I just think they want to handle things their way and in their own time. We might be bucking a system they've worked out over a century or two.'

I knew it was an argument without end, so rather than discuss what could happen I brought up what would happen.

'Tomorrow we're going to school.'

A person can respond to a sentence from left field in many ways, but when the person is angry, the person tends to stay angry. I think that's one of Newton's thermodynamic laws. She barked, 'What the Hell are you talking about? School?'

'Kid dies, it's school where the response is most likely to be. Willa Maes was a school standout, and white or black, I'm sure he was more liked than not. Some of the kids might have been jealous of his ability, but more than most would have been glad for him getting out, especially those smart enough for college, but so damn poor college may as well have been Tierra del Fuego. And from what Wiley and Davis said, the kid was a good kid. It's going to hit his schoolmates hard, if there's even one who hasn't heard about it. Regardless, it's going to be the topic on the lips of admins and teachers. Nothing scares an adult more than the inflated emotions of teenagers, because that makes the kids unpredictable. So we're going there to see the *what what*.'

A bit more amplification of what I had in mind, a few mollifying kisses, another beer for me and the night calmed to a decent finish. Except, of course, I couldn't sleep, thinking. Everything I had thought, though, was everything I've already said, so not going to repeat it.

We both dressed in the better clothes we had packed for dinners with Watt and Annigail once we hit New Orleans, recognizing that the likelihood of actually joining them becoming less and less. We hopped in the rented car and drove to town. The regional high was on the northern, whiter, edge of the school district, and as there not being a lot of major roads in that county, so there was hardly any need to ask directions. Besides, the car had a built-in GPS.

We arrived before first bell, which normally would have sent kids scurrying from homerooms, but wouldn't that morning. I had learned about the changes to the normal bell schedule after taking a gander at their web page back on the *Sweet Discourse's* computer system, so our arrival was exactly timed to take advantage of the disruption. Trying to break into a normal routine in some place as calcified as a public high school would have earned us blank stares and soured expressions from the staff.

What the web page already had on it was a declaration about honoring Willa Maes, an event for which I wanted to be present. So, all students would be shuffled into the school's cavernous auditorium first period after homeroom.

That homeroom period hadn't changed since my dad was in school. Kids in their seat for roll call, which was now done from laptops, rolls no longer being used. However, there was the same crackling loudspeaker calling everyone to stand for the pledge. We were in the office selling ourselves as a pretty senior girl intoned in measured, rehearsed cadence, *I pledge allegiance...*

Officious office people hate to have their routine interrupted, especially unexpectedly, and June and I were more than interruptions. We looked like parents, the worst kind of visitors in a high school, the least wanted. *In locus parentis* meant no loco parents to them.

We were approached immediately, but suspiciously, by a middle aged woman who probably had a kid or two still in that school.

'Hello, we're the van Hijs, and we're moving to the coast of Florida, and thinking of here.' I saw the slightest raise to one June eyebrow. 'We were hoping for a chance to see the school.'

'Not a good day,' she said.

'Oh dear,' came from June, 'we're only here today. We are on our boat, and we're expected in New Orleans later today. Just stopped in yesterday, but of course there was no one to call, and well, you see we'd really like to see the school so we could have something to tell our children, a boy and a girl, you see, senior and sophomore...'

June had chatted to the end of pledge, when she found herself interrupted by the woman who showed her the palm to her right hand. 'Hold on.' She looked over to her shoulder at the senior handing over the microphone to a well-coiffed woman in high heels who had the most officious manner of anyone within sight. I assumed the principal, and I had assumed rightly.

She snatched the microphone from the child almost as if she expected sticky-jelly fingerprints. Not a single eyeball for us, though. 'Attention, children, this is Mrs. Anderson, your principal.' The officious dwell in the obvious and expected. I had to chuckle. My principal had felt it necessary to remind us of who he was every time he spoke. 'Immediately after homeroom you are to attend a special meeting in the auditorium, seniors to file first, C wing followed by D. Then Juniors, etc.' My *et cetera,* of course. As Mrs. Anderson droned, I summoned back the attention of the clerk who'd strayed from us.

'We'd like to attend that. We're willing to stand in the back. Then maybe when it's done we could visit some of the classes?'

'This isn't a good day.'

'Seems like any normal day to me,' I said. Good cop, bad cop, *action.* 'We're only here a day. Maybe we'll ask the principal...'

'She won't, she'll just, you wait I'll ask her.'

Parents do not understand how much power they have over school administrators of every level. Wicked power, all deriving from the fear of lawsuits. June and I just smiled. That's a far more frightening countenance than an angry face. Anger might smash a few rocks, but Patience will tear down the Grand Tetons.

And so we got into the auditorium.

I suspected the classification system had also not changed, and I was right. Seniors up front, juniors next, and so on, teachers standing like unarmed prison guards at the end of every third aisle, some actually holding tissue boxes, just in case. One thing you have to say for teachers, female ones at least, they are the most attuned people to the various moods of varying children of anyone on the planet. Unfortunately, no one listens to them, at least no one in the front office.

On stage, composed at a podium, rattled the vapid principal, while beside but behind her hung a truly distraught middle-aged man with his head down and hands clasped. I took him to be Willa's coach. On a seat too small for him was the police representative, the worst kind of rep, a slovenly, mean-eyed, superior John Wayne who had a love of fascism evidenced in every gesture. Finally, there were several others, all but one looking confused at why they were on stage. The one who did not, I recognized as that pastor who'd come with Wiley onto my boat Saturday evening.

I pointed him out to June, who nodded, accepting my suggestion we keep in the shadows. I didn't want him spotting our glowing faces.

June's nails bit into my forearm with every mention of suicide. This was harder for her than I expected. I'd noticed that opposite were three dark men, the janitors, listening intently, every now and then shaking their heads back and forth.

They interested me, but I had expected them. I couldn't imagine that they suffered the concluded career of the young ball player any better than June did, and for other reasons, maybe they suffered worse. But years of practice hid their despairs from all but the most observant and understanding.

What I wanted to see was not so easy to spot, so I tugged on June to stay put while I inched closer to the senior rows down front. I scanned the heads. Just off center aisle were two white, and whitened, boys who kept their eyes locked forward, but above the proscenium. Why they did seemed obvious to me. The farthest one, a dark-haired kid of seventeen, who looked like he'd been shaving since the third grade, or at least his second repeat of the third, something about him felt familiar. But I couldn't then say why.

Beside the two who worked overtime trying not to be part of the enforced attention to what I knew was a crime, was a good looking, sandy haired kid who had the glow of good health that came from access to sufficient nutrition. As an undergrad I had to teach a semester in a high school, student teaching, and it was there that I recognized the single greatest factor separating kids who did academically well from those who did not was the nutrition factor. The 'A' kids were always taller, healthier, and oftentimes fatter, than those destined to serve the A kids their burgers and fries.

Anyway, the good looking kid sat upright, attentive to everything being said at the podium, which was then being gripped by the white knuckled coach near to tears. Curiously, but not surprisingly, the boy was smiling. That smile gave me my clearest, cleanest emotion in a long time, which was the urge to punch the kid in the face. Sometimes you just know, and at that moment I just knew, I was not looking on innocence.

Equally expected was the girl beside him. Not expected, though, was how she kept cold distance between herself and the boyfriend, which he obviously had to be.

As I watched those four, I wondered which of them had tied a left-handed double half over a clove hitch. My money went straight on Goldilocks.

A teacher stood next to me, a man who exuded bored indifference to what was going on. Pretty sure he maintained the same indifference to his profession, and certainly to anything his wards might want. One of those pricky, passive-aggressive, shit-eating wannabee writers who definitely kept a small collection of electric guitars in his basement just waiting to be dragged out into thunderous applause on a stadium so that his rock-and-roll screamers could send forth adulation. I leaned toward him and said, 'All this for some kid didn't think his life worth it.'

He eyed me suspiciously. I knew how to grin as a like-minded cynic. He bit. 'No big loss.' That took even me aback, but then he said, 'Gets me out of class.'

'Heard he played a mean game of baseball.'

'Kid's fastball clocked over ninety. Yeah, you could say good. Where you from?'

'Philly.'

He shook his head oh-so-knowingly, like he'd been there. Probably not since a school trip to the Liberty Bell, if ever. 'Thought so. From not here, I mean. You'd've known.'

'I spotted that kid down there, third in from center, third row back. He's a ball player too.'

'Yeah. How'd you...'

I shrugged myself a little taller. 'Played myself, made Triple A for the Phils. Blew out my knee. Catcher. Means I can spot a pitcher anywhere. Am I right?'

'You are.' Nothing impresses a wannabe like a person with a real career. Not that I ever really caught a pitch. 'Ronnie Perks. Not so good, and a bigger shit. He's a better quarterback. I'm sure he's glad Maes hung himself. That kind of shit.'

'Got himself a hot girlfriend.'

'Hot ain't the word.' There are a few truly off-limits topics that even a crappy teacher avoids, and one of them is to talk with a parent about the sexuality of a student. Might be a parent himself, maybe even Daddy to the Hottie. Bad Rock Star Teacher recognized he'd brushed the line. He turned away from me as the principal, finishing up with a dab at a non-existent tear not gathering at her eye, stepped back to the mic to brush aside the coach. 'Now, a moment of prayer. Reverend?'

My old acquaintance Pastor Something or Other, I still didn't catch his weirdly pronounced last name, took the spotlight. *This ought to be good.*

I could tell the man sensed the almost complete split of white to black faces in the audience. He instinctively saw his only two choices, go black, or go white. His choice wasn't an honest one.

I knew he didn't buy suicide, but he sure sold it, and all the attendant Holy Evils that go with it. I decided not to like him.

Heard enough. I got a name, would have preferred the girlfriend's. I edged back up to June, gave her a nod, and that couple wanting a look-see at the Regional High unexpectedly, and happily for all concerned, disappeared.

Once she and I cleared the door, June raised issue with something I'd done. 'Mr. and Mrs. van Hij?'

'It popped out. I didn't want to spring my last name on you, and I didn't want to use Kingswood without checking first. It just popped into my head. But it brings up an interesting point. Who are we, here?'

'The Nolans. Anybody checks up on you, at least you are real.'

'Who'd check up on us? And how?'

She loaded up her official face. 'Excuse me, but may I see your ID? That's how. I can always claim just married and haven't changed over yet.'

I suppose any man broaching any part of that circumstance which required conjoining names has the same gut-queasy feeling I then had. We'd been together in the same house for almost a year, and things were nice, but I'm not one to presume much. Anyway, June seemed unaffected.

So, I had one name, Ronnie Perks, and a clear association with three kids I felt sure had names that I was going to find out. My gut pointed to Goldilocks as *a person of interest* merely because I suspected Willa Maes had been done in by several people his own age. If the strenuous avoidance of the two boys — who had concentrated their attentions on the proscenium woodwork over the principal's head — hadn't convinced me, that smile on Perks had.

Since I also had thought the hanging party had to be more than two, that group of four fit my profile like a cookie slipped back into the cutter.

Wish I'd never seen the smug grin on Perks' face.

Ugly.

Eight

Meanwhile, back at the ranch, or rather back in the marina, there was an itchy fellow overly stimulated by the prospect that a sucker had announced himself as ready for plucking. He spied June and me as soon as our rental turned into the lot.

Before I get to Bennie Running Fast, let me say one thing about that marina: it struck me again how peculiarly empty it was. Springtime in southern marinas, even on the steamy Gulf Coast of Florida, always have boats in them either ready to come out of the water, or to go in. Not often was there a need to yank a boat out just because the owners won't be around until next season. There were maybe six cars any given time we were there, but when we arrived there was just two of them. One I knew had to be Bennie's. A man who spent his life tooling around in a car will always buy one of those dino-sized beasts with wide leather seats. The other was equally expensive but far less comfortable. Had the look of money on it.

That marina had four full sections where boats could tie up either for the night, a week, the season or the year. Two of those sections hadn't so much as a drowned dinghy in their slips. That was peculiar, but this marina was in Nowhereville. Still, there was something wrong with the picture.

Anyway, Bennie, in the same faded Bermudas and wrecked sweatshirt he'd worn the day before, huffed his way over to meet us, big grin on his little face, hand stuck forward, a wink and a howdee for June. I put my metaphoric hand on my literal wallet.

'Yer all are sticking around today, ain'tcha?'

'We like it here. We're due to meet my sister in New Orleans, but we got time. What's up?'

'Yer was serious about maybe doing some development?' I didn't say yes immediately, I was afraid Bennie might pee himself. I frowned, though, and squeezed June's hand. Pretty sure she frowned as well.

I said, 'I'm always serious about land. You're not talking about that six square, are you?'

He almost danced like a bear, if teddy bears danced. 'I am. And I am going to set yers up with some people, well, one, actually, first. Won't be hard, he's up in the office now. But I gotta know if yer serious. And by knowin' what I mean by serious, I mean yer better have the shekels.'

I learned a little something about business from my father, who had owned a few printing shops and a world-class lithographers up in Philly. And I had learned a whole lot from my immensely wealthy brother-in-law, Watkins van Hij, whose name I'd purloined back at the regional high. Both of my educators had a simple dictum about business: *find a man who wants something and charge him money to get it.* Sounds simple, and is, more often than not. But Watt put a twist on my Dad's version, which he said always worked: *find a desperate man and he'll pay you anything to rid himself of the desperation.*

What June and I saw dancing before us on the dock was a man who wanted something. On the surface it was my money. But something didn't strike me as exactly a direct line from my wallet to his pocket. Bennie showed more than eagerness, he smelled of desperation. Hid it well, no sweat on his brow, but the dance and jog over to meet us had an urgency that shouted out *Bouncing Bennie wants off the hook*, whatever that hook was, wherever that hooked had snagged him.

He was practically begging me to set one of my own in his jaw. But did I want to?

I had had in the back of my mind that Bennie might be useful to developing a cover for our sticking around the marina, and this was promising, but entering into a backroom deal might also be a big distraction from what we were really interested in working.

June had pointed that out as we readied for bed the evening before. I didn't want to blow the opportunity for a cover, but I also didn't expect him to be ready to exact my entrance fee first thing the following morning.

I had to put him off, but not let him slip the hook entirely. One tugs the bait ever so slightly.

'I have shekels plenty. You've seen my boat. But I have to see spreadsheets before I commit anything. And we've already made plans for this afternoon. Set it up for…' and then he set his own hook.

'Ricky Perks's ready and waiting just t'there, over to the office. Come on, he's a great guy. Won't take but a minute to shake a guy's hand, right? Two minutes, maybe five. Just to crack the ice.'

Perks.

Familiar name.

'Sure, what's five? Perks, you say?' June gave me her curiosity look. I'd forgotten to mention a certain name once we'd left the auditorium, so she couldn't get my ready interest in Perks. My head nod sent her on back to the *Sweet Discourse*.

Bustin' Bennie spent a few seconds more than may have been polite watching her walk away, but watching June from the back was never something I could tear myself from, so I cut him some slack.

He spun on his heel. 'C'mon.'

Ricky Perks. The socially anti-social. Why does the universe keep churning out guys like him? I smelled bully as soon as I walked into his office, had no difficulty picturing him shoving a waterboy into a locker, or asking a homely girl to be a prom date only to leave her waiting for him to show up. The Ricky Perkses of the world are the piss in the punchbowl.

Although it was I who had been invited, he looked up at me like I just farted over his lunch. Poached egg eyeballs, a whiskey-made nose, lips that looked like they'd been better off on a junkyard dog.

70

I guess you could say I took an instant dislike, but if I hadn't, once he smiled I felt a lifelong skeeve move into my attitude closet. Same smile as good-looking Junior's. Still, I donned my own Heya smile, thrust forward my hand for reception by what I was certain would closely resemble a fresh placenta. I wasn't far off.

Bobbing Bennie did the intros. 'Heza one I told yers about, with the new boat and all.'

Ricky Perks had a unique ability to let the gleam in his eyes go back and forth, like the highlight in a robot's visor. Then came that smile. 'Never saw that make. What is it?'

'An *Henriques,* from Jersey. New in the water half a year.'

'Custom?'

'Of course. But it's a model. There are others.' I almost felt that talking to him about the *Sweet Discourse* got unremovable crud on her hull. But I digress, or rather I think that point has been made. Pushing on. 'Although I do a charter with her out of Largo, she's my tax write-off. I'm sure you know how that works.'

He leaned forward, elbows on desk, fingers intertwined, glint in eyes going *zoom* left, *zoom* right. 'Yeah. I'm all about tax write-offs.'

'Bennie here tells me there's a big square of dirt with opportunities that should be growing on it. Anybody allowed to pick from that field?' *Gardening metaphors, Drew?*

'Not just anybody. Person's got to have the right boots to walk land down here in Florida. But,' he said, glancing out of the window that looked down on the boat slips, 'Docksiders might do fine.'

He tapped the requisite flat humidor on his desk, offering. But I declined, though it was not an easy turn-down. I do like nice cigars. I suspected he kept the same stockman for cigars that Bennie had. Anyway, he shrugged and left the box unopened. 'So why you want on my land?'

'Obvious reasons. But mostly because I love land. I have plots up and down the thirteen colonies, and a few from here. Ocala, mostly, but some swampland I got for a song after Andrew and Hugo got done giving them a bath. Part of the reason I'm headed to Orleans. Dirt is still dirt cheap, I hear. Gotta love hurricanes.'

He leaned back. Obviously I was playing Golden Oldies to the man, and he knew the notes well. Actually, the idea of making dough off of poor people further decimated by those storms was repugnant. There'd been a wholesale ripoff in the boat industry after those storms went through, people selling hulls for a song. But, in for a penny, in for a pound, although I think I may be misapplying that notion.

'We'll see, Mr...' he raised his eyebrows. I reminded him. 'Right, Mr. Nolan. We'll see. What I am most interested in is what you back things up with.'

I gave him a long, thoughtful look. For all his wheeling and dealing, he was an amateur at negotiations. Grilling a perp was as much negotiation as anything, and it was one thing I had been good at. I knew from experience that Perks' *ad hominem,* his Docksiders/boots suggestion that I appeared insubstantial, would require a response. We were already in a tussle.

I weighed, though, whether I wanted the man to feel himself shoved back against the ropes, needing to defend himself. The best defense against attack is to refuse to acknowledge any blows as having landed effectively. And sometimes the best offense is often to show that, by not coming back in an attack, you could, you would if provoked, and would win, painfully.

No desk is without a pen and a scratch pad, but I did not see one. I knew he'd have both somewhere, so I asked. He gave. I took the pen and wrote one name on the small square of notepad. *Watkins van Hij.* I then slid the loaned items back towards him.

My brother-in-law, as I said, was rich as he needed to be. More importantly, though a fairly quiet man about his power, he knew that its most effective use was in how others supposed it. That name rippled through financial markets all over the world, let alone the east coast. If Perks didn't know it, he would know it.

Either case, he did not reveal what he knew. His mechanical glance at what I had penned told me nothing, except that there was no need for further discussion regarding either my interests or my access to shekels. Burstin' Bennie fidgeted like there had better be a toilet in his near future.

I stood. 'More later?'

'There is always that possibility.' I had to take hold of the placenta paw once more. But that time his handshake had some muscle in it. My own ain't no old lady's, and I met his squish with my squash. There went that junkyard dog smile again.

How he managed it I do not know, but Bennie stayed quiet the whole walk back to the *Discourse*. His boat was beyond mine. As I turned to my finger dock running along the starboard side, I thought to simply bid him *Afternoon*. But time had a ripeness to it, and I thought a swift blade under his chin might just lift his head off enough to get him to speak plainly and straight. 'He's got you by the short and curlies, doesn't he?'

Buffaloed Bennie almost lied, but he saw I was not a stupid man. I had been playing a kind of stupid until then, but no longer. Jerked him up like I suspected it would. 'Yeah. But it's ain't so bad. I can still get a piece out, if things go. I got a few more friends in business than just him, and they're bluefins compared to that piker. But I do have a bit of coin tied up in the deal. He's getting a lion's share just to help me shake it back loose.'

'How's it work?'

Just then, probably from having heard my voice, June poked her head out of the forward hatch cover. I couldn't see her, but I could hear her. 'Hey, you two want something cold?'

I could see that Baleful Bennie not only wanted something stronger than a sarsaparilla, he needed one. And maybe one with a fifth of whiskey chaser.

He followed me into the salon. I wondered if the laser-eyed confidence man up in his office had turned his eyebeams onto the two of us then disappearing behind a closed door. *Screw him if he was watching.*

June joined us, and I had to take a second or two filling her in. During that, I could see Ben Wilkins, sans booze, needed a moment or two to himself, for reflection and projection, before dumping his heap on us. June took me aside to ask questions about the meeting, which I answered, leading her to ask, 'Think you can handle him?'

The question could have been as much for Ben to consider as for myself. The old man had probably conceived himself a consummate deal broker, but Perks had broken that. I knew the layout. Ben had been the homely Prom girl waiting for the doorbell to ring, and worse, he'd paid for the tickets. I wondered if he had everything tied into the situation.

'I know enough when to put on the brakes, things begin to stink.' I turned to my guest. 'Think I'll need brakes riding with Perks?'

His faced said it all, however the say-anything-but-get-the-deal history of the man put the lie to his lips. 'Nah, it'll be fine.'

I didn't care. Not like I was actually going to buy land in Florida. I wasn't born yesterday.

'So how's this work?' June asked.

But I had my own form of the question. 'So how's this really going to work?'

Bennie laid it out superficially at first, but June had her own history. She'd been an Uncle Sam tax investigator with a law degree to boot. A lawyer *and* an accountant. It's a wonder I ever let her into my tent.

She said, 'I suppose he wants to develop the land for housing, or whatever?'

Bennie smiled at her. 'Ricky Perks doesn't develop, he siphons. Soon as all this closes, he'll get a developer in who'll make money for Ricky, and they'll lay a pipeline down that'll flow cashola towards him like a sewer.'

June frowned.

'Let me explain it better. Yers noticed not many boats, right?'

We both nodded.

'What yer don't see is this marina's full of boats. Almost completely full.'

Now we more than frowned. We looked at one another. 'You seeing ghosts, Ben?'

'I see exactly that. Back when Perks was a kid this was a fishing hole, trawlers and shrimpers here, no yachts. Perks was the mechanic, and while he worked for the old owner he had a deal, there's always a deal with Perks, haulin' old hulls so he could rip the guts out of them. Started his own parts yard inland, getting the niggers to haul out what he couldn't resell and burn it in their woods.'

'So he made his bones in a junkyard?'

'Hell no. Once the niggers,' he saw June's expression, 'sorry, y'all. Habits of an old swamp stomper. Anyway, once they got going on it, he let 'em keep the business. Old parts is a filthy business, he said. What he got more interested in was the titles, legit titles. His boats might stop being holes in the water, but he kept up the registrations. That keeps the titles active. And the titles just kept getting upgrades.'

'I think I'm following,' I said, 'June?' She shook her head.

'What I mean is, he claimed to be fixin' boats for resale even when they was charcoal out in the pines.'

'But why do that?' she asked.

I remembered what Perks had said he was all about. I sat back, stunned at the purity of the idea. 'Tax write-offs.'

'Exactly,' Ben said. 'Taxes.'

'You should know this, Hon. Government lets businesses take write-offs for boats. Perks sells a boat, or rather boat title, at a less than marketable price, holds the mortgages, thereby acting as a banker, and...'

Bennie jumped in. 'Even better'n that. He gets people not tax savvy but fairly well off t'get involved, them thinking what a great deal, and then he holds it over yer head until he gets what he wants, like something they got, or maybe can do for him. How yer think this land deal's gonna go through? He got more'n me by the short and curlies. Can yer say judge? Prosecutors? Man ain't stupid.'

'Huh,' was all June said.

I could see a whole lot of trouble in this scheme. But I guess if the people involve are otherwise fairly clean and legitimate, they'll probably not be investigated. I could see it working, for a while.

'Oh I'm damn sure the whole thing'll fall in on his head soon enough, but trust me, Perks planned for that. He'll scrape his way out.' Suddenly Bennie's eyes narrowed, as if he spotted something on the horizon only he could see. Didn't have to wait long before he pointed it out to us. 'Like I said, though. I got people, friends, just might trap the rat.'

I didn't want to know. Hell, I didn't even really want to know what I just found out. While I cogitated on the news, though, June asked him, 'How's he keep this marina legitimate? He's got to show income.'

'That's the best part, Miss June. Every month, every one of them slips gets paid for by poor suckers with a ghost boat in 'em. They don't dare put a real boat in anyone of them. Nobody, once they been burned, wants to get that close to Ricky again.'

'Except you,' I said.

'I'm still in that rat's nest. Once that land deal goes through, yer won't find me using anything less than a spy satellite for keeping up with Rickie. Kate and I got that planned.'

We saw Ben out. I watched him go, to make certain the old man didn't take the long walk off our short pier. Before he left, though, I did ask him why my coming in on his deal might help him.

'It won't. Sorry I opened my yap.'

Wish I could have eased Ben Wilkins' unsettled mind, since it didn't matter to me one way or the other that Perks senior was a crook. I was not interested in a payoff, but a cover.

I was after a murderer, not a conman.

Nine

Still, all garbage stinks the same, no matter what goes into the pail. Here I was looking into a murder, I find blackmail and fraud. Fools and money had been getting parted forever, and would forever, and I wasn't interested in stopping the ritual, but there are people who get all giddy at the prospect of catching a con. June was nearly tap dancing once I got back into the salon. 'Can you believe this? Federal fraud? I have got to call…'

'What you got to do is stop and think a minute. And there's something I forgot to tell you. I think the scumbag down there in the office is father to the creep who maybe hanged Willa Maes.'

You would have thought I just told her she was adopted, and her real mother was Godzilla. Boggle-eyed and in mid-tap, she asked me, 'What?'

I filled her in on what I'd learned from observing the four kids and talking with the crappy teacher back at the regional high school, weaving in my theories about who tied knots, pointing out that there was almost a perfect number involved, if I had it right about those two scared stiff boys, the angry girlfriend and that obnoxiously self-satisfied snot of a jock in the middle of them. Bothered me a bit about the cliché nature of the group, but that's one thing about high school kids. Teenagers work overtime keeping clichés from fading out of existence.

It's not like they have a whole lot of choice varieties for modeling themselves after, not in today's clichéd media-managed world.

Of course, my suppositions were all conjecture, and pretty much based on prejudices about high school kids common enough among adults. Not that I forgot what it was like being a teenager; Hell, June and I had been teenagers together, and it wasn't like we weren't still acting sixteen. I felt like a Hardy Boy hanging out with Nancy Drew, but with better sex.

Still, I felt mine were good conjectures. All, and always, devolves upon Means, Motive and Opportunity. Justice relies on those substantiations when she comes to nail those who run afoul of her expectations.

Means? Easy. Perks owned a marina, Baby Boy Blonde Ronnie would have had easy access to exactly what was needed for gathering all the gray cotton anchor rode he would have needed, and somebody floating down at these docks would have taught him a clove and double half hitch. Motive? Unclear, but I felt pretty sure it was a teenager's motive, which almost always was Jealousy. Not that teens aren't capable of mindless hatred, a paradigm picked up from a mean-spirited parent, which I suspected Daddy Perks to be. But even actions based on Pure Hate wanted for a trigger.

People kill for reasons, unless they are truly deranged. Might be a reason here and gone in a flash, something arising out of anger, defensiveness, accident, whatever. The law looks more kindly on the sudden killers, self-defense, unexpected discharge of a weapon, vehicular manslaughter, and as rightly it looks with a cold and dispassionate heart on those killers who not only have a reason, but who used reason to kill. Assassins, murder-for-hire, creeps who kill to cover up other dastardly deeds. If a killer's motive is thought out, well-planned, that he has icily determined a person will die, the law in some places is equally serious in making sure the killer dies as well. Might be physically, might be socially by putting them in solitary for life, but one way or another the idea is to get them gone from us, and as surely as possible.

Although Perks' motive — and I had no reason not to assume that Ronnie Perks lacked one — most likely would have been jealousy, but his wasn't the kind of jealousy that flashed. Like I said, that lynching had been planned, and executed according to plan. That it got swept away by the authorities, and rapidly, told me that somebody involved had connections.

Through his father, Ronnie Perks had not just connections, but agents. I had seen one of the self-satisfied oafs up on a stage.

As well, what the boy also had were cohorts. And though I knew who they might be, I had to know who they were. And that meant digging.

'June, this kid I think did the killing, he has a girlfriend. Like I said, something had to get Willa Maes to the rope, and I can't imagine, if I understand anything, he wasn't so stupid as to be a black boy willing to go into the woods with three white boys, even just to drink beer. If it turns out Maes and Perks were best buds, I'd have to re-evaluate. They might have been teammates, but both were pitchers, and Maes outshone the Perks kid like the sun to a star. I'm thinking he didn't follow three white boys into the woods, he followed...'

She was right on it. 'The sister of a cousin of a girl who was the friend of a waitress's daughter.'

I had to laugh. 'Yeah, something like that.'

'I think I need to make a new girlfriend.' She didn't exactly say that to me so much as to the air over her head, the way teenagers speculate on how tight Boy X is with his present girlfriend, or how she'd look with her hair dyed. Didn't last long, but she was Nancy Drew all over, which curiously made me think of having sex. Acting on that impulse would have been bad timing, especially after she came back down to Earth to say, 'Seriously though, you know I can't let this land swindle crap happen and not do anything.'

Something told me Perks senior wouldn't get that exit strategy he had planned. But if we were going to tilt at windmills, best we were to consolidate on the one bigger one in front of us. 'You know, sounds like Bennie Boy has the stopper working.'

'What could he have that tops my hand? I have the Feds." June's eyes sparkled. 'You know they called just last week to get me back.'

'Thank my lucky stars for vacation plans, then, huh?'

'Thank your lucky stars I prefer your sheets to spreadsheets.'

That I did. I really did. Maybe what I had in mind wasn't bad timing after all.

We'd gotten back to the boat about noon, my meeting with the man upstairs had taken no more than a half an hour, but it was almost one-thirty before June got around to making us lunch. Hey, not a chauvinist pig here, it was her turn at galley duties. Actually, she's a lousy cook. Her favorite recipes usually involve car keys and a credit card. Single in New York? What could I have expected? A James Beard finalist?

My plan was to go find the local county library and read sports pages. If Willa Maes was another Willy Mays, except a pitcher, then somebody somewhere wrote about it. And by doing so, I was certain Little Ronnie Following-in-his-Father's-Pecker-Tracks Perks got a mention or two as well. I suspected the column inches on the two boys was not similar.

June discussed the many ways she might get to the waitress's daughter, thinking maybe to go back to Denny's and then follow her home, hoping to catch an eyeful of the junior member of that set. I said, 'Too complicated. Occam's razor.'

She was getting a little tired of that principal, having heard it a few too many times, especially when she clipped recipes that she never used out of Redbook magazines that she never read. The Principal of the Razor states pretty much that when you have two competing theories explaining a situ, the simpler is better. I take it to mean that in any given action plan, simpler will be more successful, or at least less plagued with obstacles, interruptions, sudden deviations and those evil little things called gremlins.

We were discussing her alternate plan to go after hours, to say she was an old high school chum of the lady *(which wouldn't work. I said every waitress there was probably an old high school chum of every other)* when I felt the boat heave. Somebody had stepped aboard.

You don't step aboard a man's boat unless you ask permission and were given it, or unless you're carrying something to persuade the Captain that you have the right to do as you damn well pleased.

Sometimes that's a gun.

This time it was a gun, and a badge.

The fat red face that poked itself into my salon doorway was somewhat familiar. I'd seen it up on stage wearing both an imperious unassailability and sheer boredom. It left the bored face home.

'How y'all doin'?'

Pleasant enough. The recognition of his face and an association of it with his profession told me to retard the comment ready to leave my lips, one that pretty much resembled *Who the Hell are you?* But with a word or two changed out.

Either June had forgotten his face and not made the connection, or she didn't care who he was. The *Sweet Discourse* was as much hers as mine. 'We'd be doing fine we knew who you are.'

'That's Sheriff Beau, honey.'

'Who? Oh.'

Sheriff Beau was southern gentleman enough to not only recognize that among women his natural superiority sometimes got underestimated, but to forgive any lady, if she was pretty enough, her momentary lapse in judgment. 'Beautop, ma'am.'

She shot him one of her laser smiles, swift and killer. 'How may I help you?'

'Oh, not me wants help. Mr. Perks up at the office had to run home, and he asked if maybe I could stop by and ask you, Mr. Nolan, to join him out at the house for a little sweet tea and talk.'

I think you could hear in Key West the bells, whistles and *Uh oh's* going off so loud in my head, but didn't alter the fact I was being more than summoned. I was being kidnapped by an officer of the law. At least, I hoped it was me.

'I can manage that. Honey, you go shopping like you was planning. I'll probably be back before dark. Can't live far, right Sheriff?' I was grinning baboon teeth. June wasn't grinning at all.

My hand had dropped onto hers, which was meant to say *I'll be fine* without me having to move my lips. But not to seem too eager, I offered *tea, coffee, a whiskey?* to the big lawman, who declined. I, however, still held a cola between my fingers, and I was determined to finish it in my own time. Then I had to find my hat, and then my wallet, which had decided time had come to play hide and seek, then I had to take a leak. May be a cheap-ass way to let someone know he wasn't fully in control, but it worked. Man was getting redder, so I finally let him take charge. I had a notion I might have to pay with my game play somewhere down the line.

Kissed the little lady whose screaming dark eyes bore into mine, and then into my back as I followed Sheriff Beau out and onto the dock.

'So, sweet tea and talk, or tea and sweet talk?' Sheriff Beautop may have had a sense of humor, but it didn't seem to have made it into his car that afternoon. At least he let me sit up front. And he kept the siren and lights turned off.

Though I had no idea what Perks had been up to in the two hours between the time I'd left his office and the moment I got to meet Offissa Pupp up close, I considered having some idea about what had taken place unbeknownst to me as necessary to the continuance of my good health.

What I did think was that it was some pull that Perks had, getting a Florida County sheriff to do cabbie duty for him. Made me understand the Devil myth, that he gets his souls by creeping in inches.

Had Perks tracked down the registration of the Henriques, found out that Drew Nolan was himself well-connected, even found out Mr. Nolan had once been Detective Nolan? What did Sheriff Beautop know, and when was he going to use it?

Of course, I had no other choices than to ride shotgun-less beside the big man, except either to turn chatterbox, or be somebody so engrossed in the flora whipping past that speech was impossible. Not much of a choice, especially since the sheriff failed to answer even my simple question *Where we headed?* with even a head nod forward. Silent it was.

My thoughts turned to the Kingpin of the County living down a country road. I suspected there had to be an iron gate and a fellow with an Uzi on patrol. Nope, I was not on television.

Perks house turned out to be a simple concrete block construct that was popular in the Fifties and Sixties. Along the Gulf Coast of Florida, still popular. One floor settled on a stack of concrete blocks against floods by hurricanes, fairly wide and, I supposed as we pulled up the cracked shell drive, amplified in its floor plan by an addition or two in the rear. Being Florida pretty much guaranteed a pool, but looking as conventional and as pedestrian as the place did, I was sure there was no chance that seven or eight hard bodies flitted about in little thong bikinis. Darn. Such a disappointment.

A regular house with a lot of sun-saddened brown. Conventional. We even rang the front doorbell. No Haitian maid. Perks came to the door himself to let us in.

'Hello, Mr. Nolan. Thanks, Beau. Come on in, both of you. My Mrs. is having a lie down. Kid'll be hopping off the bus any minute.' *Junior didn't have his own SUV with spinner wheels? What gives?* 'But maybe we'll be out of here before he comes stomping in all piss and moans.'

I cocked my head and raised the eyebrow? 'We going somewhere, I mean besides here?'

'You're interested in this land of opportunity, Mr. Nolan. Only fair you should see it.'

I nodded my head, *got it, sure sure.* 'Drew. Friends call me Drew.'

'Friends already?' The junkyard grin had been absent, not even the unnerving eye gleam, until he said that. But both were there, then gone, in a flash.

I knew a head pressman at one of my father's print shops, who operated a web press that printed newsprint circulars. This head pressman was, by all accounts, the biggest dick and Hitler in all of pressdom, but once he stepped through the door to his own house he was as gracious as, well, fill in your own idea of what makes a perfect host. Night and Day. Shook your hand, sat you down, fed you incredibly well and much, asked all the right questions that said he'd had an interest in you for a while, and listened like everything you said was of interest to him beyond all else. Back at work, you were a pissant turd the size of trouble, and in his way. Night and Day.

Perks wasn't exactly in that man's class, but he'd had a lesson or two from him. Made me even more nervous than had the man's flesh-eating grin.

He carried on his chatting as he busied with the house, straightening a couch pillow, moving an ash tray, pouring out the tea he'd been drinking, washing out his glass before setting it on a drain board. Then he began talking about his son, only half heard, as he left us to go down a hallway to the rear.

I'd lost the thread of what he was saying when I lost the volume he'd said it with, and only half re-tuned to the man as he headed back to where Beautop and I stood. I used the few minutes between Perks' going and return to check out his property. It was a married businessman's house, which meant except for a few pictures with him in it, there was nothing in the decor that hadn't been chosen by the missing missus, or dropped by a kid. Except one cabinet.

They are called étagères. Why, I have no idea. They're tall, glass-fronted trophy cases I'd seen often propped by a door, near a sofa, or shoved into a corner. They hold the precious, inexplicable icons of personal history, and many I have seen hold representatives of a housewife's fantasy. Overpriced pressed glass bowls to suggest she was princess enough to own real wheel-cut crystal, quite often some Disney artifacts that said *Inside I am still a scared shitless little girl who misses her daddy*.

I'd seen one étagère that held both expensive and inexpensive timepieces, a collection that had to have begun with Grandpa's hand-me-down Timex, which got developed by an accidental and whimsical purchase of another at a yard sale, and subsequently inflated by well-intentioned friends and family who happily decided they'd never again have to think of a gift to give the old man on holidays.

What makes the collections inexplicable is there often is no rhyme nor reason, no connectedness to the objects other than personal, nostalgic attachment.

All of Perk's prizes were baseball paraphernalia. Or rather mementoes of forgettable baseball games that his son had played in. That surprised me. He didn't seem the doting father type.

One baseball stood alone on a shelf, all items above it arranged so that the little toplight of the étagère would rain a pool of white onto it, like a Hollywood Jesus light, clouds parting, hosannas murmured, angels weeping, all in awe. I thought it might be the boy's first homerun hit, or something of that nature, but the ball appeared far too old, approaching that waxy, grey-brown look of those I'd seen in Cooperstown. I thought to ask about it, and would have, if Perks hadn't come into the room with two long barreled pistols in his hands.

One always says to oneself in that situation, *Oh shit*. I did. And I almost did.

But I needn't have worried, even though both barrels were carried in such a way that, had either gone off, I'd have had one bad belly ache. 'Thought we'd take a few pot shots out there. Nothing for miles, except poor people who have no great love of white men shooting firearms off nearby.' There was old Junkyard, grinnin' and scarin'. 'I assume you shoot?'

Truth be told, any chance I got to avoid shooting a gun I took, ever since somebody decided I needed a hole in my shoulder. But I'd stood at the targets plenty, even more than was required back when I was required to shoot paper men with big black circles on them.

There's many who wore blue that not only managed to retire without ever taking a gun from the holster unasked, and many, many more who never wanted to draw one out in the first place. Doesn't mean there aren't John Waynes out there, but they are few. A very few.

Unfortunately, they are also the one's without a healthy fear of firearms that keeps most cops humble and helpful.

Don't ever say to me 'Guns don't kill people. People kill people.' Because, if I don't shoot you then and there, I'll respond with 'People with guns kill people, asshole.' Funny the effect being shot has on a person.

Still, I accepted his invite, so away Mr. Drew Nolan went with Officer Beau and Mean Dog Perks to plunk at unsuspecting trees, and maybe defenseless critters, with little chunks of metal that come out of a gun barrel way faster than you can imagine.

People along the Northeast corridor, especially those who don't ever leave town, have no idea how big this country is or how much bigger than Disneyland Florida is. And how much of what's out there is uninhabited. Old timers prefer it that way, but some of their more enterprising neighbors, of which Perks was emblematic, think anywhere a house can go up a house should go up, especially if it nets him a box of cash.

I asked Perks about Perks. Typical story, grandparents in the fifties discovered Miami, got sold a bill of goods on a stretch down by Fort Myers, parents fled the cranky old grandparents and moved to their own stretch of nowhere somewhat north of there, and young Ricky had to figure out himself how to survive. He survived. Did okay. Wife, kid, business, off shore account.

'Saw the baseball, the kid pic of him sliding in safe. He a ball player?'

'Yeah.' That's all I got. Wondered if maybe there was an Oedipal rivalry there.

Along a particularly empty stretch of road he said, 'We're there. The land starts here, run's about four miles down, four miles in. That enough nothin' for ya?'

I'd been in places where nuthin' was an overstated case. I knew what was in there, could see what was eventually going in there. I'm not a raving ecologistical tree hugger, but I couldn't help but feel sad that what was presently in there had been home for centuries to a lot of things that wouldn't have homes much longer once the unknown judge drops his gavel on the contested ownership case. 'Ben Wilkins told me this was almost sewn up. That the case?'

'Let's just say there's little left to worry about. That wheel's greased, and rolling.'

'So, why you want me in? And how much?'

'Didn't say I wanted you in, now, did I? Thought it was you wanted in.'

Sheriff Beau, who'd been as mute as a stone troll, chuckled.

'And I said I might. I just wondered what I'd be buying, what you want my money to do. Pipes to be laid, foundations poured, that sort of thing?'

I thought naïve might be the way to go, a thing I was completely able to pull off.

We began passing a few houses cut into the woods, homes built in an architectural style that said *we plan to survive no matter what blows through here.* Solid block, low-brow roofs with plenty of eave to block out the near-tropical sun, up on block pilings to survive flood but just high enough to offer prime shelter to friendly cottonmouths that sometimes slithered out to where the kids played. A few had the expected broken-down autos shoved into a weedy nest of palmetto, a surprising number of them Pontiacs.

'What about these?' I said, pointing to a particularly hovelish hut.

'Don't care. They'll go. Squatters, all of them. I do things right, they'll want to move.' *Do things wrong* I suspected he meant.

'Turn next house, Beau.'

There was a woman hanging wash on a stringer in the back yard. She watched us barrel past on the dirt road pushing into her woods. Didn't like what she saw, by the looks of her.

Road didn't improve farther we went. End of the first half-mile I thought we'd left the country. Probably wasn't but minutes later, but after what felt like an hour I spotted one more cinderblock house, more decrepit than the one at the entrance. Beyond that we came to an unexpectedly cleared knoll, a slight rise. Beau took us to its edge.

'Time for some gun fire.' Perks said, popping open his door.

'Rick's a good shot. Doesn't miss much,' Beautop said. And that's all he said. To myself I said *hmmm* to that.

Perks'd been there before. There was a set of cedar stumps, sections cut from the trunk, lined at the far side of the knoll, cans and glittering glass strewn around. Beautop went to the trunk, popped it open and fetched out a trash bag with obvious contents. The clink and clatter of empties. Sheriff fished out a few, took them to the stumps and set them up.

One of Perks's guns I recognized, the other not so much. Every gun collector in the world probably has at least one Colt Peacemaker, and Perks, whether a collector or not, had his. A Peacemaker is heavy, stupid heavy, and when Perks held it forward for me, saying, 'Take this one,' and I did, my hand dropped considerably. Hadn't held a pistol in a while.

I was not one of those cops, when I was one, who fell in love with all things firearm. I can recognize a number, but I didn't know the gun Perk's had kept for himself. More modern, more deadly, a patterned wooden grip, metal flat black, kind of gun popular in movies set in foreign locales, the kind bad guys turned over sideways, showing they're stupid.

I said, hefting my pistol, 'I recognize the Colt, but what's that?'

Perks looked at his gun like he couldn't figure how it got there in his hand, but then he said, 'Smith and Wesson 41, seven inch barrel. Does a good job.'

'Oh.'

'Guess you don't shoot much, do you, Mr. Nolan?'

'Not much. Not a fan.'

'That surprises me,' he said, suddenly whipping the Smith and Wesson toward the row of cans. Beautop hadn't come halfway back before Perks popped off two rounds, a can down with each. The man with a badge nearly pissed himself, but still kept his yapper sealed. Takes either consummate control or absolute fear to stay so composed. Maybe I'd misappraised the Sheriff.

Nah…

'Try it?'

'Go nuts,' I said, waving Perks on.

Had I known what he planned to do next, I might have taken the gun. We stood facing each other, me appraising him, him appraising me, neither of us too successful at hiding what we were doing. Like two banditos facing off in the red dust of a western desert, except we were in a shaggy clearing in a thick scrubby woods of western Florida.

His gun hand came up. Pretty sure he never flinched an eyelid, though I am equally sure mine opened a little wider as that strange, long-barrel gun rose. I'd been at the wrong end before, and I still don't like it. Leveled out at my chest, then Perks lifted it a little higher. Soon I'm looking down a dark hole, and I'm totally unaware of the Peacemaker in my own hand. Which was good, for me as much for him. Time slowed, time stopped. Light darkened to a small quarter inch opening down which a lead bullet hunkered, itching to get out and get the job done.

But then, him shouting, 'Toss it, Beau,' he aimed over my head and fired.

Pop pop, a dead beer can. 'Again, Beau.' Two more shots, my ears by then bleeding, but that was all on me that bled, and two more dead Budweisers.

Nobody laughed, nobody found anything funny. Leastways me. Perks then simply turned, took aim at the cans Beau had left set up on the stumps, and said, 'I got a proposition, Mr. Nolan, and it's one I hope you won't…' *pop.* '…refuse. I ain't the godfather. No horse head in the bed. Just a simple,' *pop,* 'businessman.'

I was listening.

'The name you dropped on my desk,' he turned and faced me, the gun hand dropping to his side. 'I could use a connection like that. What I want is access, not your money. Of course, your money won't be turned away.' He took the Colt from me, raised it in the air, and fired. Damn things are more a disturbance to the peace than an insurer of it. 'I think it's your turn, Mr. Nolan. Don't disappoint.'

Couldn't help myself. I may not like guns, but I know how they work. I know what they can do, and what they are intended to do is leave an impression, either on the mind or on whatever got aimed at.

Four shots, four dead cans.

All Perks did was reload.

Ten

June was happy to see me. Sort of. Why does worrying oneself simple make some people so darn mad? All I got was a cursory *you're back* and a disappearance into our stateroom. I just stood there for a few moments, wondering *What the Hell?* I didn't wait long.

She thrust her head out the doorway to our room, an expression that said I might never get to call that our bedroom again. 'Bennie was here while you were gone. Man's loony scared, and he scared me. He heard you went with that man. They know, Drew. And they don't like what they know.'

What the Hell? Honey, I'm home!

'Knows what?'

'Knows who you are, at least what you were. A cop.'

Maybe I should have hit only one can. *Crap.*

'Oh well.'

'Oh well? You're playing with a rattlesnake, and he sees you like his lunch. You think this is funny?' *Was I grinning? Didn't think so.* 'I'm calling Robertson whether you want me to or not.'

Robertson was June's old boss, once with the FBI before moving to the Fed. Nice guy, a bit too much starch in his shirt, which was surely made from the same cloth as they use on the American Flag. One of those.

I shook my head, repeatedly.

'Why not? Maybe when Perks gets his by the Feds, Willa's case'll get turned the right direction.'

I couldn't see a flaw in the argument, except we had no more evidence than an old hunk of rope and an old man's say so. 'Guess I should go see Bennie, calm him down.'

'They're gone.'

'Dinner?'

'Gone. Pulled up stakes. Flew the coop. Jumped ship, or whatever you nauticals say.'

'Slipped his mooring.' She did not appreciate my assistance. 'That scared?'

June stepped from the room. 'What do you think?'

'What did he say exactly?'

'Exactly? Didn't say so much as screamed at me. *He a cop? A goddamn cop? I brought Perks a cop. You couldn't say something about being cops...* and more of that. I asked him how he knew you were a cop. All he said was *Beau* and pointed his finger at me like firing a gun. Took me an hour after he left before I realized he meant that sheriff you went with. That's it. I saw him shove Kate down the dock and onto the boat. Ten minutes, they're out of here.'

I considered for a minute that they both, Beautop and Perks, knew I was a cop and settled the weight of that into their like-minded appraisals. The whole gun show, drive to nowhere. Effectively intimidated me, and I thought they were just trying to scare a prospect. I realized they were trying to warn a cop.

I then had choices to make. Go get Wiley and get the Hell out of there? Convince Perks that I *was* a cop once upon a time but no more, and maybe not even with the cleanest badge? Let June call Robertson? Or just tell Perks I'd lost interest in his proposition?

My self-preservation instinct said *Go get Wiley and go,* but then I had been a cop, and there were residual instincts there. I really just didn't know what choice to make, then. 'What you want me to do? You scared?'

She said, 'I'm not an old man. I trust you.'

Felt a little bit like she was passing the buck, but it was a forgivable pass. She was a numbers girl, and though personable, nowhere near the misanthropic cynic I had been. I knew people, and I knew that Perks was not someone so stupid as to bring actual harm to a former policeman who was so well connected as one with a Watkins van Hij for kin.

And besides, I might not like Davis, but there was something in him, in the knot of folks who'd come to my boat, in Wiley's eyes, that said justice must be brought for Willa Maes. Maybe Davis was right, I was suffering the myth of the White Messiah, but I was there, and I was in it. That I was white? Couldn't be helped.

What I decided was not to worry about Perks, for the time being, and not let him get behind me, either. One eye on Junkyard Dog while I rummaged on his turf. After all, he was just cover. Best to let it drag.

How, exactly, I wasn't sure. I said all that I was thinking to June, who didn't seem completely happy about any of it, but accepting of all I decided.

'Okay, then, Andrew. Let's stick to our plan. We go find the library, I leave you there, then I go to Denny's and...'

I had held up my hand.

One thing all marina dwellers learn is life is open-air. You want to keep things private, you learn to keep your voice down when down in the hold. Or, if you're out among the boats, you keep things unsaid. June had learned that rather quickly, especially since she had a phobia about exhibiting dirty laundry. Not that we exhibited very often, but those first three months had their trials and errors. Her trials, my errors.

But I hadn't raised my hand to quiet or stop my lady. There was a rather loud discussion exploding shore-side, one of them a young voice. I went to the salon door for a look, which I am sure so did any others in the marina.

Two men, one young and fitting the voice, the other older, grizzled. The boy — whose head and face I could not see for the thrust of a dumpster blocked my view — argued with what I supposed was the dock master, the one I'd have to see to pay my temporary slip fee. He appeared to me a man cut straight from the same cloth that bosun's mates were ripped from. Arguing with his type was as useless as kicking a bollard, but the kid, being a kid, thought volume would give him a chance at making a point.

Wouldn't. Didn't.

I'd first met the older man soon after tying off. As there is on a ship, there's a hierarchy to harbor rats. The dock master, though answering to the owner and/or the general manager, had absolute say over everything that touched the water. Same with a bosun's mate on a ship, who had all hands and the ship itself to worry over. You want a good marina, or boat, you want a mean bosun's mate for a dockmaster. Not an unfair one, just one who could crush you with one hand or both lips.

I'd spotted the salt stains on his character immediately. The kid was his unfortunate victim at the moment. By the vociferous nature of the dock master's commentary about the boy's worthiness as a human, I understood that kid to be employed under Perks, and he'd run afoul of procedure. Exactly how, didn't hear.

A few snaps and finger jabs from both on both later, the boy stepped into view. I should say *stomped* into view. More important than that distinction, at least to me then and there, was that he was one of the boys I had seen with Ronnie Perks the Lesser in the auditorium.

I wanted to get me between him and the marina exit, providing the dock master let him choose to live as well as leave through the gate rather than by the water he was about to get thrown in. They were far enough down marina that I could walk up to where my car was without interrupting.

Or so I thought.

Spotted by the dock master, who stopped his harangue. Boy, however, didn't quit the scene. They watched me without really looking.

But the harangue really was over. Pops went up to the office, Junior walked a bit down to the farthest dock and picked up a length of discarded dock line. Not watching him the same way they'd not kept an eyeball on me, I got to see how he made the loops.

There's an unwritten but often spoke rule about how things get done around boats. All things go clockwise. Most people are right handed, and will usually take a line in the left hand to pull in the line, looping evenly-sized coils into the right. Do it, and soon anyone gets the habit.

Lefties are natural. The boy was a southpaw, and the loops he was making had practice behind them.

I felt like a spotlight was shining on his hand. I think I found my clove- and double half-hitch maker.

As he was not planning a quick exit but remaining on the docks, I didn't have to make for my car, so I feigned talking to myself like I forgot the keys, slapping my head and pockets, jabbering while shaking my head and imploring God for a good explanation of Why he'd made such an idiot, and turned back. I started down toward my dock, but shifted direction and went straight at the boy, readying a question.

'Hey, I guess you work here?' Always good to start a teenager thinking you're an old idiot by stating the obvious. 'You happen to know where there's a library around here? My wife's got a question, and we bet on it, silly ass bet, I cook and bring her beers she wins, other way I win, which is why it's silly, since she does that already and I got nothing to win. But you know, women. We're looking for an answer, so we thought a library…'

'Use the internet?'

'What?'

That alone shouted stupid geezer. 'I said look it up on Google. Every answer you need.'

Although I'd found what he said about answers often to be true, teenagers everywhere are convinced they have both built the world for old farts like me, and have to explain it to us, often with condescension and derision.

'Google.'

'Here,' he said, pulling out his phone. 'What's the question?' Does every kid have the Library of Congress in his pocket these days?

'Who caught the basket catch?'

He glared at me like I'd just said his dog was a homosexual. He also went a bit whiter. I had my knot tyer.

'We were listening to the baseball game on the radio, she's a bit of a trivia nut but I know baseball, and she said Jackie Robinson. I said…'

'Willy Mays. You win.' He shoved his phone back in his pocket and started walking off.

I called after him. 'She won't just believe me. You mind telling her? Get a chance, swing by the *Sweet Discourse*, over there. Buy you a Coke you do.'

'Yeah, if I do.'

'Do. By the way, what's your name?'

'Kevin.' It was a reflex, he was done. I let him go. Kid felt the hook, but didn't know I'd let out plenty of play. Time to set it, and reel him in.

On my walk back to the Henriques I had to fight down self-congratulation at my instincts about who killed Willa Maes being right. But I only enjoyed a few moments of it, because I felt sure June would have kay-boshed my satisfaction quickly enough. Not that she regularly enjoyed slapping me down, but I have been known to get a bit cocky and a might superior among those with whom I had no real right for superiority.

Truth was, even in high school she was smarter than me. In most things.

Besides, wasting time on congrats over what I had done only stole time from thinking about what I had to do.

There's a delicate balance in using information to get information. Use too much, you lose control of the inquisition. Use too little and the repository of what you need will ignore you, or worse, flee.

I had the boy rattled, bringing Willa Maes into the air between us, but I wanted him scared. I didn't want him scared of me, but rather of the consequences to what he may have done. Let him scare himself. Always works best.

All June had to say was, 'I wish you'd quit running off to pursue your own agenda. I feel like Ginger Rogers here, dancing after Fred.'

I didn't know how to help that. Things seemed to be happening without my efforts. There's an old saying that Opportunity knocks only on the door of those prepared to open it. What I'd been through since the day I stumbled on a dead policeman back in Philly, all the training, the routines of cop work, the presentations given to detectives on the force, my work with the international police oversees, and several thoroughly upsetting adventures that began with my getting shot, all these things made me think I was prepared to open a door. At least the doors opening then.

Ricky Perks coming out of a back room with a pair of guns had rattled me a bit, but I doubted this affair would ever have those guns lowered on my corpus again. All I was doing was asking questions, putting two with two.

On hindsight I think it is better called what it was, sticking my nose where it shouldn't oughta be stuck.

Had it not been for my lovely shipmate and not so lovely first mate helping people through a horror, my nose would have been pressed into the fresh air rising up over my flying bridge as I motored carefree to places unplanned. But, there was June, and there was Wiley, and there was a dead boy, and the air coming through that door of opportunities may have dropped with a foul smell to it, but those were the opportunities that I needed, 'cause there sure wasn't no evidence falling from the skies.

Turned out wasn't the Coke, wasn't his curiosity about my fine new cruiser, wasn't a need to find and make a friend in his darkness that brought Kevin to the stern of the *Sweet Discourse,* but a slip that had been slipped, and suddenly. He had gone past to the Wilkinses slip to secure whatever might have been left dangling. I spotted him working when I climbed up to my flying bridge for a before-dinner beer. Waited until he headed back to call down to him.

'You, Kev, how 'bout that Coke?' I held aloft my drink of choice, 'Or something better?'

Yeah, sometimes I break the law.

It was a good enough offer, and though he tossed a glance landward to see if Mr. Dock Boss was watching, he came aboard. I came down. 'Junie, fetch me out another beer, would ya, Hon. We got company. Y'all come up an' meet my new friend here.'

She'd been briefed, knew her part. Kevin and I could both hear the radio chatter. She came out carrying two bottles. I knew neither was for me. Uh oh, broke the law.

He drank with experience, but not with restraint. He accepted the second with no hesitation. Don't care how often a kid takes the opportunity to drink, none of them can hold it, and almost all of them see booze as a ride to a destination, and that was a place called Drunk, a place where Stupid needs no defense. I could see he wanted to drive there fast. Only needed him halfway where the road signs all read *in vino veritas.*

'Tell her.'

June put on her most disbelieving face, which momentarily intimidated the boy. His reaction to my command and her big-eyed stare told me the kid crumbled easily in the face of adversity, especially if that face was on someone with natural authority. Someone like the boss's kid.

'He's right, ma'am, it was him.'

'Him who?' she asked.

Poor kid, having to fight already dismasted. 'It was Willy Mays. Sorry, but it was.'

'Humph,' went my Junie. Then, bless her cruel and evil heart, she said the next thing in a faux Southern accent. 'I still sayin' it wa'n't no Willa Mays.' She feigned bad loser and went below, tossing yet another 'Willa Mays ma waht ayass' over her shoulder.

It worked, overtime. Kid's hands shook so badly I thought he was going to drop his beer onto the deck, or at least a load of bladder juice. Playing the good cop, I invited Kevin up onto my flying bridge. He shot a nervous eye in search of the boss.

'Don't worry,' I said, soothing him, 'not like there's a ton of folks here calling after you. I'll square it with Ritchie Perks, he shows up.'

'Ricky, Rick. He don't like people calling him Ritchie Perks. Not even Rich.'

'No? I would have sworn.' I can imagine why the varmint wouldn't like the associated pun. I had the feeling Perks loved money, but felt ashamed of it somehow. The lack of display. But then, Bennie had said the marina owner had himself an exit strategy. I assumed the offshore account. Plenty of them a short boat ride from the Florida coast. I wondered if his getaway included Mrs. Perks and the little Perks.

'It ain't Mr. Perks I got to worry about. Weren't for him, I'da been killed by that bastard a few times already.'

'The dock master?'

'Sweeney.'

'Like the barber? His first name Todd?' Too obscure a reference for the kid.

'Huh? No. I think its Calvin. People call him Cal. Or Cow. I never could figure which.' He grinned at his own moment of pleasure. Cow indeed. More like Bull.

It was a long day in an empty marina, and I suspected the Dock Master didn't hang around all day *and* night. Saying so out loud finally induced the boy to accept my invite to go aloft. Once up, we both did the look-over on the place. For him it gave a sense of freedom, or escape, from all he had to do on the docks. For me, the flying bridge provided a confined space to go at the boy, like a canvas-floored boxing ring does for the pugilists. Except I was the only one donning gloves.

Time to have at him. 'So you like working here?'

'It's a job. But had to quit baseball to come work. Don't like that.'

'You play baseball? Babe Ruth?'

'Naw, high school. But we were going to take state, except...' hoisted on his own petard, I think the phrase is. Wondered how'd he'd avoid the recent news. In case he had a way, I snatched at him.

'Except? What, you quitting wrecked their chances?'

'Me, naw, ain't that good. Kid died... killed...' I could see it almost lodge in his throat like a fishbone, but he was a trooper. A lying, murderous piece of crap trooper, but one nonetheless.

I pushed. 'Killed, what? He killed somebody?'

'No, sir. Didn't do that.' Voice was dropping faster than the sunlight, but not his moxie. How he could muster the lie was beyond me. 'Kid killed hisself. Hung hisself. Committed suicide.'

'Hanged.' I can be cruel, but I was reeling in a fish destined to be tossed onto a dinner plate. 'It's hanged. You said hung. Curtains get hung. People get hanged.'

'Right, yeah.'

'They sure he hanged himself?'

Swift, expected irritability. Like shoving thorns under Kevin's cuticles. 'A course they's sure. Why wouldn't they be?'

I said, 'I don't know. Not like I'm from around here. Was he a colored kid?' Wanted some soap for a tongue washing, saying that, but when in Rome... Kevin nodded. 'Don't hear about colored kids hanging themselves, especially down here in Good Old Boy country. Plenty of people to do that for 'em, I hear. What you really think?'

Kevin was about cuticled to the max. He almost shouted, 'You know what I think? I think the damn asshole killed himself, that's what I think.'

But I wasn't done, 'What for? They say he pitched good?'

Unexpectedly, I had just then given Kevin a reason to switch gears. Maybe he didn't like Maes, but it was plain that he admired him. The pitching.

Kevin, cooled, more calmly said, 'He was damn good, yeah.' Then he shrugged, resigned to something. 'But he didn't know...'

'Know what?'

'Nothing. I don't like to talk about it. He just done it. Funeral's maybe tomorrow, so I heard.'

'You going?'

'No,' he said.

Had he said *Hell no,* or something worse and more vulgar, I would have really doubted his humanity, and would have really feared for his salvation. Not really, for who gives a damn about the salvation of murderers? And I ain't Christ. Anyway, had he said anything other than that flat, straightforward *No,* I might have pitched him off my boat and into the drink. But, just *No.*

Then he continued, same low tone. 'We don't go to their funerals, usually. They don't want us there.' Then he brightened. 'Besides, we got a game coming up, home, a big game, might go to dark, from the ceremony speeches and all. We got lights. Mr. Perks being on the Council and all. There'll be something like that then. For him.'

'For Perks?'

That got him irritated again. Irritation is good, I wanted irritation. Irritation makes you go off center of your feet. 'No, for Wi... that kid.'

'A tribute? Kid must have been well liked.'

'Yeah.'

'Kid got a name?'

Kevin hesitated before saying, 'Yeah. Maes. He was Willa Maes.'

I raised an eyebrow, 'Like the fellow did the basket catch? But you said Willa Maes. You say Willa, not Willy?'

'Ain't Willy. Was Willa, like your Missus said.'

I was beginning to doubt my own humanity in making him run over his teeth the name, over and over again, so I changed the subject, played out a little more line. 'You should go to that funeral.'

'Yeah. My girlfriend wants me to go.' The sudden soured countenance on him caught me by surprise. I had a suspicion, and another piece of bait to draw Kevin to it.

'Girlfriends. Not easy your age. In your lap one minute, in somebody else's next. Or at your back instead of at your side. Trust me, I know.' I had hoped June hadn't heard me. Careless infidelity wasn't what had broken us up way back when. But that's a story for another time. Still, the idea I had driven into Kevin's psyche found a home. He fell back against the seat back, whooshing out a sigh.

'Yeah.'

'Your girl a good one?'

'I thought so,' he said, all the teenage angst from doubt welling up in his replies. 'You can never tell, though.'

'Found her out?'

'No. Just stuff I heard. But you know how it is.'

All teenagers think all love as feverish, sweaty pressings and pushings of the flesh, no matter how old they are. The only variation on loving that kids can accept is what happens between one's parents, where no concept of bodily activity is ever permitted. Try suggesting to a teenager that his parents screw, watch denial take them over thoroughly.

'So, what position you play, in baseball?'

'Outfield.'

'This dead kid, what he play?'

'Pitcher.'

'Got a replacement?'

'Yeah, sort of. Ronnie Perks.'

'Perks's boy?'

'Exactly.'

'Can't pitch for shit, can he?'

Kevin finally had a moment to enjoy. The grin was sincere as he shook his head.

'Outfield, huh? Easy place to quit.'

'I coulda pitched. Wasn't for the Perkses and coach being so damn lucky to get a speedball hauler like Maes, woulda been me pitching. And nobody but me taking them to States.'

'You pitch?'

'Did. I got a few closers, but coach said outfield, so it was outfield. I'm better than Ronnie. But then, he's a Perks and I'm just a guy works for his dad. Still, got me this job when I needed it.'

'Yeah,' I said, 'I know how that works. You want another beer?'

'I do, but I don't. Thanks.'

No problem, kid. Any time.

Kevin who works for Perks managed the climb down and walk the walk back up the floating dock to land, but I doubted he'd be worth his wages for at least another hour.

Two down, two to go.

The Death of Willa Maes Moment was coming clearer. Wasn't Ronnie Perks' girl who had turned her attentions onto Maes, a "colored boy from the sticks," but Kevin's. And it ate him up. But he wasn't the type to do anything about it except sulk and be all passive-aggressive in his interactions with his girlfriend.

If Ronnie Perks had any of his dad in him, that boy would have spotted an opportunity right away to fire up his cronies enough to do something not only stupid, but heinous. And he'd have convinced them it was just to scare the Pro-bound pitcher, not kill him. That they did kill the boy was, to them, an accident.

To Ronnie, however, it was probably a very desired conclusion.

Guess who was going to be pitching in the State game? And guess who planned to be there, watching.

Eleven

Question for me: To whom might I profess anything, should I piece the whole story together? And when should I tell it? All, really, that I had in my possession was solely speculation, but the circumstantial evidence tilted me toward being dead on in my suspicions.

Which scared me. I'd been dead on before about what I thought had been going on, only to find out how pretty far off the mark I was, so far that I might as well have been on the other side of the planet.

It's what I discussed with June while she fried up a couple of eggs for dinner. At least she said they were eggs. Wasn't sure when she slid them under my gaze.

'What? You not hungry?'

'June, have I told you lately I love you?'

She laughed, which is a whole lot of why I did love her. Add to that her wisdom, for she reached the hook where the car keys hung.

'I'll get my shoes.'

Laughs aside, she did see things my way. What kept both of us there was the serious lack of any other theory that included the knots as part of the explanation. Or just the nautical ropes, the coincidence of Willa Maes and Ronnie Perks both being pitchers, the telltale grin during the *In Memoriam* at the auditorium that Ronnie Perks had worn, the reaction of Kevin the Wharf Rat to the rainfall of Willa Maeses that I had brought down on his head, and the affections of some unknown white girl for a black sports star.

Nope, right track. Just maybe, though, the footprints were done in disappearing ink.

So, to whom to tell what, and when to say anything?

My guts told me that I was unlikely to find any evidence beyond the circumstantial, and that if any justice was to be served, it would have to be through a full confession of at least one person who'd been involved. And even then, the way Perks seemed to have his county tied up, a subverted group that included a County sheriff turned into a fetchin' dog, and a judge able to drop his gavel favorably, for Perks, on a state matter, even then I wondered if anyone who *could* give a damn *would* give a damn.

I was glad that I had June there with me, or else a frustration would have fallen on me and I might also have become one of those who seriously didn't give a damn. I'd been there before. In fact, I pretty much lived in Casa de Whatever year round. Consequence of Largo living. And as a consequence, my sense of justice wasn't as noble as June's, nor — possibly — as naïve.

Don't tell her I said that.

But she did believe in Justice, capital J, so by proxy — and for the sake of peaceful cohabitation on a boat — then must I. If the injustice of Willa Maes' death weren't enough, there was Richard Perks's manipulation of her beloved tax code. Not the complex one that drove accountants into a padded cell and straightjacket, but the one that said no matter what one thinks, our country depends on everyone paying up a fair share.

Of course she was not so naïve as to believe everyone acted according to fairness, but she did think there were many, many Americans who did their share, and probably more, and they should be protected from the machinations and underhanded practices of the few who didn't.

Gotta love that in a woman.

June was tap-tapping away on her touch screen smartphone, seeking a decent eatery that was not a Denny's, nor any fast food chain for that matter. I wasn't much of a gourmand, but I still relished a juicy rare steak, and they are getting quite rare in chain restaurants. Cost of gas driving up the cost of food, and driving down the quality of beef, I am afraid. Anyway, as she tapped and tapped, her phone both rang and sent to the screen an ID photo that had her shriek, scaring the crap out of unflappable me.

Her first words alerted me to who called. 'How's Roly Poly Noly?'

That was her name for the first addition to my immediate family in several decades. In fact, all of the decades since I was born. I haven't life enough left in me to type down all of the poor rich kid's names. Had they been embroidered on a blanket he would have smothered under it. Suffice it to say Daddy Watt had gotten his wish, and the boy was named quite a bit for him. But no one these days allows a child to be referred to as Watkins, or even Watt, much less Wattie. So the second in the long string became his. I didn't argue, for Nolan is a fine name. But when June came out with *Roly Poly Noly,* I feared for the first thirteen years of the child's educational career.

I called him, simply, Noles. As in Holes, but with an N.

Curiously, Roly Poly Noly didn't offend either Papa nor Mama. I'd even heard my sister Annigail use that reference, in a revoltingly cutesy kind of way. The poor child was less than half a year living and already he was doomed to carry great weights. Couldn't wait to get him out fishing, to save his tiny soul.

People on phones have no respect for those nearby who may be eager to eavesdrop on their conversations. June hopped up and dashed out of the salon, perhaps a kneejerk reaction to some innate notion that cell phone use indoors came nowhere near the clarity and reception of out of doors. I lost my connection, but then it was just Annigail.

Or so I thought up until five minutes after she left me. That's when she stuck her head through the door and said, 'Get more than shoes on. We're dining in Flor a Mar. They got a late start getting away, and they're using a friend's slip for the night. We're to come to dinner. On Watt.'

'Isn't he sending the heli?'

A private joke that I thought June would have found funny, but she shook her head, no. 'You're driving.' Sometimes the more tuned in June gets, the more tuned out she gets, you know what I'm sayin'?

I'll never get used to seeing my sister breastfeeding. And she'll never get used to my embarrassment. I mean, in the lobby? The people who stared? But, as had been said many times, the rich may give offense wherever they might go. Not that I think breastfeeding is offensive. To the contrary, I like it just fine. But time and place? And she was my sister!

Anyway, there she was plugged into my two-foot long next of kin, beaming like she invented boob milking. Motherhood agreed with her. She'd been off the sauce religiously since first awareness of conception, and it showed. She was naturally plumper, but now healthier, a richer depth to her complexion, and agile humor in her eyes. She'd always been quick to humor, but it was often at either mine or Watt's expense. Since having a baby boy, she'd softened a bit on menkind. But just a bit.

'I can see your tonsils, Andrew.'

What could I say? I shut my mouth. June just planted herself in front of Annigail, arms akimbo, knuckles on the hip, waiting. But she had wait aplenty in her nature, for then Annigail would become a motherless woman until way past dessert.

Hmmm, I said to myself. *Hmmm.*

Watt and I did the ritual handshake, stood about awkwardly not looking at each other as Annigail unsuckled the child. June purred like the kitty she was, a new man in her arms. We were then called to our seats.

The van Hijs were never made to wait, but Watt thought it ungracious to take his seat at the table without offering his guest, his female guest, first selection. And since June had their heir to the fortune, she could have sat anywhere she wanted. Watt would have bought the restaurant for her. And not *just* because she carried little Nolan, either. June had planted a big, fat Cupid's arrow in the man. Of course she'd done the same to Wiley, and into Frank Whitcomb, my pilot friend, and into everyone at our home marina, and even into Paquita, Watt's enormous cook.

Me? I was slaughtered a century ago back in grammar school.

Takes about a dozen minutes at least to get over the gratuitous chit-chat of reuniting friends, even though we'd only left them a week ago. They had a house southwest of me, on Islamorada, just east of Key West. Eventually Watt — getting tired of hearing about the virtues of cloth diapers, breastfeeding and manual-versus-mechanical milking machines — leaned over his hors d'oeuvre plate to ask me, 'So, what's new, kiddo?'

Both June and I looked at one another, neither of us wanting to begin or even say. She finally took the lead, sort of.

'You tell them.'

Watt's eyebrows rolled north about as far as I had ever seen them, and I gave him a sharp look. 'Not what you're thinking, Brother.'

Annigail, now a mother and therefore imbued with the powers of a god, and by that I mean at least uncanny omniscience, merely said, 'Oh, Christ, Andrew. Not again.'

What was there to say thereafter?

Through the hors d'oevres, the soup, the main course, desserts and even a cordial for June, scotch for me, nothing for Annigail, and an equal nothing for supportive Watt, I mostly talked. June said a few things, not so much as clarification but in the expression of certitude as to why we'd both jumped feet first into the piss.

For June it was indignation, and not the self-righteous kind, either. The sense of injustice kind.

For me, there was far less firm ground under my reasoning.

'Even if I know everything,' I said, 'even if I actually could find something like physical proof, be damned hard to bring anything to light. I'm a boat captain from Key Largo, and that makes me already suspect. June, maybe, being a lawyer, but I still don't see those kids suffering anything except some long festering guilt, maybe some mental breakdown, loss of hair, nightmares.'

'But,' Watt put forward, 'you'll continue anyway.'

'Damn straight,' June said. As I said, certitude. 'At least on the fraud and coercion charges. He's got a damn judge, for Chrissakes.'

He asked her, 'That surprise you, June?'

'No, but it doesn't mean I get to look the other way, if I can help it. Evil succeeds because good men do nothing.'

Watt frowned, perhaps thinking that his vast wealth, at least in its beginnings, may have depended on a few shades of wrong being further shaded to out of sight. But, then, being the unquestioned authority that he was almost always allowed — he was married, after all — he leaned even more forward to say something. I knew what it was, and held a hand up to stop him.

'I know, I know. The one who knows has the responsibility. But why the Hell does it always have to be me that learns this crap? All I want is a nice boat, a calm sea, and bait for my hooks. And you're right, Annigail, what *am* I doing back in the piss? Crap like this happens the world over. I had enough of it as a cop. Creeps just keep on coming.'

Then Watt said, 'That's the point, Andrew. Crooks must get caught. Shakespeare was right, murder will out, but too often criminality emerges too far after the unprotected are irreparably damaged. That's why we need people dedicated to pushing the criminality of others into the light. Even left on its own, criminality is inevitably doomed. But should the urge to discover crimes, to illuminate the truth, to bring wrong to the light, if that ever succumbs to frustration and dejection, then the corrective measures, or as June has it, the Wheels of Justice, will stop. And that does no one any good. We have a whole world of that history to learn from.'

'Just be careful,' Annigail said to June. I think she meant to include me. I think.

'Watkins, you're sounding like a downright liberal.'

'Not at all. I believe I am as fiscally conservative as the next fellow bloated with inherited wealth. But the van Hijs are descended from those Dutchmen who preached that blessings come from blessings. All the good that is mine must be used not just to further itself, but to aid the fellow who hasn't been as blessed. Which leads me to this. Do you suppose perhaps I should offer a scholarship in the boy's name?'

Now I leaned forward. 'I think his people would be about as insulted by that as they were by the lynching. I've had that little darkness lit up for me quite a lot recently. This is not a white man's burden, it's theirs, and they want it to be theirs. Which is another reason I don't feel completely right about pushing this.' I felt my excellent lunch get a little sour in hearing myself pitching *us* and *them*. 'But in for a penny, in for a pound.'

'Oh you men,' Annigail finally interjected. 'It's not that complicated. Do whatever you can to get whoever killed the boy to confess, and let the system take care of the rest. You both are acting like everything rests on your shoulders. If you can help correct even the tiniest wrong, then just do it.'

'Spoken like a new mother,' I said. Watt probably thought it, but him saying so would not have been wise.

That ended it. But didn't change anything. Taking care of the creep Perks was definitely accomplishable, and June would see to that. Just *Who* killed Willa Maes, and *Why*, and *What* that would bring justice and retribution upon their heads, that was pretty much on me. And the people whom I thought would most want to find out had said they wanted my nose headed away to New Orleans, like I had planned.

'Anything you need, just ask,' Watt offered. And that brought up the one point that had been sticking in my craw, that I had used his name with Perks. Hadn't mentioned that yet. Didn't beat around the bush.

My father said two things related to my misappropriation, which had become a misappropriation in hindsight. In foresight I thought it had been a smart move, though that was before the intimidation routine out at the shootin' range. *Most valuable thing a man has is his signature,* Dad had said, and more than once. Maybe almost as often he said, *Takes a lifetime to make a reputation, and minute to ruin it. And don't need to be you to wreck it.* Had I thought of them, foresight may have been clearer sight. Nothing left to do now but clean up things.

Fortunately, Watt laughed. 'You know how many people have traded on the van Hij name over the last three centuries? Probably all of them that had the chance. Don't worry, Andrew. This fellow Perks sounds like a piker. I'm still a racehorse compared to that flea.'

We parted, plans reset. It was still early in our not-a-vakay-in-California week, and I felt things would wrap for us in a few days, Thursday at worst, and we would meet them in New Orleans. Although it was May, the city still had its blooms, and despite the devastation from Hurricane Katrina and her sister Ruth, New Orleans in bloom was always well worth at least the two days we could give to her.

On the drive back I said out loud what had been rattling around in my brain. 'Am I being selfish?'

'About what?' June had been all up inside her own head, and it was the first break in a long silence for quite a while.

'Thinking I should back out of further search.'

'You think you can remain indifferent?'

'Not the right word. It's insouciant. Indifference implies disregard for something that can't matter to me. Insouciance means I should care, but choose to disregard it.'

'Thanks, professor,' she said.

'No, seriously. It's the difference that I'm having a problem with. You can't care if you're indifferent. Insouciant, which is what I'm feeling, is a direct disavowal of caring.'

'Fact is, Homer, you do care.' Funny she should call me that out of the blue. He was the fellow who wrote a little tale about a man blown off course, dooming him to wander around the sea and getting his ass into continual trouble wherever he went until he finally got so far inland that people didn't recognize he was carrying an oar. Was that me?

But, fact was, she was right.

Now, to find other people who gave a crap. Maybe Willa Maes people didn't care, but Wiley cared enough to bring them to me. Maybe that's where I was to go next.

'I should call Wiley. Think the funeral was today?'

'Only one way to find out,' she said, digging for the smartphone.

Our friend said, 'Jus' sittin' here 'round a barbecue, talkin'.'

She mentioned the Maes kid. 'Yeah, most 'bout that.' She asked, she listened, her response was, 'So, tomorrow, then. We heard there was a game, and...'

He complained about the reception, so she shut off the speaker phone. 'Better? Some? I said there might be a ceremony for him, at the... Oh, you heard that? Nobody? I guess that doesn't surprise me. Drew misses you almost as much as I do. You sure? Tomorrow night? I can understand that. Sure, we were planning to go to the game, we have news, can Mr. Davis... the high school? No, that's fine. The boat, then.'

She said a few more words, mostly to comfort the big man, much as she could. I'm sure the words worked some. Finally she ended the call, sat with the phone in her lap for a few seconds. 'He sounds so sad.'

'I'm sure. What about tomorrow?'

'He said nobody's going to the game. None of his people, anyway. But since they're staying away he suspects he can get a ride down to the boat. I think he needs to touch her. Been too long, you know?'

I knew. Boy did I know.

'Anyway, he told us do what we have to, go to the game, he'll meet up with us on the *Sweet Discourse* when we're done.'

She took my hand, gave it a shake, and reminded me that I was a good man.

Willa Maes, this Bud's for you.

Twelve

Full belly spelled sleep, but only for my driving companion. About half-way to the marina June's head tipped back against the headrest, her eyes closed and mouth open. I felt certain that little Roly Poly Noly cherubim flitted about her dreams hand-in-hand with some sugar plum fairies. A few times my own eyes had wanted to close, but I had too much experience in taking a wheel in my hands with too little sleep in my head to ever let that become a problem.

But my head, full of bad as my belly was of good, said some thought-clearing activity was needed. June popped awake as I bounced us into the marina's lot, so I suggested we take the *Discourse* out for a little night cruise. A bit of a preggers moon was well risen over the tree tops, promising to stay high long enough to spill some pretty glitter onto the rippling dark sea. I wanted some of that magic. Clears the soul as well as the head.

I had all of the remaining ingredients for making the night magical: a good pair of cigars, an opened but not too much touched bottle of Bordeaux, plenty of gas, and a really nice boat. All that I wanted June to bring to the party was her silk-soft crown of hair, to be felt by my cheek once she rested her head on my shoulder.

The night air was gentle, the partially starred sky allowing only a couple of high cirrus. I had stocked up the jukebox with some New Orleans music, but I felt myself more in a Chet Baker mood. Something slow, something cool, something blue as velvet. Maybe a skosh of Tormé, or a tumbler full of Ella.

But, then, there's what you want, and what the universe will allow.

Soon as I stepped on board I felt something was wrong. I'm far from mystical, but I felt mystical about my boat. I knew her, even though she'd only carried me over the waves for fewer than six months. I had felt her essence before I even saw her, back when I had been talking to the Henriques Yachts people, and again beside her birthing cradle at their shipbuilding facility. Like talking to a babe in the womb.

Everything looked right, nothing felt right. I told June wait on the dock. I carefully stepped up onto the gunnel and then, with the feet of a cat, dropped down onto her deck. I kept a gaff in a holder just above an outrigger base, and carefully slipped it out from its catches. One hand on the gaff, the other on the doorknob. Slow, then fast, I was inside.

Where it was dark, more dark than I'd expected. All the lights were out. That was wrong. Worse, there was a soft big lump dropped right on the salon floor, and I went ass over teacup because of it. Banged my head, hit my forearm on something sharp, lost the gaff that went flying, which — a second later — came out of nowhere to smack me hard on the back of the head. *Mother F!*

The big lump turned out to be Harbor Rat Kevin, asleep after crying, crying because of a beating he'd been given. He jumped up, once I accidentally woke him, then dashed out to the deck. But seeing June, he stopped. June called his name, and he started warbling repeatedly, *Sorry, so sorry* into the night air.

I thought he would jump from the deck to the dock, but I don't like to snug my stern in too close, so the leap would have been difficult. He hesitated just long enough for me to recover my consciousness, get to the salon door and bellow, 'What the Hell, asshole?'

June, more nurturing than I, merely asked him, 'What do you mean, breaking into my boat?'

Darnedest thing. Boy started crying again.

Finally got out of him, 'No place else to go they won't catch up and kill me.'

Well, Hell. First up, *Who* were *They, Why* would they, and *Why* come to *me?* I mean, us?

Then I saw the blood on his forehead. 'June, maybe you could get the first aid. And a beer. For me.'

Kevin was kind enough to help her on board, and as soon as she landed he started to go. I still had the dull-tipped gaff, and time had come to use it. 'Whoa, son. You're going nowhere.' I guessed that had enough Daddy sound in it to stop his forward motion, but the gaff around his arm insured it. 'You're in no shape to put that face in front of your mother. Get below, and let her do what she can.'

There still fell tears, but not in such copious amounts. He shook off the gaff, then pushed past me. I was left on the deck to stew for a few over the remnants to my projected pleasant closure of an up til then pleasant evening.

The hook was more than set, I thought. *Damn fish is running to the boat.*

When I joined them, June was sweeping into a waste can the tissues and pads she'd used on his dried blood. Kevin kept an eye on me like a twice-struck dog. I had little to say. Let him run a bit more.

'Sorry, sir. I'll go soon as...' he looked at June, who kept her eyes down. She'd seen my face. Fake anger. I was actually incapable of the real kind. To take myself that seriously would have cracked me up. No, just a game.

'You broke onto my ship, and you stowed your stinking carcass across my threshold! Caused me a bloody migraine, a knot the size of Gibraltar on the back of my head, and here you are, further co-opting the remains of what had been a nice night. And why? Because you got into a little scrape with some of your classmates? Tell me why I shouldn't kick your ass overboard?'

Nice speech, Nolan. I'd seen one too many movies. But I wasn't there yet. 'Well? What you got to say?'

I remember myself at seventeen. It was the year that I felt more scared than I had ever been before, or since. Pissed off at my parents about something one night, I had driven to the Delaware River, to park and steam, but spotted a rowboat and stole it. Fog rolled in as the tide ran out, and I thought what a wonderful nothingness to get lost in. Pissed off teens think stuff like that.

Mid-river I had shipped the oars and laid myself down in the bottom, wrapping two kinds of fog about me. Despite the real fog, boats were active, but I didn't give a damn if one of them ran me down and drowned me. That kind of pissed off.

The anger had passed, at least enough for me to get sensible, which took much longer than it would an adult. Of course I fell asleep. Drifted quite a while. Once I sat up and saw that I had gone way farther than I should have, I rowed for what I thought was shore, but the strong current had swept me really way downriver.

By the time I heard any waves striking shoreline, the night had gone solid dark. Worse, wherever I did touch a bank, I found only sticky, unsupportable mud. Nowhere to gain firm footing, nowhere to come ashore, and no way to get myself home and safe.

I grew exhausted, the river still bearing me south. I grew more terrified that I would drown and die on the river.

Kevin had that look on his face, the terror of having no certain place to land, himself in a current sweeping him away, deeper and deeper into unsafe waters. My suggestion that I toss him overboard had cut to the bone.

'Who are They? And what could you have possibly have done that makes you think somebody wants to kill you? And what makes you think I'd be somebody who'd listen to your crap story and still give you sanctuary, especially after you broke onto my boat?'

I did know who the most likely assailants were, but I couldn't let Kevin know that I knew. Besides, I not only wanted him to tell me who, but to confess why. For that I needed...

'Andrew, back off the poor boy. Can't you see he's scared enough of somebody already? Doesn't need you screaming down his neck.' She even put her hand on the poor boy's arm. Any woman any time can sucker a fellow into thinking she was his ally.

Poor boy my ass. I was dead certain I was dealing with a murderer, or at least an accomplice. Hanging Willa Maes may even have been his idea. I knew I was crushing him with each word, and despite June's Good Cop defense of *the poor boy,* I knew she knew what I knew, and she would have wanted me to tighten the screws to get that confession. *Well, screw him.*

'Woman, you back off. I stop in at his god damn marina and pay an inflated fee just to park my ass for a layover, I expect some consideration, not some damn employee breaking into my boat just because he got himself into a little hot water...'

'It ain't a little hot water.' He actually sounded pissed that I'd underestimated his predicament. If he only knew how out of the frying pan and into the fire his ass had landed, he'd have chosen another place to cry himself to sleep.

'So convince me.'

Kevin, naturally, hesitated.

'June, call the cops. I got not time for this. I'm going to check the cash box. Maybe this fellow needed a wad for some crap he'd want shoved up his nose. You a druggie, kid? You carrying now?' Experience said what teenaged kid didn't have a joint shoved in one pocket or another.

'I can't. I just thought you'd help me. I thought so, you two...'

'What?'

'Ain't you cops?'

That surprised me. Kevin didn't give off the idea that he was a perspicacious individual. Wharf rats usually aren't, being the type to pay little attention to anything not affecting them. I suddenly had a sense that if he hadn't been part of the hate crime, he'd have one day made a bigger prick of a Dock Master than the one who presently stalked marinas.

'What gave you that idea?'

'Sweeney.'

'Who?' Kid was successfully knocking me off rhythm.

'You know, he runs the docks. He said you was a cop.'

Yeah, cleared that up. Who the Hell didn't know I was once a policeman? God damn, Bennie. Or had it been Loose Lip Kate?

'No kid, I'm just a charter fisherman out of Largo headed up to Orleans. Just laying over here while my first mate visits some relatives. Other than that, and some interesting business prop with your boss, I got no interest in being here. I was a cop. Just ain't no more. Can't help you. But I still know when I should call one, and that time seems now, unless you start talking.'

Kevin was almost all done in. But he clung to his little rowboat with all his might. In a choked whisper, 'I can't.'

'Not good enough, son. And how bad could it be? You screw your best friend's girl?'

He looked like he was about to spit. 'Best friend, yeah.'

'That what you did? I doubt he'll kill you. Might add a few more knocks to that stupid head of yours, but people don't kill you over a girlfriend. Not at your age.'

'Oh yes they do.'

'Hell, girls are a dime a dozen.' June shot me a raised and hairy eyeball. I forced myself to ignore her. 'So that's it? You porked the wrong babe? I was seventeen I might think that was a good thing. Who's the kid took up the hobby of clobbering you?'

He studied me, then June, then me again. Was he safe in my salon? *You betcha.* 'It was Ronnie Perks.'

'Boss's kid? Well, that's not good. He work alone? That seems a nasty knock, not a knuckler. And if he's gonna pitch the state game, I think that trumps being pissed his girl's cheating on him. I doubt it was his knuckles did that.'

He nodded.

Now I knew plain as day that Ronnie's girl didn't crawl between the sheets with the cousin, no matter how pissed off at Ronnie she might have been. There were bigger issues in the air, worse things between them than a little teen-aged jealousy. I wanted me some of the real argument.

'So, who's the kid Ronnie got to work you over?'

'Nobody.'

'Kid, we gonna dance all night? I'm tired, and you ain't pretty.'

'Gregg Whitaker. Ronnie only took me down. Hit my leg with a pipe. Was gonna hit me in the face with it, but Gregg got hold of it. So Ronnie just kicked me in the head instead. Then Gregg took over. But he was hittin' me like he didn't want to, we're friends, and I got my chance to get away, and I didn't know where to run but here. Then I saw your boat with the lights on inside, and I thought you was inside, but you didn't answer and I know how to get in a boat.'

I made like I was considering better locks, but what I was actually doing was recalling the dynamics of the morning in the auditorium. If anyone had gotten pissed at anybody, it probably had been the girl pissed at her boyfriend Ronnie, for getting her mixed up in troubles he had a father that could help him to get out, but maybe not her. As for Ronnie or with Whitaker at the auditorium, there had been no icy distance then. Possible that Cousin Kev had gotten used by the girl to piss off Ronnie that night, but that didn't feel likely.

Still, I kept playing him, letting him think he had control of the game. I asked. 'So who's the mattress?'

'What?'

'The punchboard? The slut? The girl you laid on top of?'

Lob that back, you little shit. He might have no moral center preventing him from lynching a black kid, but I knew he was one of those twisted Bro Code believers. That meant don't crap on your friend's girlfriend if she was blameless, even if she was a cold blooded co-conspirator to murder.

Talk about cognitive dissonance.

The name he gave me was a lie. I reminded him of my past profession by shoving the gaff against his gut. 'The real name.'

He let it out in another tiny whisper. 'Bonnie Lou.'

'What?'

'Bonnie Lou. Dennison. Bonnie Lou Dennison. Cheerleader.'

All names accounted for. Realized then I never got Kevin's last name. Interrogation not over. So I asked. Surprised me.

'I'm a Perks.'

'You his freakin' brother? You screwed your brother's chick? Oh, Kevin.'

'Cousin. He's a cousin. Not even first.'

'Cousin. Your cousin breaks your head over a girl? Kev, this sounds fishy. I think there's something else. I really do. My cop nose is twitching like mad. Something stinks, and it smells like garbage. You smell garbage, June? And on my brand new boat, too. I think I'm getting pissed off.'

One thing I had been actively engaged in while standing in front of the door to the salon was the continual slapping of the gaff against my palm. Rhythmically, but off time. When I said *pissed off,* I raised the gaff against my shoulder.

'Can I just go? I'm sorry. They probably went home. It'll be cool. I'll cool it with Ronnie, I swear I will.'

'Where'll you go?'

'I can sleep in the shed up there. I'll be okay. Seriously. I just want to go.'

'I bet you do. But there's still a little matter of you breaking into my boat.'

'I told you, I just was looking for help, you guys maybe, that's all.'

June spoke. 'You should take him home, Andrew. If there's more, that's his business. Give the kid a break.'

'For you, sweets, not for him. I'll tell you what, Kevin, you come here tomorrow and see me.'

'I don't work tomorrow. It's Ronnie's day to work.'

'Thought there was a game?'

'That's later. His dad makes him work three to six. He drives, so he can get here and to the game. And Wednesday. But we both work Wednesday, me longer than him. He makes Ronnie clean the showers and toilets Wednesdays.'

'Even if he wins the game?'

'Yeah.'

'Actually, that'll be good.'

He must have realized I'd asked him to do something. 'Why you want me to meet?'

'I'm gonna stick my nose in your business.' Kevin jerked a bit, his eyes on the gaff. 'He won't bother you after tomorrow. You just keep out of his face for a while. And keep your woodie out of his knothole.'

'Don't do that. I can handle Ronnie.'

'Yeah, looks like you can.' I pointed at my sweets, who had been bustling about with coffee in the galley below us. 'I'll do it because she wants me to, that's why. Don't you worry. I can handle teenage punks.'

That was something Kevin Perks knew like he knew his last name. Knew it in his quaking bones.

And there were a few other teens I wanted to know it as well.

Thirteen

During that night, rain began. Rains in Spring and Summer on the Gulf Coast frequently bowl in twice a day like a pissed-off drunk looking to smash something. They come down like clockwork, once at nine in the morning and again at four in the afternoon. But those rains, falling so often and so regularly, are forgettable, may even go unnoticed.

Not so much a night rain.

The unexpected spritzing after midnight woke me, but didn't keep me up.

That rain fell — or rather whisked a gray soup about the harbor — all the way past dawn. The day would prove, as the rain continued, enclosing, confining, though hardly embracing.

I wondered if they would cancel the ball game.

I doubted it. More likely, it being Florida, the water that had fallen would rise up again into the air as stinking, greasy sweat-inducing humidity, making the air thick as cotton shoved up the nose.

At first light I saw the rain beading on the plexiglass hatch cover overhead, silvery islands, mercurial and shifting. The kind of rain that falls not hard enough for sounds, but thoroughly enough to subdue all the sounds in the harbor except my favorite, that clock-like clang of a snaffle striking an aluminum mast on a sailboat securely tied in its slip.

That rain never rose to a howl. It merely whispered, and it whispered *sleep. Sleep,* the rain and snaffle said, so I did. We did, though not before I slid my hand onto the radiant warm skin of my lovely June. Not sure, but I think I slumbered with a smile on my face.

No dead boy, no vicious junkyard dogs grinning with drool, no crying harbor rats, no cursing old men, no accusations, no responsibilities, no feelings of unassuageable guilt, no self-recriminations. Just two bodies, naked and smooth, murmuring through Dreamland on a floating home, and every now-and-then rocking the bed.

Don't get no better than that, and it don't ever get left alone.

Thankfully I had time enough to wake, again touch June, have June with her thigh touch me, time enough to come together in the way people dream of coming together on a boat on a rainy morning. Time enough to pee, time to make coffee, and time to drink a cup or two. Time to find my humanity and sense of poetry, before there came a knocking hard against my hull.

Real hard.

June had not yet dressed, and it was a long and saddened eye that watched her jump up to dash away in search of modesty. I slid aside the curtain and saw a bulk in a dark blue slicker dripping on the finger dock. The hood obscured the face, but not the roast beef-sized fist that reached again and struck the hull. I went to the salon door, cracked an opening, and yelled out, 'Yeah?'

'Perks wants to play cards.' Sheriff Beau. 'About eleven. You play.'

I thought he'd asked a question, maybe even two, but I wasn't sure.

'What cards?'

'Cards you play with money. Bring some.'

I had by then decided to extricate myself slowly from the deal, especially since it included intimidation by gunfire, but I hadn't yet prepared for myself a good extrication speech. Thought a simple departure would do that, or Perks's suddenly relevant discovery that I had been a cop.

Some people do think *Once a cop always a cop*, and those people tend to be crooks of one sort or another. It's Newton's Fourth Law of Thermodynamics: A crook in motion stays in motion. And two certain things about Perks: he was a crook, and he would think about this ex-cop that I was still in the cop business.

June missed the exchange, spending her time diving into an old sweatshirt of mine and a scraggly pair of khaki Bermudas of hers, so I filled her in. Only took one sentence.

'You want to?'

'Hell no I don't want to. But I'm thinking I better.'

She mused a moment. 'Maybe you should duct tape Olivia to your thigh.' Yes, June had a tiny pop gun and had named it Olivia. Cute little monster, and not something I'd want crawling up my thigh.

'Maybe I should not.' Taking Olivia to the party would lead to her asking Perks's Peacemaker to get up and dance. Not a Boogaloo I wanted in on.

At some point before the eleventh hour rolled up, June said, 'Think it'll rain all day?'

'Probably.'

'That's so sad, the funeral and all. And the game. They'll probably cancel it, and his memorial. Rescheduling a memorial service seems so, well, crass.'

'The funeral we're missing anyway. It'll go on. Rain and funerals, tea and toast.'

'I know,' she murmured. 'I wanted to see Wiley. The *Discourse* seems wrong without him on it.'

I could have taken that two ways but I had enough concerning me that I didn't need to feel put out or jealous. And there was the rumpling of sheets an hour ago.

'Rainy days feel like transition days. Not like yesterday, and tomorrow won't be like today.' I was feeling philosophical. 'Maybe that's why it always rains when there's a funeral.'

'Does seem like that, more often than not.' She poured herself a coffee.

There's an attitude that comes along with boating, something from the years, centuries, of people living and working on boats. It's a sense that ritual is necessary, that maybe ritual saves lives. Change is not welcome, though change is always expected. Much of what goes on in running a boat is the predicting of change, whether it is the direction and magnitude of the wind, the swells of the seas, the shift of clouds overhead, the mood of the crew. Sameness is safeness. And safeness, on the water, is paramount.

Take coffee.

The coffee maker is ubiquitous in households across the nation, probably other nations, but it isn't what *should* be used to make coffee. For me, coffee must be perc'd, because the aroma of percolated coffee perfumes a morning, especially a rainy, enclosed morning like that one, with a fullness and richness that no sterile, unattended coffeemaker can match. It calls one's attention to the possibility of relief from the tasks at hand, which in itself calls attention to the tasks, and we perform them better with the increased attentiveness.

And for me? The percolator is always a white Corningware coffeepot strapped down on the burner by a jury-rigging of Bungee cords. Sitting in port, no need for the Bungee. But watching June tip the pot over her cup, one finger on the glass percolator knob, said to me *That's how it's done.* Just like my mother did it, Dad, my grandfather, me.

Continuity. Ritual.

But some continuity is not good, and thinking about the distant funeral, since June mentioned it, led me to think of the kind of continuity Willa Maes had faced, would have faced, and his people would continue to face because not enough people think change is prudent. The funeral ritual screams *us* and *them.* Nobody wants a hated face involved in the transition from a hated life to the eternal joy of rocking away in the bosom of Abraham.

Going to play cards with the creeps wasn't part of what I wanted to do in celebration of Willa Maes transition, but it might help with June's personal crusade against that kind of corruption which systemically makes life just that much harder for actually nice people.

Did I want to go? Hell no. Would I go? Hell yes.

Besides Perks and the sullen sheriff were three others, none of them liveaboards like Bennie Wilkins. A major and necessary skill of poker players is the ability to size people up in a usable way, and that's done by not only sifting through the obvious evidence like facial features, clothes and the always evident tells, but in what topics are chosen for conversation, by the speed and directness of response to something said, and just as importantly by declining to respond at all.

Sheriff Beau's greatest asset in playing poker was his seeming indifference to his hand. He never rearranged his cards, barely looked at what he held. He showed zero interest in winning when he did, and less disappointment when he didn't. That made him a dangerous person, because that made every event one of potential unpredictability. That went double because he did nothing unpredictable at all. So, I said to myself, when Beautop did move, move out of his way, and fast.

Besides Perks, running clockwise with the deal, was a fellow whom Perks introduced, with no emphasis, as Flagler. I assessed him as a man of arrested development. Seventeen if a day past, though easily in his late forties. Impulsive, emotional, probably a frustrated womanizer who'd never leave his harridan of a wife, and sooner rather than later getting up from our table broke.

I eventually learned Flagler owned trucks, short haulers, and several tractors, such as front-end loaders, backhoes, bush hogs. Not full road builders or graders, just enough to pick up side work available from larger concerns who pushed blacktop into the swamps.

After him sat the kind of man I always referred to at a poker table as Doc. Well to do, well dressed to show how well to do he was, and not a stitch claiming more. We all wore shorts, me barefoot, others in sandals, and all with a Tee, while he wore Dockers and a buttoned-to-the-collar Oxford shirt, striped. Doc wore glasses, wire-rimmed and certainly bifocaled, but the seamless kind. He did rearrange his cards, but continuously. Hearts weren't sorted with Hearts, Spades with Spades. His sorting was done more to confuse somebody who *thinks* he knows how to read another's hand. He was the kind of guy who took pleasure in taking money from guys like Flagler.

Whether his name was Doc or not did not matter to me. He was Doc.

Then me, then the Sheriff, and finally before returning to Perks again, a lawyerly type by the name of Fredericks, or Frederick. And nothing else. I called him Fred, the two times I called him anything. He didn't respond with much more than a glance up and a card tossed away.

The card play was irrelevant, and I knew that. What mattered was that, when Perks turned the conversation to the land deal, none of the four others flinched. I did, though.

'Thought about taking you back out to the property for some more shooting,' he said, looking past me, 'but this damn rain. Just ruined all my plans. But maybe not yours.'

Thank Heavens for rain.

'I saw what I saw, and don't need another lesson in soup can assassination to see what I needed to see.' Two could play his game, but he had been the man with the guns. Remember, *Olivia* stayed home with June. 'But what I haven't seen is what needs to go in the kitty.'

'So,' he said, picking up his cards from the Sheriff's deal, 'you're in?'

'Not out. All In remains a possibility, even though who brung me to the game has split for parts unknown.'

'Oh, just a little trip with the wife. He'll be back.'

Everyone knows there's a Dead Man's Hand, aces and eights, in poker. But there's also a Dead Hand, and I'd just been dealt it. A three of Clubs, a six of Diamonds, a nine of Diamonds, a queen of Spades, and an ace of Hearts. It's allowed a person to toss away his whole hand, but that makes him a chump. Stupid to fill an inside straight, and Flagler was smiling. Still, what's a few strips of green paper between friends. I kept my hand and called.

Lost it, but to be expected. Trick was, they never saw my cards, only that I was willing to play with the cards as they had been dealt.

Flagler lost his pair of Jacks to Perks's trip treys. Of course, the Sheriff had dealt.

As Fredericks picked up the 52 for his turn at the deal, Perks stood and asked anyone if they wanted a beer. Three okays, not one of them mine. He brought me one anyway. It pooled in the humid air a small lake that I had to keep my cards from drowning in.

Over my hand I looked across at Perks. 'So, what is the opening bid?'

'Fifty thou a share, four shares available.'

'And four shares makes me?'

'One of the boys.' Damn junkyard smile. 'And that's to buy a seat at the table. More to play. But, just details.'

'What about the perks?' I hate irony that's merely coincidence. Watt had said go ahead, and it seemed then necessary to suggest that card.

Boss man asked me, 'Is it in your hand?'

'It is. I might go four shares. Suppose three of them van Hij.' He showed no reaction to my suppose, though Flagler and the lawyer did. A slight shift in the seat, but evident. Doc, no. Then I added, 'Or not. Maybe a share, mine, and he says maybe later.'

It was how Perks reacted that bothered me. He just shrugged.

'He says that, I say not this time,' he said. 'Always a next hand, though. Might be a bigger pot.'

Finally, something out of Sheriff Beau. He chuckled.

Made my frikkin' skin crawl.

Two hours into play, I'd had enough. So did Flagler, but for a different, and worse, reason. Doc mentioned an appointment and I could feel the steam go out of the play. Perks looked up, packing the cards in his fingers without dealing, and said, 'Well, looks like the rain's letting up. Might get a few shots off still. You in, Nolan?'

This time I had an extraction plan ready. 'No.' Stood, shook some hands, left.

The rain had left, but so did the clouds, and that meant the near tropical sun shoved his face in our business, and our business was wet, everywhere. The result? Humidity, the bane and usual condition of a waterman's day. Living on the Keys you get used to it. But Gulf Coast humidity when the sun shines on rain sends every fool diving for air conditioning. Sent this fool.

I was dripping by the time I walked from Perks's office to the *Sweet Discourse*. By my watch it was just past one-thirty. I was hungry. Got June to put down her book and take up her purse. 'We headed to Denny's?'

'Yes we are.'

My reason? I wanted to know who the girl who had the hots for Willa Maes might be. That meant another chit chat with the fake-red-hair waitress Ginny. Besides, they do make a decent chicken fried steak with over-easies.

I carry with me everywhere a small 2x3 inch notebook, lined pages, for keeping notes. Usually notes for what I had to buy: shackles, new line, piano leaders, bait, beer, et cetera. But I also used it to keep track of things I knew my brain would scramble if I didn't write them down.

Quotations, and in this case, the relationship that went from Box Red Ginny to Willa Maes. It looked like this:

(A) Red-haired waitress Ginny → (B) Daughter of Ginny [DoG] → (C) DoG's friend → (D) friend's cousin** → (E) white girl →→*Willa Maes* → Kevin Perks (?)

* Girl may be dog, but who cares?

** (the girl cousin had a brother who played baseball)

While waiting for my Denny's eggs and chicken fried steak I made another list.

1. Killers: Ronnie Perks, Kevin Perks, Bonnie Lou Dennison, Gregg Whitaker
2. Motives:
    a. Ronnie Perks
        i. Pitching at state? Medium Weak.
        ii. Doesn't like black people? Weak.
        iii. Jealousy: Stronger.
        iv. All the above: Strongest
    b. Kevin Perks
        i. Natural follower? Weak.
        ii. Peer pressure? Weak.
        iii. Also jealousy? Stronger, but weak.
        iv. Doesn't like black people? Weak, and weaker
        v. Kiss-ass wimp? Probably
    c. Gregg Whitaker
        i. Whatever Ronnie wants, Ronnie gets? Possible.
        ii. Full blooded psychopath? Strong.
        iii. Doesn't like black people? Who knows?
    d. Bonnie Lou Dennison
        i. Doesn't like black people? Who knows?
        ii. Liked a black person now dead? Rumor has it.

iii. Has little Ronnie p-whipped? Possibly, but
      only if the hanging was her idea. Was it?
      Auditorium mood says nope.
iv.   Is afraid of Perks? Strong, likely.

June asked, 'What are you doing?'

'If I am on the right track, and Bonnie Lou was found out by Perks for picking up with Maes, in whatever fashion, that's gives Perks reason enough to want Maes hurt. Add that he's probably a racist son of a bitch and second on the pitching roster for a team headed to States, more than enough reason. That makes Bonnie Lou guilty by association, but is she associated, or involved?'

'How would she be involved?' June wore skepticism. 'If she had a thing for Maes, she wouldn't want to be party to his harm. And you say she's a cheerleader type, although you better remember I was a cheerleader two years. You're still right, there is a type. If she's one of those' June used the finger quotes, 'type, then I'd bet our last dollar she'd never get involved in anything that would compromise her future. Maes would have been a dalliance, an exotic, a kind of reverse bad boy for her. But she'd know, or think she knew, the Perks kid was where her bread was best buttered. And if she had been in any way intimate with Willa Maes, and the kid found out, he would have dropped her like a hot turd. But you said they were sitting together at the auditorium.'

All that made sense to me. 'They didn't look happy with each other, or at least she didn't look happy with him.'

'Then let's look at everything differently, because one thing I know is girls, and what they do, and can do, to boys. Ginny's daughter has a girlfriend, or said she had one to her mother. I think that, what did you write? DoG? Nice. Anyway, she could just as easily be not only the one who had a thing for Maes, but she could have been the girlfriend of any of the two other boys, that Kevin kid, or the other one.'

'Whitaker.'

'She might have stepped out on one of them with Maes, say maybe it's Kevin. Might be tough for her to date an African American, especially around here, but she'd want to score him, especially if he was the rock star everybody says he was. And it's not likely this girl is anything special, if she was doing Kevin Perks. Girls love the light, and she'd have wanted it on her, even if it meant compromising what people down here think is so damn necessary.'

I could see her dander raising, and pointed it out.

'Well, dammit,' she shouted. 'Doesn't it make you mad?'

'Insofar as it doesn't make me screw up the investigation, yeah, it does.'

'Okay, I see your point. But what I'm getting at is maybe the white girl is Kevin's girlfriend, and he goes pissing and moaning about the situation to Ronnie, who most likely tells Bonnie Lou, who'd maybe even know the girlfriend and could get it confirmed. That wasn't that big of a school.'

I said, 'But there goes Perks's motive.'

'No it doesn't. If Perks is anything chipped off the block, he'd see an opportunity. The stupid Bro Code you're always talking about.'

In a snap, I got it. Perks had reason to be shed of Maes. He would take the opportunity to step up to help his friend and relation. Obviously there was some kind of Master-Slave relation between Ronnie and his cousin, because of money, because of lifestyle. Because of baseball, for chrissakes. Kevin may have been reluctant to go along with Perks plan, but Perks was smart enough to make it seem they were only to scare Maes, but once things got underway, Kevin would be too deep into it to back out.

June, no longer red from anger, glowed from the neatness of having yet another column added up. 'And that's how they got Maes in the woods. Bonnie Lou.'

Which lost me.

'Andrew, easy. Remember us? How we happened?'

Oh yeah.

I had two best friends back in high school, Brian and Joe. Brian had zero interest in anything that wasn't round, covered in leather and was useless unless it crossed a goal line at some point. Basketball, football, baseball. Hell, he even would play field hockey with the girls if they had let him.

Joe, on the other hand, although he was also sport-minded, was skirt-minded to a much greater degree. Although the women had his number, Joe still managed a number of dates among the classes behind us. One of those underclass girls had a sister who had a girlfriend who was named

June Kingswood. The same June Kingswood I was presently studying with both ears, as well as with both hands and both lips.

Girl learns from Big Sis that June thinks I'm cute. I am oblivious. Big Sis's little sis tells Joe, and Joe sees it as his mission to drive me crazy.

No, she isn't.

Yes, she is.

You're crazy.

I'm tellin' ya, she'll go out you ask her.

You're crazy. Look at her. Go out with me? You're crazy.

He wasn't crazy.

Point was, girls can get guys to think any idea they want them to think. June wanted her interests known, and she knew the line that would get it to me. Kind of an Underground Railroad, to which lovestruck suckers become the slaves. That would have been me.

'So you think somehow Bonnie Lou uses what she knows about Kevin's girlfriend to lure Maes into the woods, where the two Perkses and this kid,' I check my notes, 'Gregg Whitaker, are waiting with the anchor rode?'

'Makes sense, doesn't it?'

I had to agree, it did.

Didn't, though, explain Bonnie Lou's distancing herself from Ronnie at the auditorium, but then if she just thought it was all supposed to be a scare, but what happened got all of them completely implicated, then she would have been completely crazed by the consequence of their prank, not all of which she had guessed that morning. Bonnie Lou would hold Perks accountable, because he would have drafted her.

Perks might have cooked up the scheme, but the other two boys went along. When I saw the four Monday morning, they each had a trapped look, except Ronnie. Actually, Bonnie Lou didn't look trapped, so she probably left the scene before they strung Maes up, and being the airbrain she probably was, she figured that exonerates her.

All of this speculation let White Girlfriend — whether she was redhaired Ginny's daughter, a girlfriend of RHG, or nobody — pretty much off the hook.

I liked June's assessment, but I wanted mine completely blown out of the theory pool.

And where I could get the information to do that was headed our way with a coffee pot.

I flipped the notebook closed.

Fourteen

First, look concerned. Second, let her know it wasn't about the doneness of my eggs, the saltiness of my chicken fried steak, nor anything she'd done or not done. Red-haired Ginny the Waitress, by virtue of her professionalism, was about to let her concern about my concern become our concern, and I took the leap at it.

'No, everything's fine. Great. But I was just thinking you might be able help me out here. I just learned a few things, and I'm trying to put some things together about some friends. You remember us, we were here, before?'

'Sure, Hon. Y'all left a nice tip. Gladda you was who was leavin' it.' Her implication? Had it been Davis and Wiley, her tip would therefore have been paltry, *them* being *those* people.

Didn't like the implication, but I could use it to help the cause. 'I hear that. But you said the colored boy who killed himself was doing a white girl…'

'Well, I didn't say that, exactly. But some're sayin' such.'

'We're visiting friends here, and I got the feeling it was their daughter who had been seeing the black boy. They weren't saying, but whenever their daughter got around us, they all acted really PO'd at each other, even with us right there. Seemed it might a been about that. I'm thinking she was the white girl, and I just can't see it.'

'Who's yer friends?'

'We're here visiting the Dennisons. Doubt you know 'em.'

'You know the Judge? They eat here all the time. Him and the fam.' She leaned in, co-conspirator in hate. 'So, you thinkin' maybe Bonnie Lou might be runnin' with a colored boy? That's a hoot. You got nothin' there. She'd never touch anything hanging a-tween the legs a one of them. She's Judge Dennison's daughter straight down to the bone.'

Dang! More than I expected, and I felt my lucky stars. I hoped Judge Dennison wasn't chowin' down at Denny's any time soon. I also wondered if he was the deciding judge Perks kept in his pocket. But with Ronnie knocking the knees apart on Bonnie Lou, that was very likely the case.

'Well, that's good news.'

Paid up, got the Hell out of there.

I'm sure June said something I should have paid attention to while I drove back to the *Sweet Discourse*, but my mind started rolling details around like they were rocks in a lapidary machine. Or rather it started throwing images and scenes up to the movie screen on my mind's eye. We've all done it, driven a car while all up inside our heads, and most of us come out alive at the end of it.

I suspected, once I came to, that June had her own movie going, because I think she sat as silently beside me as I did her. Glad she wasn't driving.

Here's my movie.

Late afternoon Saturday, maybe even after the game last Friday, sultry hot tropical air, boys done, pulling off their sweaty cleats, a few of the girlfriends hanging around waiting for boys. Locker room, talk, Ronnie Perks pleasant and best bud to his target, a slender but well-muscled cinnamon skinned youth destined for greatness but not yet consumed by it. A good kid, name of Willa Maes, after the great black ballplayer, a bit shy, not immune to the girls of his own race who purred when they called him by one of those private neighborhood nicknames. Butter? Playdough? Maybe Poodle? Something they grew up with but nobody in the regional high school knew much about. Willa Maes. Born with the good fortune to have that last name, with more fortune to have that right arm, a spring-loaded rocket rifler and a pair of talented fingers trained to the horsehide.

Maybe a pretty kid, too, which doubled because of his shyness. A dimple or two that popped out when attention from a white girl penetrated a little deeper than his social training had said *Aw shucks, go 'head and 'llow it, permit yo self some attention. Doan' it feel nice?*

Ronnie? Okay, asshole sometimes, but then there was his Dad, and everybody knew about Mr. Perks. Not like when his people talked about that white devil they did it in murmurs and whispers so the kids didn't hear. Oh no, the kids were *supposed* to hear how big a dick old man Perks could be. *How they gonna learn?* Ronnie, dropping down on the wooden bench between the lockers. Bonnie Lou prepped for her role: *Hey, Maes. My girl's gonna wanna talk to you, and she's making me make it okay. So she talks, you might wanna listen. I don't like what she's helpin' set up, but hey, ain't about me, now is it? You go listen to Bonnie Lou, but that's all you gonna do. You got that?*

And Willa, a black boy from where white boys don't go to play baseball, hearing a white boy say he better listen, all the alarms going off, he listens. But then Bonnie Lou, pretty, she's got that kind of way that stops shy boys from stopping them from anything they want to do, when she says, *Hey, Poodle,* or whatever nickname he never expected to come out of her mouth, he hears more than alarms.

He hears maybe for the first real time the sugar-smooth voice of good old Satan warming up for a conversation. Pretty Bonnie Lou goes on to say the one thing he wanted to hear, but was afraid he'd never get to hear, even though he's the best pitcher in forever, *Y'all know Cindy Sue, doncha?* Or Bobby May, or Ronnie Bob, or one of those classic hick combinations the South can't shake off any better than a dog can ticks, *Y'all know Cindy Sue got a thing for you. Me, I can't see why,* bats a set of eyelashes calling attention to her baby blues, *why she'd have a thing for such a skinny little thing like you,* maybe even slides a just a bit too moist a palm over his forearm, *but she does, and she wants to see you Satiddy over to the Babe Ruth ball field, y'know, one by the woods there, that is you can shake loose about noon? You don't say to nobody was me told you, her secret is my secret, and now, honey, it's our little secret. Y'all go see her if you're a smart boy, noon, Satiddy. Okay? You want, me and Ronnie come with you, case you're shy?* At which Bonnie Lou slides that hand down the smooth dark muscles that never shake at the touch of horsehide, but which quiver under the touch of the cheerleader. *You jus' tell Ronnie you will and it'll be all set.*

And the poor boy, all alone with his secret and his passion and his swelling, he counted off the minutes, cooking up reasons he was headed to the Babe Ruth baseball field near the woods all by himself, though it was Saturday noon and his boys, and maybe more than a few of the girls, expected him to hang with them. Running through his head? The soft lips, the little girl voice, baby blues and shy ways of cotton candy pink Cindy Sue, because he had noticed her, and had noticed him noticing her.

Poor kid, doomed. The long mosquito-riddled walk under a hot sun, the dropping arrow rays of the west Florida sun firing up clouds of gnats over milkweed and bottle brush. Poor kid, doomed. And — surprise of surprises — Bonnie Lou herself just up there ahead, and Ronnie Perks, pushing out not just her curling lips but her hips, and Perks's fingers maybe touching a part of Bonnie Lou it just ain't appropriate to touch in plain view of anybody, of Willa Maes for sure. Maybe the Poor Boy doesn't see Kevin Perks shaking behind a knot of palmetto, or Gregg Whitaker — *Damn, that asshole?* — crouching as low as he can get behind a toppled-over yellow pine, a ball bat twisted over and over in his sweating hands, waiting.

And Ronnie Perks, pulling his wet lips off Bonnie Lou's mashed and ruby-red, turning to face the confused but hooked Willa Maes with that same dog-tooth grin everybody remembers having seen at least once on old man Perks, with a directional nod of his head tells the Poor Boy *Cindy Sue's sweet little white body's waitin' for ya, Boy, and is she ever hot.*

He passes them, to head into the forest by the Babe Ruth Field, all goes dark. Maybe he smells the cheap perfume of Betty Lou Dennison, or the cold sweat on Perks, or perfume and sweat both on both, and he gets a tingling sensation that maybe all's not right with the world, but he goes into the woods anyway, dragged by the fresher and sweeter scent of what possibly could happen if he put himself in the hands of a plush young teenage white girl all ready for him in her summer dress.

Bonnie Lou and Ronnie watch him walk into the woods just far enough. Perks follows. He doesn't tug his girl after him, but he expects she will follow.

And if she followed Ronnie into the woods, Bonnie Lou Dennison soon gets to see three boys working hard to put the fear of white into the heart of black, sees the length of old anchor line Kevin's stolen from some forgotten gunkhole inside some forgotten boat. She gets to see the baseball bat, a bat with blood on it that later would become part of a raging bonfire in some other woods or field, a fire whose raging would become emblematic of the frustration and pent up rage turned loose out of three very drunk boys. That would be later.

Then, however, she'd be watching Ronnie and Gregg Whitaker lifting up the difficult body of the dull eyed and slack-lipped baseball pitcher, see Kevin slip the looped anchor line around the Poor Boy's neck, Perks laughing, calling him the names they'd never have called him without that probability of getting their throat cut down the road on some future dark night.

And then she'd get to watch Kevin go make that clove hitch and double half, Ronnie and Gregg holding a kicking Poor Boy even higher, him scared, them successful, but then Ronnie lets go of Maes, and maybe Gregg too, seeing how he followed Ronnie into everything good or bad, and Maes drops, the body frantic, thrashing, kicking and clawing, and Bonnie Lou Dennison goes wide-eyed and more white than she'd ever been, aware — as Willa Maes was surely aware — that any more minutes of that and there'd be no more minutes forever.

And maybe she'd cry out to the boys, *Okay, that's enough, that's enough,* — but for them, *Oh no, not enough.* And then she'd see the Poor Boy had gone limp, and maybe she'd see on at least Kevin and Gregg the look they'd wear for the rest of their lives, the one they would wear during a ceremony in the school's auditorium: that consuming face of hidden terror rooted in who they really were.

But she'd also get to see that dog-tooth grin on her boyfriend not go away, and maybe over her screams, *Cut him down, cut him down, what are you doing?* she'd actually form the last words *Oh my God!* which said all ever needing to be said.

Maybe she didn't follow the boys into the woods. Maybe she didn't see, just heard later. Didn't god damn matter. Didn't matter one God Damn at all.

Guilty, every last hating ugly damn summabitchin' one of them.

I felt my hands tighten around the wheel. If maybe there was a bat, and it hadn't been burned in some backyard bonfire. But that hadn't appeared as part of the evidence, only the rope and the body, and neither was any longer evidence. *No,* I thought, there's only what lies in the heart of four committed to evil and conjoined because of evil.

How to dig that out for all to see?

We pulled into the lot at the marina and I sat there a moment, or what I thought was a moment, the engine running, the air conditioning rattling out its conditioned air. Then June said, 'Drew.'

'Yeah?' I turned off the car engine.

'It wasn't my cousin found her boyfriend hanging by a lamp cord.'

'I know.'

'It was after you, though, college, my junior…'

'S'okay, June. I guessed that.'

'It was awful. Awful. For a long time.'

'I can guess.'

'I wanted so much to find you, talk to you. But I didn't know…'

'I know. S'okay, June.'

It wasn't, and if she had found me, then used me for some solace and some comfort, it would never have become okay. There never would have been June and me sitting together in a marina lot with my hand atop hers. But what else was there to say? 'Really, I understand.'

We sat for a few more minutes, but with the car off, her hand under mine, the heat went past oppressive to almost intolerable.

On our walk to the *Sweet Discourse* I spotted what I first thought was Kevin, but realized quickly enough was Everything-to-gain, Nothing-to-lose Ronnie Perks.

Walk the halls of any Center City police headquarters, you're going to meet up with a killer. Most'll surprise you. Weed out the drive-by punks, and they are fewer in the statistics than you'd imagine, you're left with two kinds of people who take the life of another. There's the overwhelming majority which are the stunned, apologetic, weeping burnouts living marginally on the edge of reason and ability.

Occasionally, and only three times in my career, a stone-cold killer would sit in chains in view of you. Their faces — and you'll remember each one more clearly than the one in the mirror while you shave or put on mascara — will stun you, and forever. They each will have a face exactly like someone you thought you knew, except somewhere deep in the eyes there'll be a blankness, a cold retraction from the integration with the living that makes you *you*.

I didn't want a closer look at Ronnie Perks, but I knew I'd have to peer into those eyes. Had to be sure.

I got sure in a split second.

Acting as though I thought he was Kevin and not the whom I knew him to be, I hailed him. Shoved June along, *go back to the boat,* and waved my hand. *Yo, Kevin, hey!*

Don't know where I get the will to shove down what I feel, but I can.

He had that cocksure expression letting me know he thought *Another fuckin' asshole boat owner wants something.* So that's what he wanted, that's what he got.

'Kev, that game... Oh, you ain't Kevin. Sorry. I thought.'

'He don't work today, and most days when he does work.'

'Well, yeah. Hey, listen, he told me about a high school baseball game tonight, and I told him I'd like to go. I am a baseball nut myself, played first, and...'

'So?' In other words, *Why you in my face, Old Man?*

'Well, I wondered, do I need tickets? What time's the game? I'm pretty sure I can find it, he said it was a home game and they were playing some Ocala team I think.'

'West Port.'

'That's it. Night game?'

'Yeah.'

I turned to walk away, then stopped. 'You think worth going?'

'I'm starting pitcher.'

'Really?'

'Yeah. Unless you lived under a rock, I'm taking the spot of our other pitcher. Killed himself.'

'What?' I feigned surprise. 'Why the Hell...'

Ronnie just shrugged, the bastard.

'Well then, I guess I'll see you there.'

'Guess you will.'

I beat it out of there.

Definitely a cold fish. Maybe prehistoric gator.

I left him, but the murder didn't leave me. On the short walk down to the *Discourse* I found myself rechecking all things again. There were three things that had to occur in killing the boy.

First, Willa Maes had to be enticed to the location.

Second, Willa Maes had to be subdued. Whip-muscled though he might be, Perks wouldn't have done it. That meant Kevin or Whitaker dropped him with something. Was — maybe — a gun? Daddy Perkses?

Third, Maes's had to be raised up.

Four conspirators. And no reason not to think maybe more, but that clouded the picture. More was unnecessary, more would have become unmanageable, and Ronnie Perks would have supposed that.

I thought hard on which of them was most likely to give up the others. Gregg Whitaker I didn't know, and seems he had the least investment except allegiance to one of the Perks cousins, maybe both.

Bonnie Lou seemed to have the least invested passion of all, except what the red-haired waitress had implied. I've seen mobs, studied them on the force, and frequently it's a woman acting as cheerleader who gets things happening. Or kicked off, at least. If Bonnie Lou Dennison was the racist Hellion, she'd be least likely to crack. Couldn't fix her in my mind, but she had slid up my criminal scale after what I learned at Denny's.

Ronnie Perks? No way. Cold fish. Most to lose, too.

Kevin Perks, on the other hand, was already scared. Scared big time.

In order to get a person or persons to do what you want, there are four avenues of persuasion. You could use Reason, to make him see reality, if he is a reasonable person. Could work with Kevin, but he's a teenaged kid, a tribesman not known for reasoning skills. I easily tossed logic as a tool.

There's appealing to Moral Codes, that sense of right and wrong, but that seemed in all of them already corrupted. Using lynching told me that. Hard to employ morality on those without morals.

There's appealing to Emotions, specifically the sense of well-being. I could put a finger on the pressure point between Feeling Good for what they'd done, and the prospect of whole truckloads of Bad inevitably coming down the road for what they had done. I could see making an approach on that. Kevin seemed halfway there, and Bonnie Lou's soured expression in the auditorium said maybe she was way too vulnerable to that.

That left the fourth, Violence. Violence usually works because it is the least cerebral, the most immediate, when it's physical. But I couldn't get physical with teenagers, no matter what they did. I'd be the one landed in jail. Though physical violence works, violence need not be physical. I wasn't looking for instant response. Mental violence moves things along fast enough. Just ask any perp in an interrogation room. The fear of violence can be most effective. And the threat of physical violence, itself only mental, can work wonderfully, especially since it's hard to prove. Of course, terroristic threats was, is, illegal, and punishable. Trick was, don't get caught. Best way not to get caught? Don't threaten where there may be witnesses.

If Kevin was the weakest of them, I wanted to scare the crap out of Kevin, but I couldn't do it. One reason? He might talk, have already talked about the nice people on the boat, and he might point. At me. Being in the junkyard with that dog up in his office might turn violence on me. Or worse, on June.

They come to hurt me, I live. Maybe not happily, but I could live with it. They hurt June, they better kill me.

Just as I lifted my foot up onto my boat, I realized the threat to Kevin didn't have to come from me. I needed someone else to join the fray, so I cast a mental eye on my photo book of possible assistants.

Immediately Wiley came to mind, but just as easily I dismissed him. Though not Black himself, he was still dark. Introduced a variable with unnecessary consequences.

Watt? No. He wouldn't, even though he could, and effectively. A new Dad of a new boy, he'd decline hurting, even emotionally, someone else's kid.

Finally, and most importantly, my assistant would have to be available, and capable of getting there and away quickly. It was the idea of instant mobility that led me to think of someone who not only could come quick, but who'd want to do it just for the opportunity to exhibit sheer meanness.

Frank Whitcomb.

Frank owned a seaplane.

Frank was afraid of very little, and that was probably a fear of having to spend any night without getting laid.

Frank was cheap, or I should say *inexpensive.* The thrill would have been payment enough, but a case of lager went a long way. And expenses, of course.

Frank had nothing to lose except time, and he was a man often willing to throw away time at the drop of a hat.

Frank Whitcomb was one of those black haired, black eyed guapos of no distinguishable ethnicity, quick to tan and always tanned to a ruddy bronze. Made his piano-key teeth gleam, but he never looked wolfish. And he had no discretion when it came to flesh, none whatsoever. He'd screw a bedbug you get a bra on it.

Soon as my feet hit the deck, I called him.

He was in. Long conversation, June popping her head out, her look of unsatisfied curiosity dismissed by me with a lift of the eyebrows, me rattling out all the details. He could make it to whatever location in a few hours. I checked my watch. He'd land mid-game, and if I was waiting for him in the *Sweet Discourse,* we could catch Kevin by the seventh inning.

And that is exactly what occurred. Sort of.

Fifteen

Never thought I'd get excited over the possibility of beating up on a kid, even though by proxy, but I felt excited. All the thinking on it was over. Time had come to be doing. June spotted the change in my mood as I tumbled out my plan to Frank, and she was kind enough, and patient enough, to wait me out before telling me that we were meeting Wiley and Coleman Davis, if he stayed, at the night game.

While I was thinking and talking to Perks, she had gotten it in her mind to touch base with Wiley, thinking maybe he'd need a friendly voice before leaving for the funeral.

Oh, poop.

I said to her, 'Maybe I could drop you, and you could fill him in. But then again, with Davis there, think it's a good idea? I mean, this is still only speculation.'

'You think Davis would really go there? Didn't Wiley say none of them were coming?'

I had to remember. Yeah, he had. But I guess he changed his mind, maybe to piss off some white people. I had to admit, June's use of *them* snagged in my ear on its way to the brain, but some things just don't need mentioning.

Anyway, minor details. We'd work them out.

What I really wanted to do with Wiley was not so much to fill him in on the *Who* and *What*, but to find out what, since last we saw him, had been happening among the people he was with. Was there talk? Was there speculation? Was there anything that said *Drew, you're on the right track?* I'd run down roads before that seemed headed to the right and final location, but just when I thought I'd arrived at my destination, all things turned south, and I was nowhere near where I thought I'd been headed.

Very disconcerting.

'More important,' I told her, 'for this to work, you have to get a moment alone with Wiles to tell him about Frank. I bring Frank to the game and Wiley spots him and says something, might mess things up. I don't want anyone to know Frank got my invite to the party. Not in any way.'

I wanted Frank at the game to see Perks pitching. He was to find Perks after the game, say what I wanted him to say, make the threat and then walk away. I'd take him back to his plane, he'd head out and be out of the picture for good. *Fwit fwit fwit,* my hands clean.

All I needed was maybe three minutes of him scaring the crap out of Perks, or even better, pissing the boy off. And we'd get that done by tipping our hand to his eyes, let him know he wasn't in control of everybody. That would send him after the others, to find out who talked.

I felt Frank could best fly into Flor a Mar, where he could tie up his seaplane, me find him, and get us both back to the game in time to do what needed to be done. But as June and I were leaving, we saw Ronnie Perks coming down the dock with a fat manila envelope in his hands.

'Hey, I thought you were pitching tonight?'

'My dad let's my ass loose. All I got to do is dump this on ya, I'm gone.'

I took it, wished him — reluctantly, but necessarily — good luck, and walked a few paces behind him toward the car lot. Package was sealed, unlettered in any fashion, but fairly substantial. I hefted it, looked at June, who nodded. We both had a guess.

She took it, and once in the car opened it, read as I drove. It was what we expected, papers relating to sale of land. Actually, it was two things I expected, but didn't think Perks expected me to expect. In the back was a rental agreement for a boat slip twice that which I had to pay Willington down in Largo, a far more prestigious location than Perks' waterhole. And there was a transfer of title to an Owens cruiser named Twinkletoes for about twenty percent of the buy-in of all four property shares. A steep bit of vigorish.

There was no mention anywhere of the lawsuit against the property. I guess Perks forgot that.

Some people get excited reading racing forms, by Rand MacNally maps, by old newspapers, whatever. Nothing excites June in print like spreadsheets and legal crap. She was engrossed in what Perks had given us, and, as I pulled up to the high school, I almost had to pull it out of her hands.

'Sorry to be dropping you so early.'

She pouted as I tucked the pages back into the envelope. She faked a whine. 'It would give me something to do.'

'Yeah, and it'd give other people something to speculate about they got their beady eyes on you reading it. No, better off on the back seat. And better in the trunk. You can read it by bed lamp tonight.'

'You really know what it takes to turn a girl on.'

'If it gets me laid.' I kissed her goodbye and set off for Frank.

Frank was already there, and already working a young girl who'd come out on the dock to watch a seaplane rumble up to a mooring. She was almost cute, and almost legal. Frank spotted me, waved, and whispered something to the girl that made her stand really straight, and really speechless.

I could only imagine.

First thing I did was stretch forward my hand, and not for a handshake, but to turn over a pair of Benjamins. Frank's a friend, but he lives by paid favors. Hasn't had a regular job since he got the pilot's license, if he ever did have a regular job. He'll do something for free, but only if at the end of it there's beer, a bed and a body in it waiting for him. I wasn't into that kind of payoff, so the two hundred was my option. There was never a discussion of cost or charge. He always accepted what was offered, so long as it was enough. It wasn't, you just knew. Took my payment without a word, just like always.

Chitchatted our way out of there after I settled up his mooring bill, some about the girl, some about the flight, some about the possibility of his taking the little girl up for a little flying, a big landing, and the other things.

'You hungry?'

'Not for food.' And he didn't mean booze. Frank never flies with an ounce of alcohol in him, or his passengers. Driving boozed on a highway isn't a great idea by any account, but at least you can pull over and sleep it off. Up there, not so much.

I was wrong about the inning. We made great time, and the third had turned out to be long string of at-bats for both teams. Score was 11-9, home team behind. We'd agreed he'd go to the opposite team bleachers, and if for any reason Perks wasn't on the mound I'd take off the Phillies ball cap that was usually and prominently on my head.

As Frank walked away and I headed to the hometown bleachers, I feared the tattle-tale scoreboard was telling me that maybe Coach had yanked Ronnie Perks, since he'd been smacked around over two innings. But then, doubtful, not with Daddy Perks watching from the dugout. That's right, sitting with Coach. Perks. Bottom of the fourth, home at bat, one out. But quick work by the opposing pitcher shut down two batters to end things.

I spotted June as the teams began the top of the fifth, all fielders running out to their posts, Young Perks taking his good old time retaking the mound. Despite the knock-around, he looked fresh, eager, up for it. He looked like he wanted every pair of good eyes turned on him.

What a putz.

The kid tossed up a ball, way outside, then got control back. He laid down a pair of hot curves before getting his third — he waved off the call for a fastball — smacked line-drive foul over the left field fence. That's where Frank had taken up position, and the man jogged the few paces after the foul ball, finding it in a crop of rough grass.

Another thing about Frank. He also played ball, once upon a time, and we argued frequently about my home team, especially when they had crunched the Tampa Bay Rays championship hopes in the '08 World Series. So when he picked up the ball and hurled it in one long arc back to the boy on the pitcher's mound, he got a few claps. More than that, he got young Perks' attention. Especially since he waved at the boy.

Eventually, Perks struck that batter out, the next popped one to center for the second, a walk on the third, and a high fly out to short for the closeout.

Not that you're interested.

I had slid in beside June, carrying a half dozen hotdogs and a carrier full of drinks. They don't serve beer at high school games, even in Florida. Frank would not be happy.

Coleman Davis reigned stiffly at the far end of my friendly trio, a dry stalk beside towering Wiley, and he didn't look comfortable. A smattering of dark faces, all old men, several times during the innings leading to the seventh, turned toward him some knowing stares. I got that Davis wasn't just a guy from the neighborhood.

The hotdogs were appreciated by all, but the Cokes stayed lined up in the carrier beside me. All we could manage was small talk, except once — before the seventh inning stretch — June leaned in to whisper, 'Haven't said anything. Take Wiley for a walk.'

I figured I would do that during the stretch, but that ritual was co-opted by the administration so that the coach could come up into the announcer's booth for a repeat of honors about the departed Willa Maes. I felt it inappropriate to take Wiley from Davis's company during that, but it was Davis himself who got up without a word, stood, the old men rising with him, and then each filed down off the bleachers. They then walked away. Wiley had attempted to rise with them, but Davis waved him sit back down, *Just doan' wanna hear.*

Couldn't blame him.

Once Davis was out of earshot I switched with June in order to talk quietly with Wiley.

'You saw Frank?' He did. 'I have so much to tell you, and looks like no time. Will say this, see the kid pitching for home? I'm pretty sure he's maybe one of them we're looking for. I called Frank to stir things up, and if it works, I'm just sure there's going to be one of them making a confession that even our friend the Sheriff can't ignore.'

He didn't get my 'friend the Sheriff' reference, so I spelled out that an opportunity arose for me to get to know some of the Powers That Been.

I covered what I could, told him that, besides the pitcher, I figured two other boys and Perks' girlfriend had been in on the lynching. But I also got him to swear to me that he'd say nothing to anybody until I was sure. No sense people going off half-cocked, even though I felt strongly about what I had deduced. Wiley swears on something, you can take it to the bank.

Also true to his word, Kevin Perks was nowhere to be seen. But I spotted pretty Bonny Lou and her appointed guardian, Gregg Whitaker. Pointed out all three. Wiley listened, head and eyes lowered.

'You bin busy, Cap'n.' I could see he wasn't a hundred percent pleased that I had been.

'What, Wiles?'

He hesitated. 'Stirrin' up things ain't always worked out best 'round here's all.'

'You want the killers out?'

'Course I does, but I ain't local. Not now, anyways. You think won't be no mud flung up on them all, once you get them boys confessin'? But you don't know, do you?'

'I can't see how. Not a single person who's a friend of yours will have to go say anything. Those boys talk, it becomes a white problem. They'll have to take care of it, and when it does happen, everybody'll see it was just stupid kids, not a race thing at all.'

'And you really thinks that?' He gave me a really suspicious look, like I'd just grown much bigger ears as a consequence of venal sinning. I got his drift, and I apologized.

'This won't be a match to tinder like it could have been. I can't see anything but good coming from this. But you say the word, and I mean you, Wiley, not Davis, not the Reverend, not anybody else. We stop. But in an hour, maybe less if Perks's pitching falls off, it'll be too late. So if you think stop, we stop now and I wave Frank off. You saying that?'

He looked off to where Davis had gone. I couldn't see him, and felt Wiley didn't either.

'Jus' not my call. But maybe fearin' some mud'll be flung no matter what is better'n buryin' ourselves like we always does. Go 'head, Cap'n. I'll handle Cole.'

'How are things, with him? He seems more invested than I'd have thought. I mean, I get how awful everything is, but he seems cut right down to the bone.'

'We all is, but him more'n others 'cause Willa was a'most a son to 'im. Y'know his name's not really Willa Maes. It acherly Dan'l Maes Ichobi, but nobody call him that 'cause his daddy Big Danny Ichobi was killed hisself 'fore Willa come into this world.'

'But why not use the last name?'

'Danny Ichobi wasn't of 'em. He come from Ocala, one of the east coast Seminoles, or was but they changed the rules about the blood. Not more'n a little part Seminole. They wouldn'ta called 'im cousin. So for Willa's mama t'get married, she just left off the Ichobi, and then didn't never get married, so it stayed Maes.'

'And Davis?'

'He'da married Ciminy Maes, that's Willa's mam, but he was in a pickle hisself then. In Kuwait, fightin'. Then when he come home no arm and all, askin' didn't seem so good an idea to 'im. And Willa was out by then.'

'How you know all this, Wiley? They been talking up a storm?'

'Family, Cap'n. Cole is cousin to my ol' lady.'

He mentioned his wife so infrequently, and probably thought about her less, that I forgot he had one. And kids, which I saw once, but they were happy under the roof of another man, even though she and Wiley never finalized a divorce. Probably because they never really got married. Just the jumping of the broom. He'd called their parting a swamp divorce. 'We said so, it was so. Not like we got more'n a coffee can a piss 'tween us. Them kids is better off.'

The major contributor to that swamp divorce was an enforced separation imposed by the judiciary of the Great State of Florida. But that's old business, and Wiley's business.

There was then movement that meant the game was about to pick up again. At the same time, arguing between two men started around behind the concrete building in which the tickets and hotdogs were sold. I looked up in time to see Rick Perks land ass down in some Florida sand just this side of the back corner.

He was back up fast enough, but he didn't re-enter whatever fray he'd gotten involved in. I heard a woman behind me say, 'What in the Lord's name has he gotten himself into now?'

I turned to see who had spoken, spotted a well-dressed and rather attractive woman standing, eyes fixed on Perks. Then I saw her blanch, then gasp, finally raising a shaky hand to her trembling lips. Of course I looked back at Perks, just in time to see Coleman Davis press himself more fully in Perks' face. The white man moved back a half step.

A few white fellows near the end of the bleachers headed towards them, and Perks' — smart enough — held up a hand to fend off their intervention.

'Wiley, go get him.'

He did, but not fast, not in any way that would have escalated confrontation. He could have run like the fullback he'd once been. His size alone would have stopped six men from tossing a punch, let alone Perks and three cronies. But it wasn't necessary. Like mad dogs they just glared.

June said to me, 'How old is Mr. Davis?'

I'd figured seventy minimum, but Perks hadn't landed on his ass in the middle of an argument because he'd slipped on a hotdog.

Once Wiley reached Davis he stepped in between him and Perks, said something, looked over at me, tossed his head towards the lot. I shook mine in agreement, holding my thumb and pinky extended as to say *call later*. They left.

I didn't know what to make of Coleman Davis and Perks not just knowing each other, but having enough history between them to engage in a public ass whooping.

Wished I'd had more time with Wiley, to make clear to him that he was to say nothing about my suspicions about Ronnie Perks, his girlfriend and friends, but I hadn't. I was sure, seeing Davis being led away, sort of, by Wiley from more chitchat with Perks, that if Davis found Willa's killer to be a Perks, there'd be a few subsequent exchanges of heated words in their future, and maybe heated up lead pellets.

But I couldn't worry about that, as that ball was already let fly. There was a more important pitch coming, and I could barely wait to see it.

Didn't have to wait long. Perks let up three more runs in the eighth, and with Daddy out of the dugout, the coach yanked him.

One thing you do when you play ball, any ball, is you stay with the team. Even if you're ejected by a ref, you stay with your team. Unless your coach says *Get your ass to the showers* because you're a big time jackass, you stay with your team.

Not Ronnie Perks.

I had a decent view of that point between the dugout and where Frank Whitcomb walked up to him like he was a pro scout. Hand out for a handshake and everything.

I saw Ronnie light up, I saw Ronnie smile, I saw Ronnie listen, then I saw Ronnie turn gray. Then I saw Ronnie turn white, and then, Frank putting out his big glad hand again, I saw Ronnie turn red, and turn rude. Wouldn't take Frank's friendly gesture.

Imagine that.

I'd written his script, and if Frank had stuck to it, it had to have been something like this:

You Ron Perks? Some okay pitching. Everybody gets a bad night. But I liked what I saw. I think you maybe could have a shot at a scholarship, maybe even a tryout, except of course for that prison time you'll be serving for your part in a little recent hanging I heard went on around here this weekend.

Yessir, not a smart idea putting a rope around somebody's neck. But don't you worry about that right now. What you should worry about is how the Hell does this man know anything. And I do. Don't move your lips. Just hold your ears still. You see, I'm not here to get you in trouble.

No sir. I just hear your Pop has been able to set himself up a pretty high pile of cash offshore, and I want a little of it. I don't see any of it, I just might have to go to one of your compadres and let them know you're about to confess what you got them to do. I was planning to go to them too, but other than the Judge, not a lot of scratch coming from there.

They just might want to stay out of jail, and they might get it into their heads to make it seem your guilt about hanging a poor black boy out in the woods was reason enough to do yourself in. All they'd need to do was confess you came to them saying you were gonna do it.

So whaddaya say, kiddo? A million worth of my goodness? Don't decide now. You think it over. By the way, you're probably thinking I have no proof. First my proof is how well you've been listening to this, all polite and subservient. But the real proof? Seems like every damn kid

149

in the world has a cell phone takes pictures. Every one of them. And some of them have close ties to an overachieving relative like me.

So, Frank the Shakedown Artist said, putting out his hand, *Friends?*

Man, I slept good.

Got Frank back to his plane, but not before insisting on feeding him. He filled June and me in on the quick conversation with the kid, chuckling through many of the fine points.

'Thought I'd be smelling that kid's back door any minute after I mentioned how bad an idea hanging a black kid was. You've gotten me in some fun times, Drew, but I had so much fun play acting in this one I'm almost tempted to refund one of these hundreds.'

He caught my expression.

'But y'all know I'm only tempted by one thing, and you ain't got it. And Miss June here, no matter how tempting, ain't never on the menu.'

'You bet your ass she isn't.'

Watching him lift off the black water, I had to envy him going back to Key Largo. No good comes to me when I leave there. But I felt things had finally moved, and in a positive direction.

There's a point in every investigation, a moment when there's a shift from frustration to hope. Maybe it's unexpected response to a chance call, or an anonymous tip, maybe it's a piece of evidence that gets matched in just the right way with another piece, maybe it's a totally unexpected confession you didn't even have to work for. But most times it was that moment when you know you have the suspect, even if he isn't in custody. Just a matter of time. You know you have him because you have the complete picture, and you have an upcoming chance to spell everything out to his continually dismayed face.

That's when you feel like saying, *Gotcha, you son of a bitch.* That's when things call for a celebratory scotch, or even several.

I got my assurance moment the second I saw Ronnie Perks lose his smile. Had he gone quizzical, had he jerked back his face and turned on his heel, I'd have been nowhere. But he kept listening, trapped by every one of Frank's words like a snake to a charmer's music. He stayed.

And that meant, *gotcha, you son of a bitch.*

And soon, I'd have them all.

Sixteen

Or so I thought. Never count your chickens until they're in the soup pot.

I had slept well, so well that I missed June rising. I brought my fogged-in self into the galley by following the quivering aroma of coffee with my nose. She'd left the salon door open, the steamy morning heat already working its way through the conditioned air forward. I could see a waggling foot. It belonged to June out on the fighting chair. Poured myself a cup and headed her way.

She looked up hearing me. 'Sign these.' Perks' title papers and slip rental sheets were shoved toward my not-yet-ready-to-think head. I managed to take, but not read. 'Where's my coffee?'

Glad I was cotton-headed. Might have mouthed some incorrect words had my brain functioned enough to form any. As it was, I took the papers, set my coffee on the coaming, looked them over before starting to do what June said I was supposed to do. 'Why you want me to sign these?'

'Because.'

Always loved that answer. Used it a lot up until I was six. 'You're asking me,' I said, lifting my hot brew, 'to sign something illegal?'

She almost glowed with hope. 'You sign those, it's proof of coercion.'

'How so?

'Like there's really a boat called Twinkletoes? No, wait. I'm going to sign it. I'll be more believable this goes to court. Ex Fed.'

'Trumps ex-city cop?'

'Trumps a beach bum. You just tell Perks it's the Woman who needs the write-off, not you. He'll love that.'

'I'm not going to tell him anything. My plan's to get him to tell me something. We never talked about my having to buy a boat, or a slip I'd be paying for but keeping empty well past necessary. I intend to shove these in his face and ask what the Hell are these for? Then he'll tell me, and you'll be recording it on your pretty little smart phone's recorder, so long as we stay connected. And I already figured you're a better agent than me, which is why his voice will be on your phone.'

She reached for her morning kiss. 'You aren't as dumb as your friends say you are.'

'I ain't is right.'

No time to think about coffee breath, or who would see us.

No time to think at all.

To make certain my plans worked exactly as I wanted, I dialed her number. She began recording our silly conversation with one of those wonderful smartphone apps that kids invent to confound the older generation. Finally freshened and clearer headed, I walked up to Perks' office with the full intent of flinging the documents on his desk.

Best laid plans and all. He wasn't alone.

Door to his office was open to the outer room. That pretty woman that had been behind me in the bleachers stood to the side of Perks's desk, a bit distraught. In a chair racked up on two legs, his head against the wall, was their son.

Kid didn't look upset, disheveled, pinned between a rock and a hard place, not even tired. Damn if he didn't look a little happy.

'Sorry, I…' I held up the papers. 'I'll come back.'

'Nolan, I'll only be… would you mind waiting? We're almost done. And close the door'

'Sure, sure.' I did as asked, and did my best not to overhear what was being said.

Yeah, right.

Couldn't get much, but I did hear clearly enough her saying *I don't know how long, but me and Ronnie're leaving. You have to do this, and are going to do this, now.* With that I heard movement, figured they might open the door any second, which they did.

No introduction of Mr. Nolan to Mrs. Perks. As she pushed past, she seemed a figure of fire caught in a bottle. Ronnie ignored me with that arrogant teenage way kids employ as a putdown of any unauthorized authority figure.

Gave Perks a moment to collect himself, entered. My plan to dramatically fling the sheets went out with the Mrs. and Son, so I tried the commiserating face. Worked.

'Everything cool?'

'You're married. What do you think?'

'Well, I'm not married, but I get your meaning. Is this a good time?'

'Sure. Maybe. Yeah, a fine time. What the Hell. Guess you read the papers?'

I nodded.

'You'll sign, then.'

'Not exactly.'

'So let's make it exactly.'

'What's this crap about this boat, Twinkletoes?'

Perks did the old feet up on the desk, rock back in the office chair, interlocked fingers behind the head trick. Man, I wanted to kick him over. Junkyard snarl, lizard-like eyes, not a thing to makes you wanna snuggle up with him. After a moment of sizing me up and down, which was unnecessary because Perks was the type to size someone up before they enter the room, he said, 'She's your next boat. And a slip to dock her in.' Straight to the point, I had to give him that. 'You want in on business here, you need a reason to pop up every now and then. There's always a percentage.'

'The house cut?'

'Now that is exactly,' he grinned. But it was a bloodless grin. Still distracted by the demands of the departed wife?

'What if I don't want a reason to come up here?'

Feet came down, hands unlocked. 'Then you won't have a reason. It's the way it works, Mr. Nolan.'

I held out, as though actually thinking about which way to decide. I could see he didn't like it, but his mood had already been fouled by the wifey visiting. 'What if I want the shares, but my girlfriend signs for the boat?'

'I don't care if John Hancock comes back from the dead to sign. Long as I get payment, and my monthlies stay regular, we're happy.'

I held out again. 'We looked things over. You really think you can get two hundred units up?'

'Easy. Florida is still retirement central for the East Coast to Ohio, and we plan a heavy push in sales to the Canucks. That's part of what your money will go do. You said shares. I take it you've contacted Mr. van Hij?'

I felt a tug on my fishing line. 'I had dinner with him night you brought me in. Money to him is like mosquito bites to you. Causes some annoyance, but there's plenty of them around.'

Perks stood. He was about to say something when I asked him, 'You'll be here? Sounded like, sorry, could help but hear a little, through the door, but sounded like you might be going somewhere, and if you're not going to be here, maybe I'll hold off.'

'I'll be here,' he said. 'Her and the kid won't. Family business, you don't mind.' Not a question, a notification.

I blew out air. 'Give me two days, tops. The money's not the problem, but I want to check with my accountant. Which is not as easy as you'd think. Tax season' just passed, so he's probably chilling in a tub of margaritas about now.'

And so ended that. I walked out, closed the door, took out the phone in my top pocket and said to June, 'Heard all that?'

'Yeah. Seems Mr. Perks is going to be batching it for a while.'

'Seems like. Check the recording, let me know when I get to the boat.'

Bye, sweetie honey sugar poopie lovums.

I was on the *Sweet Discourse* in five minutes, and back in bed with June in nine. Or rather on the bed. We do our best discussing there.

She started the questions. 'So this Mrs. Perks is going somewhere? With Junior?'

'Seems like it.'

'And you think they're thinking of leaving the country.'

'I do. Makes sense. Heat's turned up, time to quit the kitchen. I hadn't figured on Ronnie going to Mommy, though. But seems he did, not the outcome I wanted. Damn, should have considered the Mommy Factor. Just never saw her until last night at the game.'

June, as do many women, had the ends of her hair in her right hand, stroking the ends between the fingers of her left. It meant she was thinking.

'Possible Daddy still doesn't know what Momma knows? Think maybe there's been an impending divorce for some while? Or at least one talked about, and she's cashing in on an opportunity?'

Now I felt like stroking hairs, my chinny chin chin hairs. 'A possibility. He didn't seem too ruffled except by the fact he was being muscled into something. Frank's putting the notion that Daddy has a stash of cash somewhere might have been news to Momma. Perks didn't seem to balk at the idea of her leaving, and pulling Sonny Boy out of school a month to go. Especially that State game over and them losing.'

She said, 'Perks has pull enough like you said, I'm sure he can get his son diploma'd without finishing.'

'They run, they're out of reach, or least out of his hair. Besides, doesn't matter. He needs to go, they go.'

'Maybe.' She kept thinking.

'Non extradition countries are so lovely. But I'd pick the Cape Verde islands. Cheap enough, nice view, people are not hostile.'

She rolled toward me. 'Canada. They won't extradite if capital punishment is a possibility. And Florida isn't exactly pacifist on that count.'

'Canada's too cold. Cape Verde for this beach bum.'

'But you'd have to kill somebody first, and I doubt that's going to happen.'

'You forget Annigail is still my sister.'

She punched me.

But she was right. Pulling a revolver from my holster was an act of will that didn't come by naturally when I was a cop. Might be why I got shot the way I did. Was certainly a contributing factor in why I quit being a cop. 'I should call Wiley. You think this sudden vacation of the Perks is reason enough for them to be convinced?'

'Reason enough to believe it, even convinced, so long as you're not on a jury. You still need more.'

'I was hoping Ronnie Perks would screw up and threaten one of his buddies, or run off with Bonnie Lou, or something. I thought maybe Perks would jolt Kevin, maybe even Whitaker, but I didn't know the boy enough. I thought maybe he'd get one of them thinking it's time to fess up. His ass or theirs, and they'd not choose his. What do you think? Should I do something maybe to shake Kevin up?'

'Like what?'

'Maybe I should let him know Ronnie Perks is splitting the country, that word is leaking out about something, and Perks's money is doing for the ringleader what it won't do for him.'

'Maybe. And maybe Bonnie Lou is the better choice. Kevin is afraid of the Perkses, but Bonnie Lou is about to get dumped.' June smiled. 'Dumped girls are capable of doing the stupidest things.'

'How would you know?'

June hit me again, harder.

But she had a point. Question was, how to get to Bonnie Lou, with school in session?

Answer? Can't.

Actually, there was one way, but I couldn't bring myself to do it. Call in a bomb scare.

They tend to clear out school pretty damn fast.

I admit, I gave that a lot of thought. The last weeks of school were exam weeks, although for seniors, exams were pretty much done. My last year we spent most of the time, if we weren't cutting altogether, playing games and watching movies. A joke. Wouldn't be disrupting much.

But still. Couldn't do it.

June, on the other hand, found the idea of doing something like that not only criminal but exciting. She'd wanted to do something exactly like that when we graduated. 'Oh, let's. Please o please o please?'

Shook my head many times, but I was a guy being begged by a soft, beautiful and emotionally soothing woman in a supine position. Like what? I'm not human?

'Not til one, at least.'

Passing the time until one was easy.

During the later, less strenuous part of having to wait, I thought about the effect the scare might have on the four kids. At the very least Kevin would get out early and maybe have a fun extra hour before work. I had anything to do with it, it would be his last.

Bonnie Lou, on the other hand, would make a beeline to Ronnie, since he wasn't in school. Spring, boy and girl, hot and sultry weather. Yeah, he'll want a last hookup before splitting for Canada.

Wondered if he'll tell her about his run-in with Frank Whitcomb. Hoped he would.

My immediate concern was with getting caught. Bomb threats are a terroristic illegality, and since 9/11, taken very seriously. But bomb threats to high schools are more common than you'd think, especially during exams. With so many turning out to be pranks, which nonetheless are always taken seriously, they are often not investigated, especially when phoned in.

Still, numbers could be traced. With everyone carrying cell phones that have Caller ID on them, tracking back to someone is a lot easier. What we needed was a pay phone — and happy day — there was still a pay phone at the marina.

That it was Perks' marina, and Ronnie Perks hadn't gone to school, we could swear we saw him there if asked. He'd catch the blame. So, so much the good!

I was getting as excited as June. Gosh, it felt like high school!

Of course, that would only work if nobody saw *us* on the payphone. It was a lazy, muggy Tuesday midday at an already fairly vacant marina. Spotted one fellow unloading tools and such from his boat onto the dock, and another occasionally popping his head into view inside his cruiser. I'd heard someone fire up engines earlier and head out, probably for a day of fishing, maybe a cruise down to Key West, who knows.

A real problem was that Perks had three chartermen docked with him, and two of them had headed out earlier with charters. If they were half day trips, and in that heat a half-day charter was about all anyone could manage, they were usually back by one. Neither were. That meant whoever was on board might be getting off board just as June was making her call. I got on the horn.

'This is Captain Kingswood of the *Legal Brief* calling charter captains fishing Waccasassa Bay. Come back.'

I kept my gain turned down, hoping I'd reach only those within close range

'Captain Conicki of the Four Marks. What's your twenty, Cap?'

'Coming past on a slow roll to Orleans. No problems aboard, Cap. Thought to troll away the afternoon. How's the fish?'

'Asleep.'

'Copy that. We might put in for the night as well. Any marinas you recommend?'

'There's one right above Waccasassa. Perks, where I'm headed in ten we get the poles in. He's always got a slip available. But watch out for the dockmaster. He's a prick. You'll go see him for a slip, so ignore him being rude-ass. Fees ain't bad for a good marina, but this ain't what you call four stars. You ain't gonna get much for what you pay for here. Still, them're here are okay.'

'Thanks for the TMI. Mighty kind. I see you around, beer in it for you.'

'Sorry, dude. Once this boat's stowed, I go. But thanks anyway.'

Boat people are not only nice, they say things straight. Usually. Got what I wanted, and that was the interval of time to place the mischievous phone call.

We had a half an hour, maybe. Didn't raise the other boat, but captains are almost always sharing the same time piece. Be two minutes between them both reaching the docks.

We discussed the tactic. Her script, my methods. Pretend to be a boy, gravelly voiced as she could manage, once someone picked up the other end. Then she was to say, *Fuckin' cheerleaders. I made a bomb. Hope I get me at least one.* Then hang up immediately.

Done. In the car in thirty seconds, out of the lot in forty. We made it to the high school right behind the fire trucks, and right ahead of the entire county's worth of scared mothers in SUVs.

The way I figured it, if Momma Perks let Baby Boy Perks out of her sight for a second, he'd be on his way to the high school the second he got the call from Bonnie Lou. Momma doesn't let go, Bonnie Lou would be headed for some car, probably hers, in the student lot. Either scenario, Bonnie Lou would be swinging those long legs in plain view of us, June and me. If no Junior, and since she didn't have a clue who I was, I planned to pull a Frank Whitcomb on her. If Ronnie did show, June was to intervene. Trickier, but so was June.

Whatever, point was to say to her pretty face much of what she didn't want to hear, which was what she had probably felt with confidence as something nobody would ever say.

Apparently, Momma Perks didn't 'llow her boy no runnin' off to get his girl, which was great. I got to play act.

Exactly as expected, the streaming yellow hair and flashing long legs I recognized not only came into the sunlight, she came damn close to where I leaned against a ride that should have been too way expensive for a high schooler. Close enough she could hear me call, 'Bonnie Lou?'

She stopped. Nobody expects a perve to come right out into a school parking lot, but she had that wary look.

'Ronnie Perks nabbed me, ast I pop on over and find you. I got a message from 'im.'

And what a message it was.

'He says you better run, girl. That's what he says he's doin'. Probably already gone. Said something about word is out. About what, damn I know, so don't ast me. Sounds serious, huh? Scared? He won't get to seeing you, Momma snatched up his cell. They stopped for gas, him come up and pays me to do this. A hundred bucks is a hundred bucks. Besides, I know you. Seen you some.' Got to use my creepiest smile, which maybe isn't so far from my regular smile. 'Anyways, whatever he done, she went and yanked him outta school. Said you tell your friends run too, and you'd know who them are. So you be sure and run. Them too.'

Her face expressed thought processes to the same degree a roll of toilet paper would, but I knew that somewhere in that head tallies were being toted up. Pretty cool character. All she said was, 'Thank you.'

I watched her walk away, punch once at her smart phone, listen, exhibit frustration, probably at failing to reach Ronnie. Lucky me, and then she stopped to make a more difficult call. I bet Kevin Perks was the lucky boy. She talked, I walked. Away, and fast.

June had already maneuvered away from the swelling crowd of parents converging on the school, and was wise enough to put my Phillies hat on the radio antenna. I spotted it, ran.

Cool. Giggling and snickering, we got away.

I repeated what I said to June. 'Hope it works like a match to a string of firecrackers.'

I put a call in to Wiley, letting June keep the wheel. 'We're thinking maybe pick you up. This is going to erupt, I know it, and I'm not sure we should be around to see it. Davis will keep us up to date, probably.'

'Not sure, Cap'n. But we was gonna call you an' invite you an' Miss June for some cookout. Cole done barbecue, and I was talkin' about you and Miss June and he says maybe you might not be so bad as he firs' guess. Y'all come on over, and we'll do some talkin'. I think you'll like him, you learn what he's been.'

'That's fine, if you think now is okay to show our faces there.'

'Sure it's fine. Cole lives out in the middle of nowhere though, but don't know how much longer. They's some lawsuit or somethin'. Don't understand how County can jus' take a man's house fum under 'im, but they's gonna. He'll tell you'

'About that, Wiles, I may have something to tell him.'

And the man did live out in the middle of nowhere, but I'd been there, or near there, before. Still, hadn't been me who had driven. Unless I drive to a place, finding my way to it again is never easy. We lost the GPS signal fifteen minutes before we found the cut into the trees down which his house stood. Fortunately a lost GPS signal doesn't erase the map from the screen.

Anyway, Wiley's directions were fair, and we eventually ran up a long strip of sand almost less than a car wide, the center grassy but the ruts cleared, all the way up to his property.

Didn't expect much of a lawn from a one-armed seventy-year old man, but Davis's property was — once we parted from the scrub pines and shrubs — grassy and well trimmed. The house stood straight, much like the man, and there wasn't a rusting hulk anywhere to be found. His car, big and polished, had been parked beneath a home-made lean-to projecting from a screened Florida room. Both men were there sipping iced tea. A pitcher and two glasses waited for us.

160

'Much obliged.'

'Why this was so sweet of you, Mr. Davis. We are parched.'

The man's gruff was gone, and so were the downturned lines on his face. I didn't figure the finality of Willa's funeral had effected that change, but rather it was him being in his sanctuary. A few pleasantries passed among us as we sipped an excellent minted tea.

He offered to show June his house.

We entered by his spotless, organized kitchen, from which I could see into a room designed for a dining table but used as a trophy room. What caught my eye, and Davis caught me looking, was how much baseball paraphernalia he had tacked onto the visible wall. And some of it wasn't about Willa Maes's career. Some old pennants I recognized.

'Big into baseball, Mr. Davis?'

'It's about everything to me, 'til now. Uh huh.' He directed me to a closer inspection of his things, many of them museum quality. I was hugely impressed.

'Played some, 'til this.' He raised the stump of his right arm. With his other hand he directed me to an aged clipping. High school standout. I checked the date, and it showed me that my guess about his age was wrong. If the clipping was about him, he wasn't anywhere near seventy. I showed June.

'Things was different then. No way no Florida school's gonna give a nigger like me no scholarship, so it was the Marines, which took away this,' again the stump, 'and damn near everything else.'

'What did you do for the Marines?' June asked.

His reply was not meant to shock her, but it did. Did me. 'I shot people close to the eardrum as possible.'

She audibly gasped, and I may have as well. I got the feeling Davis had answered that question so often he felt the only proper answer it deserved was the bald-faced truth.

'I went for th'Navy, but they did funny recruitin' here for years, Miss June. Recruiter said all us was t'get down back where they was maybe forty kiddy animals, them stuffed kind, all out in the weeds. I was first to go shoot. He hands me this rifle, an old M1 from Korea or maybe even older, and he said just shoot some rabbits. I got down on my belly and dropped three was hidin' in the weeds. That recruiter nearly crapped hisself when I got up, walked out and came back. Had me three dead rabbits. He meant for me to shoot them kiddy ones. He didn't even see they was any real rabbits. Navy lost me to the Marines, Marines lost me to the SSP. That's Special Forces, Miss.'

'You were a Marine, though.'

'Oh, yes I was. Semper fi. See, I could spot fleas making love on a bunny's butt, and I grew up in these swamps. I was already fit as they wanted, and y'all couldn't find me with a searchlight on a five lane highway if I didn't want me found. I was pretty good, and they was pretty happy to show me some best ways to make a man dead. Did it for over twelve years, until one day I'd pissed off the wrong soldier.' He cupped the stump end of his elbow in his left hand. 'Us SSPs get a little superior, Miss June, a little cocky. See, I played baseball, and I could put a pitch between a spider's eyes. I took down a pretty good team in a platoon match in a humiliatin' way. Things my arm done was made worser with my mouth. One feller got his opportunity, an' he got me right through the elbow with his own kind of fastball. No mo' arm, no mo' SSP, no mo' lot a things.'

'He shot you?'

'Good shot, too. I think.'

'Oh my God,' she whispered. 'Where do these people come from?'

Cole smiled at her, but not in a warm and friendly way. There was something in his experiences wouldn't allow warm smiles. 'They come from next door, ma'am, most often. Anyway, coupla years later I come home. What home there was.'

Wiley, from the kitchen, said, 'I tol' y'all about him and Ciminy.'

'You didn't tell I was a damn slow fool, did you?'

'No sir. Din't tell 'em that.'

June and I both had the lifted up eyebrow. 'Happens t'us cripples, get thinkin' we're not all man left, once parts go missin'. Ciminy was waitin', but I was delayin'. Delayed so long after while, wasn't no reason 'cept help raise Willa to ask her what I shoulda done, but spilt milk.'

I nodded. I felt we'd strayed into the too personal for comfort, and turned toward the one wall I'd not yet inspected.

Many items on it were about pro ball. Black and white publicity stills, a few news shots, a St. Louis jersey in a frame, even a letter signed by pitcher Bob Gibson, though not addressed to Davis.

I also recognized a tall piece of furniture in the corner, an étagère. Not as fancy as what Mrs. Perks had in her living room, but as filled with personal treasure. All old. I would have guessed the stuff to be everything he had kept from when he was a kid, had it not been for the date on the clipping. It was older than his childhood.

There was a pair of cleats on the bottom shelf, a dry, gray, wide fingered glove behind them.

Spread fanwise above those were a number of score cards and game tickets. Oddly, the top shelf held only a stand used to hold a baseball, but no baseball.

'You holding out for the foul ball you'll someday catch?'

'No.'

No long answer?

He knew I wanted an explanation, and may have had good reason to remain quiet about that empty ball stand. But he said, 'There was a ball, once. Stolen by a son of a bitch.'

'Hmm,' I said, scratching my hand. 'Saw an old ball in a holder exactly like that, at Rick Perks's house. Collecting old baseballs must...'

'You was in Perks' house?'

His forcefulness of question disarmed me a second. 'Yes sir. We were doing some...'

'And you saw a baseball right out in the open? An old one?'

I nodded.

'That son a bitch.' Dark and deep as Coleman Davis's complexion was, I could see the red rising under it. First thing I went to was the kicking onto his ass that Perks had gotten from the old man. I couldn't help but keep an eye on Davis's face. I had truly put him into that spirit best summed up by *So mad I could just spit.*

Occurred to me if he did, that spit would melt iron.

June touched his arm lightly, but he shook her off with fury. I didn't like that, but then I knew in my bones he didn't actually mean anything by it.

I've been that hopping mad, and at the same worst time, which was among people I didn't know. Anger like that which approaches madness is best given private space to burn down. Wiley, though, knew his friend and gave us a head toss. We went back out to the Florida room, all three of us, to leave Coleman Davis be.

June and I sat in silence, grateful to have a tumbler of minted tea to occupy our hands. I listened for the evidence of explosion, the kind that smashes ashtrays, dishes, pictures once hung on the walls. My Dad was famous for those explosions, and they still scared the crap out of me.

But there were none. There were only minutes ticking on my digital watch. I'd reached the bottom of my glass and went for the pitcher when he returned.

'Tell me 'bout that baseball,' was all he said.

Seventeen

Which I did, but there wasn't much to tell. I remembered the ball as old, though without much in the way of nicks or bruises on it. It had red stitches and the horsehide had changed from its original brilliant white to a creamy gold, as if steeped in weak tea.

'Was it signed?'

'Not that I saw. Might have been'

The old man crept through his thoughts in spates of silence, though his expression never changed from that of the one who must win the arguments he was having with himself. He stood for a long while at the bottom of three steps leading down from his kitchen door. Something must have concluded, for he took a seat on the top step. We gave him all the time he needed. None of us had anything to say anyway.

'That was my ball,' He said at last.

Soon as I'd seen his reaction to my mention of the Perks' ball, I guessed at some relation he must have had with it. Once he'd made that claim about the ball, it being his once and Perks's presently, I began a debate with myself as to whether or not I'd have to tell him about Perks's son, what he had done. I had no idea where, and especially when, to begin revealing my discoveries. Thankfully, I didn't have to say anything then and there.

Davis came down off the step, saying the food was ready. Wiley had taken charge for us, and he jumped up to get June and me a plate. Conversation thereafter was forgettable, must have been since I forget what was said. I recall I kept looking for an opening to bring up what June and I had found out, but my instincts were telling me that no opening presented itself because I wanted my opening to stay shut.

Fact was, I was afraid of setting down a can of worms at the picnic. I didn't feel exactly comfortable around the one-armed man. Further fact was, I didn't feel comfortable anywhere we were except on my *Sweet Discourse.* So when June nonchalantly dropped a small question into the conversation that could have led to all things Perks, I wanted to stomp on it.

She'd said, 'You give that baseball Drew saw to that marina owner person?"

I made a little inward gasp, a kind of gulp, the kind that hurts the inside of your chest the way a too-large bite of hotdog will make as it finds its way to your gullet. There was a split second between what she said and my thinking up what I wanted to say, all during which Coleman Davis fixed a poker straight and hard iron stare on my girl. But I needn't have worried. She didn't invite what I felt surely would have wrecked our afternoon.

The man breathed in deep, dropped his eyes, then began.

'I told y'all I went t'get in the service 'cause they din't give me no scholarship. That's half a lie. Actual truth, I went off 'cause of a woman. What am I sayin'? A girl. Connie. Constance.' He choked out a small laugh. 'Constance. Wrong name for that one. But then, maybe she was. Just not t'me.'

Ever listen to a man talking who didn't consider that you might be in the room with him? That was us listening to Davis. We were simply reason to put what rattled in his head to rattling in the air. His talk gave us a job, though, and we did it. We listened. Not a peep until we were sure he was done.

Of course, gave me a chance to do two things, which was to listen and to not talk.

Davis went on. 'I'm talkin' 'bout the Connie married Ricky Perks. She made an end t'us come real quick. Don't take much for understandin' what happens to a nigger boy puts hands on a white girl, specially in this county in this state, back then or now. I guess lucky they only took one arm. Bad, mighty bad, lovin' wrong. Really bad, lovin' the wrongest one. And she was that. She liked it fine when it was nobody around, but that didn't stay that way near long enough f'me. You tell me one woman can keep her trap shut about the man she's pressin' herself on? Sorry, Miss June, but that's how's it is. She let it out, our secret. Got the shit beat outta me, sure, more'n once, but they didn't knock all of it out. Not all of it. I had shit enough left t'make it t'the recruiter, and y'all know the rest. She said I come home, she'd be there. I come home alright. Took four years, after me losing this.' He raised the stump. 'I got back, but wasn't no home I wanted to come home to. She had went and gone married Perks, something sure t'put a big F U on everything we ever had. Wasn't for Dave Ichobi, Willa Maes's daddy, getting killed, might never stayed. Y'mind,' he said to June, 'pouring the last of that tea for an old man?'

Later, way later, after all was said and over, when Wiley walked us out to our car, we learned from my first mate why we'd guessed so wrong about Coleman Davis's age. *Got the cancer, Miss June. Ain't brought him down full, but it will.*

But that was later.

Davis sipped his sweet tea, started back up again.

'Ain't a lot of work 'round here, but when there was a war on, there was need for scrap parts. We had ourselves a graveyard of boat parts ripe for pickin'. Marinas up and down Florida, all the way to Miami, been usin' our bay for a boat graveyard. So Rickie Perks come to me, we wasn't exactly friends but we didn't hate the other like we do now. This was before I took up with Connie, and he asks me help set about pickin' at the bones for whatever he could sell. Was making money. Money makes for good times, and we had a few of 'em. He had me to his house, I had him to mine. We was in school then. Not together, separate school for niggers. It was me goin' t'his house when I first met Connie. Kept it on the down low, us two, and we managed some getting' together. Wasn't a lot, but it was burnin'.

'One day I find Rickie in my house with me not there. Nobody there. I got a older brother, and my mama was still alive, Daddy dead from fever. None of us was home, but there was Rickie, standin' in that kitchen in there like he had the deed in his pocket. Didn't like it, but Rickie, he's always smooth. Made me to think somehow was *me* made *him* think it okay he wait for me in there even nobody home. I said it wasn't, though if was just me it would have been, then. My mama saw he was a snake, just hadn't shed that last bit of people skin yet. But the good money covered that up. Why he was there with nobody there? It was that baseball.

'You seen it. Nothin' special, right? Y'all be wrong. Y'know baseball, Miss June? I guessin', Nolan, you sure do, and I know you do, Wiley. So y'all oughta get what it's gonna mean to me when that baseball be taken by a shit-eatin' worm like Perks. Sorry, Miss June. Not much goodness in him f'better words. Not from me.'

Time for another sip.

When I get pot-boiling mad, all the blood in my neck seems to turn into concrete and I eventually lose my voice, especially if I was to use it as much as Cole Davis planned.

He went on. 'Y'know about Willy Mays, Miss June? Can't be American y'don't know Willy Mays. Best ball player ever was, and he was one of us. A negro when we negroes didn't have so much as pissin' room in this country. He was the king, you see, best we could hope to be. Among us, that is.

'See, Willy did things no nigger was let to do in that white man's game. Hope I don't make y'all uncomfortable, but I want y'all t'get what I'm sayin'. Back in'54, my Dad worked the grounds for the Giants. Later for St. Louis, which is where I come along. But Giants then, and he knew Willy Mays. Before every game Mr. Mays handed my Dad a chunk a chaw, that's tobacco for chewin', Miss June. Willy says to my Dad, *You keep this half for me for after the game. I'll have this piece chawed whiter'n those faces in the first base bleachers. I see you next, I'll be wantin' some fresh.* Dad never said whether Willy Mays chawed his first half that much, but come game end, my Dad was right there with the last half.

'Giants went t'the Series, and it was on September 28 that year Willy did something made fistfights break out. You all heard of the Basket Catch?'

I did, June didn't. Wiley, of course. I jumped in to give her the what up about it. "Basket Catches had been around for decades, Hon, outfielders often claiming that holding the glove palm up at belly level gave them a split second closer to getting the ball back in play." I showed her.

Davis wasn't talking about *a* basket catch, however, he was talking about *The* Basket Catch. The one that stopped the Cleveland Indians from any chance of taking the series. I remember my own father sometimes talking about The Catch, and he hadn't been a fan of it.

There's one rule a six-year old hears forever once he's caught his first ball. It follows every baseball player from his first catch to playing pro ball, all the way past retirement when he's playing catch with his grandson. It's a rule that never changes, is never ignored. *Keep your eye on the ball.* Willy Mays used the basket catch with his back to the plate. He says he knew where the ball was going the second he heard how it was hit, but keeping your ears on the ball isn't the rule.

Same time he did that, baseball was changing. Had been since Jackie Robinson, and I've heard more than once Willy Mays referred to as *That son of a bitch Mays,* and sometimes they put an unnecessary and ugly adjective right before Mays.

Breaking a rule means not being in your place, and there was a lot of talk about knowing your place in those days.

That last notion was explained to June later, but she knew then enough to know the catch meant something very important to Davis.

I was getting a clearer idea.

'Mr. Mays gave my Dad a baseball that day, for holdin' his half a chaw every game.'

Suddenly I knew Perks had taken more than Davis's girl from him, and more than an old baseball. I knew enough about the event, though, to have suspicions about the ball in question, about whether Davis believed one of those lies a father tells his kid to seem bigger than maybe he was feeling at the time. My dad told me a few, even though he had a circus of famous people working in his shops every day, so didn't ever need to fabricate.

I said, 'Thought nobody knows where that ball went. Nobody thought it was important.'

Davis leveled an iron glare at me. 'Catcher that day was a boy name Wesley Westrum. He caught all four them series games. He knew Willy's catch meant somethin'. Put the ball in his shirt, and when Willy come in with the inning over, he gave it to him. And Willy gave it to my daddy. See, Miss June, Mr. Westrum knew his baseball, and he saw Willy didn't just make no great catch. He saw Willy made one of the greatest catches of all time.'

She asked, 'And Rickie Perks, your friend, he came to steal the ball that day you caught him, knowing the story?'

'He didn't come t'steal the ball, Miss June, he came to switch it out. Like I said, son of a bitch. Wasn't but a long while 'til my mama saw it was gone. I knew what he done. Ball didn't have no name on it, but Mama showed us a name on the one she found. Perks put a name on some old ball. Didn't have no proof, but weren't nobody coulda done it. I put it to him, but he said was me musta lost it. He went around everywhere tellin' people I's the one lost that ball, lost it against a five dollar throw in craps. I had t'put blame down on him so my mama wouldn't get mad, but she was more'n mad an' she didn't want t'hear nothin'. Right after was when Connie says I been messin' with her. They beat me down good, and things with my brother never was the same.'

He got up and poured himself another glass of sweet tea, not asking me or June or Wiley if we needed a refill. Wasn't nobody there in his mind except himself, sorry for himself all over again. Not even coming back to sit down, not turning, not even speaking loudly enough to insure we heard him, he finished.

'I was in second year waitin' for a furlough to come see my mama, but she died, Same fever took my daddy. By the time I did come back, f'good, and I only come back t'hep out Ciminy with Willa, I'd got so lost in my hide I didn't care nothin' about the baseball. Which was half a lie. You don't forget some things, especially seein' that bastid drivin' Connie in a better car every year, and me only a part one-armed man.'

June's eyes were brimming, and she saw I'd seen them. She rose and walked down to where our car was. We three men watched her go, but none of us went after her. We'd have none of us wanted someone coming after us to mess with our misery, so we extended her the same courtesy.

'Ronnie Perks didn't just steal from me, a poor old dirty nigger boy livin' out in th'same trees his grandpa's grandpa fought snakes and skeeters in. No sir. He stole history from us, from my people. That history was in my hands, mine, to protect. I didn't. I lost an arm protectin' people didn't even want me there, f'people who don't even care I be breathin', but I didn't protect my own. So wasn't just me less a man for the missin' arm, I's less a man for not havin' not give up everything t'protect what little bit a great history us niggers got.'

'But did anybody know you had that ball?'

He nodded. 'All us did, some a them did. Daddy was a talker. But nobody, once it was known Daddy's Willy Mays ball'd gone missing, nobody ever said a thing about it. Sure not Perks. And now y'say Rickie Perks got it still, and he got it on display in a glass case, and nobody who ever gets to lay eyes on it even knows they's lookin' on history.'

My turn to nod. 'Probably tells people it was a ball dropped foul at a Marlins' game.'

'Probably, Mr. Nolan. Most likely. Like I said, he's a son of a bitch.'

'He's worse than that, sir.'

And then I told him a story.

Eighteen

Could there be a more broken man? I started out by telling him what we'd discovered about Perks's tax fraud scheme, and that maybe we'd get him snatched up with it, as well as the District judge overseeing the case that endangered his home and land. He seemed, at first, enlivened by that news. Perhaps, in light of him dying with cancer, which I did not then know, he may have been more delighted for his neighbors than for himself.

June had come back during the early part of my story, anguish dealt with. He took June's hand in his when I told him how she had worked for the Feds as a forensic accountant, and he rubbed it as you would rub oil into a new baseball glove. Wiley, not known for facial composure, although he could remain physically stoic everywhere else on his huge body, flashed anger, amazement, stunned silence, confusion, you name it. He knew Davis's rubbing June's hand was being friendly, but it was a thing he'd never presume to attempt. Was Miss June that the one-armed Davis was touchin'.

Anyway, I felt I'd droned for an hour, but it hadn't been even half. Still, I covered every detail. When I came to my spotting the four in the school auditorium, I had felt it necessary to keep my say so flat, toneless, lest any form of self-congratulations enter into my mouth about what I'd done. This was news best delivered flat, me as far removed from it as possible. Wasn't possible, but the attempt was necessary.

I stumbled mentioning Ronnie Perks, knowing his name would cut deepest into his heart.

Saying Kevin Perks, though, earned a surprised look from him. Maybe he'd considered Kevin the good Perks. Nothing came of mentioning Gregg Whitaker, and a sour *gotta spit* twist to his mouth when I described what actually happened in the parking lot with Bonnie Lou Dennison.

I said, 'I think the kid's'll know the cat's clawing its way out of the bag. Seems Perks has plans on moving his son offshore, if I'm guessing right about what I heard Connie Perks' say to her husband. Kevin will run, he has any smarts, but he's got nowhere to run except to Rick, and likely Rick'll help him some, maybe money. He is cousin...'

Davis interrupted me. 'Second cousin. That boy's daddy is a cousin t'Perks's daddy.'

'Right,' I said. 'He said that.'

'Maybe the boy might think Rickie might gonna hep him, but Rickie Perks ain't one t'think a nobody but Rickie Perks. No obligation on 'im, never hand out t'hep. You was sayin' maybe Connie Perks never said nothin' t' Rickie, so the boy come to him f'hep, this all be news. Don't know what Perks'll do, that situation.'

June asked him, 'How are things with you, with Mrs. Perks, now?'

'I got a dead heart.' I saw my romantically inclined June tremble. 'Miss June, it been twenty years. We seen each other, can't help that, no mo' said between us more'n a tip a th'hat. I know you want the lady side. We didn't quit likin' th'other when we quit, she quit. Was we couldn't like th'other, not here, so we hadda stop it. Maybe for her, she never quit, but like I said, my heart been dead since th'elbow come off.'

Wiley, who hadn't been as silent and non-participatory as I may have been implying, asked me, 'What y'all thinks t'happen now, Cap'n?'

'I can't guess a straight course, but I think this'll be like tossing a match into a box of fireworks. Or weeds. Maybe a grassfire of people knowing what happened will force out a call for justice, and with the stink from Perks's dirty dealings, there'll be a hunt for those involved. But I can't say for sure. I just know that white people will hide their guilt with everything they got, but they'll work overtime to clean up any mess that embarrasses them. And this'll embarrass big time.'

'White messiahs,' Davis muttered.

I know I had a confused look at his seeming non sequitur, and thought June might. Would have known had I looked at her, but I only had eyes for Davis. Tend to react to a challenge like that. 'You think that's all this is?'

'Not all, but pretty much. I said you t'stay out our business. We'd figure it out, and maybe figure out what t'do. But you didn't. Be lyin' didn't say was some stuff I appreciate, the baseball and the lawsuit, but y'all consider your part as done as it's gonna get. No mo', Mr. Nolan. No mo'. That's a nice boat, Miss June she a nice woman, and this friend here, don't come no better'n him. Done. Take all y'all got an' get outta here. This our troubles.'

I really had a hard time hearing my good intentions put forward as bad intentions, and I admit I was a little pissed at his lack of gratitude. In time knew I'd cool, understand, but right then I felt like chucking the whole damn mess — baseball, deeds, papers, hanging rope, everything — at the one armed man dying of cancer or not. I stood up. 'Pleasure doing your business. I think we'll take your advice.'

Junie, Junie, Junie. Love ya, but sometimes…

My lovely looked up at me standing there face-to-face with the one-armed man, and she started laughing. 'Why is it men always got to bring every story down to a fistfight? Will you two sit down? I still got tea.'

'No, June, I think maybe Davis here is right. We should go. No welcome like an unwelcome.'

That's when Wiley exercised his right to be part of the little tête-à-tête. 'All same t'you, Cap'n, I', stayin' on a bit. Ciminy ain't right yet, and she an' Cole go way back, an' I go a piece back wif her myself. Y'all head on up and catch up with Mr. Watt like you was gonna do, and I'll be waitin' on the dock when you heads back down.'

'We still got a few loose ends with Perks, Wiley,' June said. 'But sounds like a plan. Okay, Big Boy,' which she was meaning me, 'now I'm done with my tea.'

She stood, kissed the cheeks of the other two, then dragged me by the elbow to the car. Wiley tagged behind, Davis merely watched us go.

'Ain't he's mean, Cap'n, but y'all heard it y'self, been a lot took away over the years. I didn't know 'bout him and the lady 'til now. He don't say much a what's in there deep. I think we got some talkin' to do with our two selfs. An' like I said, Ciminy ain't right yet, but he ain't right at all.' It was then that Wiley told us about the cancer. 'And this what here you been tellin' him? Gonna drag him under faster he held on an anchor. I be fine, Cap'n. Brought plenny a money. Y'all pays me too much.'

He smiled, and I had to smile. It was what he always said come payday. And I couldn't pay him enough, some weeks. Like that week.

Halfway back to the marina I remembered Kevin saying it was his day to work with Ronnie, but I was pretty sure he'd be there alone and pissy about it. More, I thought somewhere between the game and then that Ronnie Perks might have had a chance to say something about Frank's confrontation, or at least mine with Bonnie Lou. Felt a little urgency driving back. We were out of afternoon, and soon light.

But, no Ronnie, and no Kevin either. Nobody on that dock except a really pissed off Dock Master and a somewhat pissed Daddy Perks. Poor fellows had to deal with the marina all by their lonesomes.

Florida has about eighteen hundred miles of coastline, which meant travel by water required a whole lot of days and even more gas, if one was to go from the beaches below Tallahassee, around the tip and up past Jacksonville to the the Georgia border. Maybe shorter than to get from Miami to Atlantic City, and that trip on a sizeable boat can takes two to four days, depending. With I-95 running like a sewer pipe from the states north to the top east of Florida, most snowbirds who own a moveable boat rarely buy a summer house on the west coast much above Sarasota. Anyone north of that usually comes from inland, anywhere from Louisiana to Chicago. If they take a boat back home, it's usually up the Mississippi.

What I'm getting at is, Perk's marina at best was a stopover for the few boats north of Sarasota headed back up north, and hardly ever one for boats eventually returning up the east coast.

By May, traffic is usually done.

But not that day.

Those poor little guys were busy. Damn near a flotilla had pulled in, and half the people appeared drunk as Hell.

Sarasota had hosted a boat show near the end of April, which Wiley and I had attended. A whole contingent of middle-states friends had decided that was the finest week to buy some boats. Like birds of a feather will do, they decided to flock together, taking possession of their boats *en masse* a few weeks after the event. Took some arranging but they finally fixed a date to do something that boaters call a Raft-Up, which is essentially a floating party made up of people who owned boats, who loosely knew each other, and who liked to drink.

They can be really fun, and really a pain in the ass to anyone around them who didn't get to drink. Like charter captains.

By the time we got to the *Sweet Discourse,* there'd already been one shouting match with a charter captain. He'd come back with an unhappy charter, no fish, and wanted to get into his slip and out of there, except one newbie had cut off his access with repeated attempts to back a shiny new yacht into a slip.

Wish I'd seen it. Heard a beer bottle missile got launched. Which side put it in orbit was unclear. My news reporter had launched a few beers into the waste can himself.

I am off topic here, but not exactly. Point is, Kevin Perks had pulled a disappearing act at the same time Ronnie had been whisked away by Momma, leaving Daddy stuck for help. His dock master didn't own the finest of patient natures, so things were explosive.

Once my own aggravation had passed — over what Davis had indicated about my sticking my nose where it hadn't been wanted — June and I made plans to take ourselves up to meet Watt and Annigail and, as June put it, her 'real' boyfriend, Roly Poly Noly.

But I had to wrap things up with Perks, and that had to take a back burner with him up to his butthole in dealing with inept and inebriated newbie boaters. All I really wanted to do was turn over the signed boat and slip rental agreements, hand him a bogus check covering my sham fees, get my copies, and make sham plans to get him some bogus money for the four shares on the return trip with Watt on Sunday next.

I was kept wanting.

It was my turn to cook, but our new flotilla best friends, stopping at our boat repeatedly with opportunities of beer and harder stuff, had had more luck with the fishies than the local charter captain. Somebody on some boat had stayed sober long enough to not only excellently fillet a dorado but griddle it to a nice doneness, and then were so considerate as to deliver a platter of it to the Missus and me. I looked into a pair of not exactly focused eyes as I accepted the plate, and decided correcting their misapprehension of my married state was a waste of time.

We enjoyed the fish and the beers passed over our transom. All the while I had kept an eye on the lookout for the comings and goings of Mr. Perks. But that was all for naught. Somehow he'd gone home without me seeing him do it.

Damn, we had wanted out, but we couldn't head for New Orleans without handing Perks the paper trap. Had to wait.

Next day, next morning, no Perks.

Left a note on his office door early, went three times up to bang on it, but nothing. The Dock Master, busy seeing off the hungover flotilla, which meant working the marina store and trying to do dock work at the same time, wasn't the most pleasant with his news. 'Fucking asshole got me here all by myself. I should quit and fix his ass for not even calling.'

I had to wonder, had all the Perks pulled up stakes?

And, I had to wonder, had the match in the fireworks done its thing?

Time kept passing, no Rickie Perks.

No Ronnie Perks. And no Kevin Perks.

I had Perks' cell number, but maybe he had mine as well. Seeing me come up on his phone, maybe he didn't have a stomach for business. Or maybe he'd taken that back door he had planned. For whatever reason, he didn't answer. Thought maybe I could find his house, but that seemed presumptuous, even though I wouldn't give a rat's testicle for his opinion.

We waited.

And waited.

Around three in the afternoon, June asleep in the vee-berth, I spotted Sheriff Beautop's official car sliding into the lot and heading around back of Perks' office. With the light glare on the windshield, plus tinted side windows, I couldn't see whether Sheriff Beau was at the wheel.

Hopped off the *Discourse* and went for the short walk.

I quietly opened the outer door, which had not been locked, and put my head in just enough to see beyond the inner door to Perks' office the Sheriff rifling the one visible filing cabinet. His movements were anxious and focus fixed. He didn't hear or see me. He slammed a drawer, but a file folder caught, preventing its safe shutting. He yanked out the file, resettled it, slammed the drawer again. Yanked open a second.

Being a cop gives you a sixth sense, the one that keeps you alive. Beautop's sixth kicked in and he whipped around to face me, a dead glare in his eyes. I knew it was instinct that slid his hand overtop his service revolver, but knowing that didn't reduce my scared shitlessness. I froze. Thankfully, Beautop recognized my face, paper white though it had become, and he screamed at me, best way an old whiskeyed voice could scream, 'What the fuck you want in here?'

He really didn't want an answer. I knew it, so I didn't give one. I just stood there. Fright does that to a man.

'Get your ass in here before somebody sees you.'

Couldn't guess who that might be except Perks, one of them, but without spending much time thinking about who, I did as I was told. Shut the door behind me.

Last man I ever expected to be involved with as his co-conspirator was that ruined fat man, but there we were. 'You're a fool getting involved with Perks. I was you, I'd get on that fancy new boat of yours and take your ass and that pretty ass you got with you and get the Hell out of town.'

'That advice, or a directive?'

Sometimes asking a question that requires a modicum of thinking on the part of the asked will confuse him. Did that time. Beautop kind of slumped, not against anything, just downward. I asked him a second thing.

'You looking for something for Perks, or for yourself?'

That he had an answer for. I just didn't expect it.

'Perks called me, said the Missus was gone, and his kid. There's a rash of missing persons this morning. He said he got a call from his cousin's wife, the kid works here is gone too. Disappeared middle of the night. He asked me come down and see if the other kid was here, and, well, let's just say I saw me an opportunity.'

'You're looking for the contracts.'

'Yeah.'

'Don't let me stop you. I'm no fan.'

He eyed me, and suddenly I recognized an ally against Perks if I ever saw one. Let's just say I saw me an opportunity, and, well…

'Let me help. Hate to see a man held by the short and curlies. I figure what Bennie Wilkins filled me in on, he's got his hand around a whole lot of scrotum hairs. And I'm guessing, yours?'

No response from Beautop except turning back to the files. In the ten we spent together pulling open drawers, nothing. He sagged even further each worthless search.

'You know, I overheard a short conversation yesterday between him and Mrs. Perks. She said that her and her son would be taking a rather immediate and distant trip. Didn't seem to fluster Perks none when I saw him right after. Why would he call you just to see if Kevin Perks was here, when he could have just called that guy who runs the docks? And why would he tell you she went away? Doesn't seem the kind shares personal business for no good reason.'

The sheriff pulled open a drawer that I'd already searched, and one he knew had already been thumbed through. 'Because she wasn't goin' right off. She wasn't to be leaving 'til Friday, way she understood it from Rick was he was gonna need time to get his hands on the money she'd need. She thinks all he makes is what's made off this marina. Some people just wanna be blind stupid.'

'Perks the one who told you that?'

He stopped searching. Closed the drawer. 'I see you was a cop. Yeah, wasn't Perks. She likes me, I like her, have for a long time. Not like you think, just likin' each other. Felt sorry her married to that asshole.'

'So you're not a fan either.'

'You could say that.'

'I guess he's got the curlies really tight.'

'You could say that too.'

'And you told Mrs. Perks about Rick's hidden stash.'

'Three on the bullseye.'

'How about a fourth? I think you're scared for Mrs. Perks. Would he hurt her?'

'I don't know. Rick never actually hurt nobody I know, but he sure likes scaring the shit out of them. I saw how you was out at the clearing.'

I told him I had wished I'd hidden my shooting ability so he wouldn't discover that I was a cop, not knowing he already knew it. But, yeah, scared me a bit, with a County Sheriff behind me also holding a pistol.

Beautop, to the best of his ability under the circumstances, laughed. 'I ain't shot this gun off my whole career. I ain't the good ol' boy you think. Might look it, but I ain't. He just likes usin' me like the boogie man.'

'So what now?'

'I call Perks and tell him no Ronnie. I don't know what to tell him about his wife.'

'You're not lying? You don't know?'

Final busted air sack sag. 'No.'

Had no reason nor desire to tell him that maybe I knew a reason why Ronnie Perks might have disappeared. Discretion and better part of valor and all that. Real reason? I might have been wrong, and I had the whereabouts of a best friend and first mate to determine before I said anything to anybody. 'I guess then you call him.'

He did. I listened. 'No, nothing, what? What they say? And they said Ronnie? Damn. Where? You sure, there? No, you let me go first. I'll go see. And far as you know nobody else knows yet? And nothing from Connie or the kid? Then you sit and you wait. This is my business now. Tell me again exactly what he said.'

I strained to hear what filled Beautop's ear, but didn't catch a word. When he hung up the man just studied the desktop. Finally he said. 'I got to go.'

'Don't leave me hanging. What was that?'

'You still got any cop left in you?' I nodded. Maybe wasn't a complete lie, but couldn't see how the truth would be the answer he wanted. 'Been another suicide hanging. Kev Perks is dead. And same goddam tree they found a kid in last week.'

He wanted someone else along. That's why he wanted to know if I had cop left. Seeing how I already knew how Perks had him by his ball sack, he didn't think bringing in his men would be as good as having me tag along. Bad enough I knew the bind he was in. Beautop didn't need to say that, but I had him confirm my analysis of the situation. He did, and we went.

I knew what we would find. Kevin Perks wasn't the first corpse I had to cut down. Behind pills and a shot to the skull, hanging is the third most common suicide of my experience.

Knowing what you'll find isn't the same as finding what you think you will. I worried that Frank pushing Kevin to scare him might have led to his committing suicide, so when I saw the very boy still suspended from a branch, I lost it some. Losing it isn't a badge of shame for a cop, despite what the actors playing grizzled and jaded TV cops might have us think. The unexpected dead make us lose it more often than you'd think. I've seen twenty year coroners lose it, though usually when it was a small kid.

Beautop let me finish, handed me a pocket handkerchief. There were already two patrol cops there, one of whom had called Beau. They had taped off the scene, but as they were doing it, people had begun showing up. They had all they could do to keep the rubberneckers out.

The sheriff handled them easily, told them under no uncertain terms they were to go far away, and to tell others to stay out as well. His boogie man act worked very well. Then he dismissed the two patrolmen, said he'd wait for the coroner and the county crime scene fellows to show, but if they could drive off a bit and keep onlookers at bay, he'd appreciate their good work.

Once they had gone, he asked if I'd cut the kid down while he took hold of the body. Kevin Perks had been strung up with a line over the branch and tied off around the trunk, just a plain wrap around his neck, a couple of simple knots. Nothing special about the knots.

It was the line that gave me pause.

Same line used to lynch Willa Maes.

I bit my lips hard and sawed through the anchor rode.

I was way beyond discretion. I was near madness. Last time I saw that rope was when I had handed it back to Wiley, asking him to keep it safe and hidden. Nothing could make me think that Wiley had anything to do with Kevin's death, but there the rope was, shortened yet again from cutting down another dead boy.

Beautop was, surprisingly, magnificent in his gentleness. I'll spare the details, but a hanged man stinks from the waist down, and he'd had to take Kevin around the legs in order to let him fall onto his shoulder. He stepped away a few paces and then laid the boy on his back, the sun piercing the cleared spot overhead. Brushed the hair away from the boy's dead eyes, pressed the lids closed and resettled the black and swollen tongue back in the mouth. I wanted to hurl again.

And still the man went one step further into amazing. He bowed his head, held his hands in front of his own face, and prayed. And not any canned homily, either, but a Direct-to-Jesus prayer asking forgiveness for what the boy had done. Then he made the sign of the cross. Old Beau was a still believing Catholic. Been a long time being lapsed, but I found myself making the same darn sign.

Finally he rose, brushed the leaves from his legs. Quickly, however, he was back down in a squat.

Perhaps he'd not seen it when he took the boy's legs to lift him, but there was an envelope in the right pocket. He pulled it clear, snapped out the note inside, and read. Then he crumpled it in his fist. 'Makes no fucking sense.'

'May I?' I asked. He flipped me the wadded message. One sentence, typed. 'Ask Ronnie Perks why this happened to this boy.'

Even though Beautop had definitely turned around my opinion of him, I remained convinced it was wise to keep my mouth shut. The common crappy knots said that there was no way Wiley had been involved, still there was the old gray cotton anchor rode. What put a crink in my scenario was how a one-armed man could possibly manage getting the Perks kid hanged all by himself. And that the message was a third-person sentence, not first person. And Gregg Whitaker wasn't the author, and it was certainly not Ronnie Perks. Ridiculous even to mention Bonnie Lou.

If Davis needed help, though, I was sure he wouldn't have needed Wiley's. There were a few living in those woods who would have jumped up to help that old man.

So, yeah, I had my definite suspicions who had hanged Kevin Perks, but I could in no way share them with Beautop without exposing myself, Wiley and especially June to the full weight and stone-deaf ears of the Law.

The one who knows, Watt had said, too often, has the responsibility.

But, I had to ask myself, the responsibility to do what?

I stayed with the body, the Sheriff having called in an ambulance and one of his men. I was told to say nothing to anyone, that I was just someone with Beautop when he'd gotten a call. I was to identify myself as a former policeman, that was all.

He made the call to June for me.

Sitting beside a corpse all alone in the woods was something I'd done before, but not happily. And there was something about the kid that wouldn't allow me not to feel. Even though he'd been part of murdering Willa Maes, I didn't see him as the evil necessary to kill. He was, in a way, a victim. And there he lay, dead under the hot high Florida sun.

And I, there with him, had nothing but thoughts.

It had been from good intentions telling Davis about my suspicions, but it appeared they had been used by the man to do something beyond bad. He'd said as much to me yesterday, about my intervention in what wasn't really my business. But it wasn't that simple. The road to Hell may be paved with them, but that's no reason to stop doing things with good intentions.

Had I not said anything to Davis, things may have taken a course toward a better justice. I knew it in my bones. What I had done was tell a crippled man, and not crippled because he'd lost an arm, the one thing that would give him justification to exact the only justice he believed left to him. I'd given him a way to react, a purpose, though a purpose to corrupt a man who had lost everything — his love, his talented arm, his self-respect, his connection to the better history of his race, and his future because of the cancer. I had done what I had done with good intention, but it sure as Hell didn't make me feel good.

Was Kevin Perks, dead under the sun, dead because of Davis's good intentions? Had justice been exacted in this killing because any Justice that the black community may have expected had been stripped and raped by the powers that be, who had called the Willa Maes murder a suicide?

Never so happy in my life to hear car tires crushing through the undergrowth. As soon as the deputies arrived, I started walking.

June picked me up on the highway.

We both took the time to cry before starting up the car again.

Nineteen

Wiley hadn't a hint of Davis's intentions, nor a clue as to where Coleman Davis might then be. After we left, Davis had taken him to see Ciminy Maes, and the last he'd seen of Davis was a nod to the man before he pulled away. As Wiley had said, his interest lay in keeping his wife's cousin company.

As for the gray length of cotton rode left to his care and supervision, I had said nothing. All I'd asked, when I got Wiley on the phone, was if he knew where Coleman Davis might be. I heard, *Doan know, Cap'n,* and left it at that. Said I'd be back in touch.

I wasn't certain what to do, but I was certain of what I knew. That Kevin would not be the last. June and I knew that when I called and told her about Kevin.

Problem was, I hadn't realized that possibility while I was with Beautop. And if I did start spouting what I knew, all manner of Hell would come raining down on me. Protecting my ass was a lousy reason not to save the lives of Kevin's fellow conspirators, but that really wasn't the reason I said nothing. Truth was, I was in some shock over the second hanging, and just didn't do the necessary two plus two in enough time.

Davis, former soldier, former sniper, which is sanctioned murder even by a sniper's definition, was on his last mission, and there was no turning him. Like people who think they hear commands from God, his orders had to feel to him sacred and right. Sure, he needed to be stopped, but going after Cole Davis by myself seemed a stupid idea. Even asking Wiley to help, which I might have considered if I didn't already know he'd need more convincing his friend might be on a mission, seemed beyond the realm of possibility. Though old and sick with cancer, Davis was still ex-Special Forces, capable enough of dragging a healthy teenager into the woods and stringing him up with only one good arm. He'd knocked Perks down pretty easily with just one arm.

Had Bromley Beautop been anything other than a sheriff I would have called him, given him the *What What*. But the shit storm was swirling already, no sense throwing the contents of my chamber pot into it. For some reason I felt myself getting pissed at my brother-in-law Watt, with his black and white very neat *One who knows* line scrawled in the metaphorical sand. But I realized it was the old *Am I my brother's keeper* debate, and there hasn't been a clear-cut answer to that one since before time.

Although I was frozen in my personal debate, preventing me from any forward action, I still had a car to drive. I didn't give *Where to* a single thought. *Where to* was back to the *Sweet Discourse*, of course.

In Greek mythology — which is where I felt was another good place to go for answers to long standing questions that had no answers — Hercules had to wrestle Antaeus, the son of Poseidon the sea god and Gaia the mother of the soil. Antaeus had never been beaten in a wrestling contest. No matter how good a wrestler anyone was, Antaeus was a god. But Hercules was a half god, and being such he was privy to what the gods knew. He was told the secret of Antaeus's strength. So long as Antaeus remained touching the ground, either the earth or the sea, he stayed strong. Hercules lifted him in the air, Antaeus lost it, and the hero became the first person to defeat him.

I wasn't Hercules. That crap-filled week was. I was Antaeus, and what had come to wrestle with me and pin my metaphorical arms to my side was the mess created by other people. But I had a place that fed my strength. Long as I kept my feet solidly on the *Sweet Discourse*, and my arms around June, I felt strong. At the moment June was a bigger mess of emotions than I had been. She had bandaged Kevin, and helping someone to heal creates a bond. A forgiveable bond.

Hence, taking myself back to the *Sweet Discourse.*

Home.

It was mine, the center of my orderliness, a tight ship, a place for everything and, more importantly, everything in its place. I wanted to touch her, see her neatly stowed map case, her well-knotted lines snugging her against the dock. I wanted to feel the rigidity of her deck beneath my feet, the polished stainless wheel that helmed her. I wanted to see her compass constantly pointing north. I wanted to hear her perfectly pitched engines, and most of all I wanted to see the boundless waters before and below her, the constancy of stars reigning overhead.

I needed *me* back, and she had the power to give it.

I did all in mechanical fashion: checked the fuel, plenty; checked her battery levels, unnecessary; went forward and released the ties to her cleats, which had been considered by both of us as June's job, but I handled it. I returned to the stern and removed those lines, again June's job; climbed aloft and fired up her engines; climbed back down and undid the forward spring line, handed it to my studious June, who studied my swift, sure movements; told her to release the spring line running aft soon as I was in my chair, again superfluous; then I started to climb upward.

My hand touched the top rung, my eyesight just clearing the deck of the flying bridge, when I stopped. I could feel the hum of her motors through my palms, her slight shift to the side from my climbing being brought back with a roll, the dropping sun warming my cheek. And I could feel June's eyes boring into my back.

They were eyes driven by concern, not burning with displeasure, and certainly not disapproval. She understood. She just didn't understand how much she understood, and she kept watch on me to take measure of me. I finished climbing, took my seat, put my hands on the throttle and gearshift, said *let her go,* checked over my shoulder to see when, not if, June let her go, and — determined, sure, and ready — I shifted.

We left.

The way clear of the marina had us turn a bit northwest, then west around a hummock blocking the mouth to the harbor, then straight on to open water. From there I had choices, northwest to meet with Watt and Annigail in New Orleans, west to nowhere but more open water, or south, to home.

I knew I was leaving Wiley behind, but he would understand. I would send Frank to get him.

By the time I had reached the first edge of that open water, and therefore the choice, June had come up to sit with me. No beer, no comment about how pretty the approaching dusk or the cleanliness of the air we were then able to breath, no warm palm touching me, reassuring me. I was left alone, to decide.

What I did was drop into neutral, the bow pointed westerly as it had during the run out to clear water. We began to bob, our forward motion decimated. By the natural pressures of what little wind there was, and by the continual roll of waves headed to a certain death on the shores behind us, our bow began to turn. North, away from home. The sinking sun began to drift to our left, to port, like a fly ball spinning in a curve to drop into foul territory.

One thing about a ball dropping foul. Somebody still has to run after it, regardless whether he has any hopes to catch it. A caught foul is still an out, so you got to try.

And the one to catch it was the person in the right place at the right time with the responsibility to catch it. Me, out in left field.

Still, though, I dropped the gear to forward, pressed down on the throttles, and took us for a ride.

Where? To anywhere but there.

We were running away from the foul dropping our way.

We didn't run for long, but we ran well into the dark. I had wanted to see the stars. On the western horizon ahead of us were a half dozen lights from cargo vessels, dancing like sea fairies at play. A glance back east showed we'd gone over the horizon. There was nothing of there to see. It was almost possible to believe that nothing was back there, or that what was there had frozen into an obsidian stillness, all life trapped in a black glass.

But I knew better, and June knew better. And wise woman she was, she understood what running away had given to us, to me: the space and time to regain footing.

'We should go back now, Andrew.'
I didn't have to respond with anything more than a turn of the wheel. But it was too late.

The time spent running outward had felt boundless, unlimited, but the time used for our determined return back over those same waters seemed compressed, shortened. I desired it cut to half, less than half.

But velocity is velocity, and hull speed is hull speed. Physics determined that our time returning be as long as it had been to reach that far horizon. All earned spacious complacency had become replaced by dense thoughts of intentions.

As compelled as I had been to run, I felt an equal, no, increased pressure to get to the Dennison and Whitaker homes, for me to warn them directly.

But as I have said, it was already too late. I just didn't know it.

I wanted help, needed it. They needed it, but the one person to whom I wanted to turn to was one whom I couldn't ask, Bromley Beautop, sheriff of the county. The reasons why not had not changed. But once I saw the lights of the marina, I realized there may have been a second. He had much to lose, if he hadn't already lost it.

If Perks was home, he certainly wasn't answering his phone.

We tied up quickly, but not insecurely, and I asked June to stay aboard in case someone showed at the marina. I also asked for Olivia, June's pocket pistol. She bore complete fright handing it to me, but I assured her with 'Last resort, Honey. Defense. You know I hate guns.'

My assurance to her was about as effective as that gun would have been. I kissed her, then got off my boat.

I found Perks house — bless the GPS — but it was dark. I had expected as much, but, still. From there I had no place to go except to the Dennisons or the Whitaker house. I sat there in the dark, watching a house that I felt would stay dark for a lot longer than anyone had planned on.

I felt small and alone, the seeping of surety continual. I looked at my watch, almost ten, and decided it was not too late to call Wiley.

'Any word on Davis?'

'No, Cap'n. Didn't know you was lookin' hard for 'im.'

'Well, I am.'

'You want I make some calls, see anybody knows?'

'I do, Wiley, but I don't.' I could hear him not nodding.

'S'okay. But you okay? Doan' sound it.'

'I think so.'

'Do that, an' you get close, call back. I be here.'

Just hearing the stormy rumble of the man's voice stopped my leaking self-assurance. Put the pedal to the metal, as they say. In twenty minutes I reached the front road to the high school. Pulled over and called. No sooner than did my *Hello* get out than Wiley handed me over to a woman. Ciminy Maes.

She had in her voice the notes that poured syrup must make, for despite the anguish and horrors of her recent days, her directions had the care and concern about me finding my way that a mother put into coaxing her son to come back home even though he'd broken curfew. I could have spent an hour in the lush comfort of that woman's voice, but I knew as soon as I pulled in front of her house I would have to shove her out of the way, because the words my voice had to convey were never to be told to her, so long as I could help it.

She just didn't need to know.

I accepted a coffee, but that was all. 'Sorry ma'am, but I have to talk to Wiley about something private, and it's urgent. I hope you understand.'

'Sure,' she said. 'Y'all go sit down in the back. There's a picnic table there. Wiley knows it. Mosquitoes are in bed, and that's where I'm going.'

Wiley reads waves like I read books, and reading faces isn't too far distant a skill either. I've noticed with the uneducated and near illiterate, they see words in things where we book smart people don't even see things.

'Somepin's happenin' Cap'n.'

I had to tell him. And I saw it hurt.

'You is sure?'

'It was the rope, Wiley, the one I gave you.' I wanted to say, *to keep safe and hidden*, but I didn't have to.

'I figured it was safe with Cole. Not like I gots lots of hidey holes around here. Maybe we shoulda lef' it on the *Descause.'*

I loved his pronunciation. When he used the whole name he said, and probably meant, that she was the *Sweet ess Cause*.

But I shook my head. No, we had done what we thought was the right thing. I told him how often recently the right thing turned to the wrong thing.

'He's going after the rest, Wiles. I know it. I just don't know how to find any of them. Only thing I can do is warn them. Bonnie Lou will know me, and if it saves her life, saves Cole from killing yet one more person, I'll have done my duty. I'll get them all to justice. How, I don't know. But this thing Cole is doing? It doesn't sit right.'

'That cause you a white city boy, Cap'n. Doan know how country work.'

'You think this is right?'

'Ain't never gonna say killin' be right, but I study up on my bible. It say *Eye for'n eye, toof for toofs,* an' ain't that all Cole's doin'? Takin' eye for eye?'

'It is. But still.'

'See, y'alls ya bein' white and city, ya got a justice way. Out here, they ain't but one side, and they's got the Law. They's got it f'lookin' out for they selfs, and ev'body t'other side jus' try holdin' on what little they got to keep. It different, that Justice. Eye for eye the way it is.'

'But you still think we should stop Cole.'

'I do. But it ain't we, not this time, Cap'n. Me stoppin' Cole i'n't a right thing f'me be doin'. Not wit her, not wit nobody.' He swept a hand in a wide arc towards the woods.

I understood. I didn't agree, but I understood that I couldn't disagree. The lessons and meaning of history was his, not mine.

'An' I cain hep ya wit a gun. Ciminy won't have none, an' not like I can go down a street an' ast for one.'

'That's okay, Wiles, seriously. Not like I have a clue where to go, how to find anyone.'

'Use a phonebook.'

'Fresh out.'

'That I can get. Ciminy got a old phone, an' I'm sure as I'm talkin' to ya she got a phone book right near. I go look, ya stay put.'

Gone a while. I was left in a soup of conflicting what to do's until he returned. Had a book, and had a light. A candle in a holder, but it was a light.

I'd studied art in college, specializing in my Masters on the northern Renaissance painters, especially Rembrandt. I think now how much like a Rembrandt we must have looked, a tired white man hunched over a tome, that phonebook our guidance in a thick dark, a black man huge in dark shadows holding the flickering light of a wax candle just high enough so that the man who could read was able.

I found no Whitaker, figuring like the rest of America who'd given up land lines for mobiles, but I did find a Judge Emery Dennison. I got out my little notebook and wrote it down.

'Y'know, Cap'n, I'd go see Cole. Go t'his house. Izzis home port. He bound to go there.'

'Maybe, but not til he's done. And no answer every call, Wiles. Doesn't it seem likely he just don't want company? He's not there. But if you want me to take you there,' shaking of the huge head. 'Didn't think so. Now I got to find my way out of here again, and find this address. Damn I wish I had GPS signal.'

But I didn't, and wouldn't have done me any good anyhow.

Going in circles it's called. Three wrong turns, but at last I felt myself on the right road, and soon I was on what some might call a main one. Looked like a back alley to any city boy, but it bore the three numbers of the county road I recognized.

Towns in that part of Florida often amounted to a bar, a gas station, a drug store, more often two, and a supermarket no bigger than a minimart. I came to such a place that was still manned. I stopped, got directions and fuel, not knowing where I might have to go later, and pulled away.

Like any Southern judge who'd risen to the District circuit, Judge Dennison had made coin enough to afford himself a faux-assed plantation house on a road with many such crap pieces. Though many by then had gone dark, all had enough light on their columned porches to show me I was in the right neighborhood. And a few, which included the Judge's, had a lighted column roadside, a light that shone on the four numbers marking its address.

But I didn't need a house number to know I'd arrived. There were people and more than a few cars, made things look like there was a party going on. But there were two cars that said, *Nope, no party*. The ones with spinning blue and red lights, with a flashing white strobe in the middle.

Too late.

Not like I could pull over, stop, hop out and say *Howdy*. I drove past slowly, a rubbernecker. What I presumed was that Davis not only had somehow gotten Bonnie Lou, but there was no need to go looking for Gregg Whitaker, either.

If, however, Davis also had Ronnie, then he had to have his mother, Constance Perks. With her, Davis couldn't have exacted the same punishment he had to have in mind for those collaborators. She was the stopper. I couldn't see what, but he would have had to do something. With an innocent in the fray, I had someone I could do something about, that was my business *because* she was an innocent, so far as things added up. Her worse crime, besides crushing everything Coleman Davis had to risk, was maybe trying to keep her son from the law, from his due punishment, from the wheels of justice rolling over him, her, the family.

But I was still at a loss as to *what* I could do. I still had no idea where she, they, might be.

Thoroughly defeated, thoroughly stumped. I felt myself going down, and not even swinging. Went down the road, turned around, headed back to the marina. Didn't even slow to rubberneck.

When I pulled into the marina lot, I easily spotted all the lights blazed in Perks office. I wondered why June hadn't called me, but then I looked at the time. She'd probably, and had, fallen asleep. Forgivable. Woke her, filled her in, left to see Perks.

I noticed the Sheriff's car parked by the steps going up to Perk's office. I assumed Beautop had returned to search again for the incriminating papers. I climbed the steps up to the outer door without being quiet. It was late, and I had no desire to be shot ever again, so I let my footfalls forewarn.

Reached the door, heard voices on the other side.

Knocked. Hard.

Beautop answered it with a forceful yank. I could see Rick Perks standing lost and vacant in the outer office. He just looked at me like, *What the fuck you doing here this late?* I just nodded to Beautop with an understanding tip of the head, who closed the door, climbed back down and waited.

About a minute later he came out, alone.

I said, by way of explanation, 'I saw lights, thought maybe you came back. He know anything?'

'Ongoing investigation. Can't say.'

'Oh come on. Does he know where Ronnie Perks is, or how he might be aware why Kevin got killed, like the note implied? I liked the kid. Kevin, that is.'

The Sheriff eyed me long time, lips grim, demeanor almost back to what it was out at the shooting gallery.

But I have my faces too. He asked me, 'Cop to cop?'

'Of course. Cop to cop. I'm just here to help.' I could lie like a cheap hairpiece.

'He has no idea. Wife came, screamin' she wanted money for tickets, he said he needed time, and where was he going to get tickets. He said Ronnie musta somehow knew there was money. Ricky really had planned helpin' 'em. She wouldn't say why she wanted out, but he wasn't surprised, 'specially after Ronnie spilled the beans about his offshore accounts. How the kid knew is beyond me, and beyond Rick. But he did. Like I told you, they weren't leaving 'til Friday, but Rickie says they disappeared late last night. Ain't nowhere he'd know they woulda gone. Twenty-four hours I can make it a police matter. But he says no, we do it quiet.'

'And that's a good idea how?'

'I don't know, but he won't listen.'

'You're the sheriff. Your call.'

'Short and curlies, remember?' Beatop started chewing the inside of his cheek. 'As for Kevin's note, he seems seriously to have no clue what it means, except to figure it out we have to find his kid. And I have nowhere to look.'

Of course I had no idea either, although scouring a million acres of tree-covered Florida in search of a couple more cottonwood flowers seemed likeliest to yield the result. 'So why's he here?'

'Because he thought they maybe took the boat. He keeps a small cruiser, a twenty-seven footer, in a slip here. It's here, though.'

'So you two just going to sit up there and wait?'

The Sheriff hesitated, seemed to be thinking over telling me something further. I urged him on. 'Something you don't want to tell me?'

'Yeah,' he said. 'There's a girl missing. Ronnie's girlfriend. Daughter of a District judge. I can't sit here. I got to get to work. There's another kid missing, too.'

'Three kids missing? You think they all ran off?'

He shook his head. Man could sag dramatically.

'Perks should be home.'

'Maybe there I can help. I can ask June, my girlfriend, to keep an eye out here. She's seen Ronnie, and besides, anybody comes into this lot this late she's gonna notice. I'll give her your number, she'll call you, and me, soon as she spots anything. I'll take Perks home. Best place for him.'

'She'd do that?'

'I ask her she will. Just give me five. I want to see her, tell her something's up. She won't press for a whole story, good about that. Do as she's asked.'

'A good one?' He seemed genuinely happy for me.

'The best.' Despite the somberness of the events, that made me grin.

Beautop shook his big head. 'Don't tell anyone. Especially Perks.'

'Like I'd need to? She radiates nice.'

'I'll see what I can get him to do. You go see your girl.'

And I did, and she was asleep again, though not how she nor I would have preferred. I woke her again, told her as much as a minute allowed, asked her to climb up to the bridge, to keep lookout, but if she had to, go back to sleep in the bunk. Hell, if Connie Perks and her son did show up to steal the runabout, I said let them. Kissed her, she kissed back harder.

'Please, Andrew, be safe. I never signed up to be a cop's wife. Don't know if I would have.'

I almost asked her when did she sign up to be anybody's wife, but that was not the time. Not sure when the right time was going to be.

Perks, reluctantly, bought in to the plan. Though he wasn't thrilled having me as a babysitter, Beautop reminded him I'd been a cop and he trusted me. I had lied to the man bald-faced, but that was the first time I felt badly about any of it.

It passed.

Got Perks home close to two-thirty in the morning. I was dog tired. So was he, but neither of us thought about crawling into a bed.

Small talk was out. What was filling up the room eating peanuts was, I felt, off conversational limits. That left the décor. I asked him about the baseball in his étagère.

'What?' He stared at it a might long. 'Just an old baseball. Ronnie's.'

One thing surprised me about the man. He seemed concerned, upset, but not moved at any time to tears.

Like Tolstoy said, unhappy families are all unhappy in their own way.

Nothing for me to say after that. We took to staring at the other, then at the rug. He offered me a drink, which I declined, but made one for himself. A three-fingered pour. Put on the television to an old Bogie movie, and I was out by the first commercial.

I stayed that way until I felt the cold round metal surrounding a little dark hole of familiar size pressed into my cheek.

I hate guns.

Twenty

I opened my eyes on a mean, mad, black pair belonging to Coleman Davis. Perks was across from me, slumped over and face down on the sofa. I could tell the revolver pushed against my cheek had no silencer.

Knew enough about pistolas to recognize a service-issue, probably Cole's Special Forces sidearm. And my quick glance at face-down Perks showed me no blood, so I figured Perks's slug-shape had been caused by a few more three-fingered whiskies poured after I'd passed out. Or, possibly, that Cole Davis had clocked Perks from behind, but I think I would have heard that. My money was on the whiskey. Still, the one-armed man proved himself a sneaky bastard. Evidence was him poking steel in my face.

'I see you a man a means, Mr. Nolan.'

I had no idea what that meant.

'But not much means. Why'n't you drag th' lady pistol from your pocket f'me?'

He pressed his gun against my cheek a little harder. I recognized that my most immediate job was to extricate Olivia from my front pocket with no more than two fingers and a thumb, sensing that his gun, already pointed in a dangerous direction, might be ready to go off much faster than June's little pea shooter ever could. Thereafter, I felt important that I keep every muscle in my body from doing so much as twitch.

I was good at my new jobs.

'Didn't 'spect t'find you here, but then your nose seem t'find its way int'my business no matter how many times I say it shouldn't. Sucks f'you. But y'get handed lemons, y'make some lemonade, right?'

I think I agreed.

'I got things t'do.' He waggled his stump for me to see. 'I could use a hand. Now get up. And get him up.'

Wasn't easy, but once Perks got his eyeful of a man with a gun, his eyes started working almost as well as his panic.

'Sit down next t'him, Nolan.' I did. 'I hear you lookin' for a missin' wife and kid, Rickie. That true?' No answer. Either the man was frozen with fear, or stupid. You answer men with guns. Period. So I answered for him.

'Don't get so damn helpful, Nolan. How many times I got to tell you that? Don't matter, I already know. See, I knew they split from you. And how I know? I got me a visit from an old girlfriend.'

You think Davis would have grinned with pleasure. No. Dead serious the whole time. But, Jayzus, the girl delivered her own son into the mouth of the lion, and had no idea.

'Surprise you? Hell, surprised me. Both 'em, right t'my house. I was really happy t'see 'em, too.'

I could imagine why, but could also imagine that Perks, if he had an idea, might not have the right idea. To make sure Perks did have the right idea, Davis continued.

'Y'sure got to know my Willa Maes was kind a grandson t'me, right? Kinda important? Almost important as that baseball over there. Fact, mo' important. Like a son. Son's're important, ain't they, Rickie? So I see your little boy come through my door tailin' after his mama, I got thinkin' how much I would like my boy back. And then I got to thinkin' how much you might like your boy back. Y'does, don't you, little man?'

Perks glared, a pair of street flares in those eyeholes.

'Y'oughta. See, y'can get your boy back. Bad thing is, I can't. Ain't it a shame? Somebody killed 'im, lynched 'im up like a God damn dog.

Your boy musta thought there he was jus' hangin' up nothin' more'n a God damn dog. He right, Rickie? You think your boy lynchin' a black boy weren't nothing more'n hangin' a God damn dog?'

I couldn't see Perks face fully, not with that service revolver keeping the two of us all neat and tidy with its working end, but I could see enough that he had no clue what Davis had referred to. Didn't need to sense it, actually. Perks said it. 'What the fuck are you talking about, Davis?'

'Y'don't know? She didn't tell you? Oh, how much she thinks a you, Rickie. Don't even tell the Daddy she was taking his son 'cause she hadda hide him. Bet you thought she was just leavin' your ass for another fella. Maybe even a nigger dog like me. You should think that. Was me she come see.'

Coleman Davis backed up until he reached the cabinet holding the baseball. In a move that made me almost have a movement, he smashed the front glass with the gun, knocking the baseball loose. It fell to the floor, rolling towards where we sat.

'Get it, Nolan. Y'know what it is.'

I did.

'Put it in your shirt. I'm gonna need y't'keep it safe.' Obedient to the end, and I hoped it would be a nice, peaceful, no gun going off end. 'Stand up you both. Time we ride.'

Perks had balls, got to give him that. Balls that made him stupid, though. Me, I had no balls. I thought it much wiser to keep my mouth shut and hands busy with whatever Mr. Davis wanted them busy. Davis sure seemed in the mood for talking, but I had no doubt there was anything useful that I could say. And nothing Rick Perks could have said would have made any difference. But Perks had a mouth, just not the savviness to keep it from working. 'Ride where?'

That's why I said he had stupid balls. *Where else, asshole?*

'You want t'see your boy? I came to drive y'to 'im. You do want t'see your boy, right?'

'You hurt him, I'll rip your fucking head off.'

'Gee, Rickie, wished you'd told me earlier. But let's hope he ain't hurt so bad he can't say hello t'his Daddy. Or goodbye, whatever he wants. Don't matter none t'me.'

I knew the point the play had reached. Perks would either launch himself at Davis, in which case I'd hurl myself out of the way of that pistol, which had to go off on somebody, or Perks would do nothing. Thank Heavens he finally had a rational thought.

Davis's car was not just a big car, it was a four door. He had me get in the driver's side, then told Perks get in the back, Davis then with him. Even though I was pretty sure Davis had the gun well pressed into Perks belly, I continued to do as told. I drove.

And I drove. I drove until the sun rose, drove south. We were soon on I-95, eventually passing St Pete, Bradenton, Sarasota, Fort Myers, and onto old Route 41. He'd been busy.

And like I said, he talked.

First he thanked me for the four names, then he filled Perks in on why those four names were so important. 'Didn't take long t'find three hepped kill my Willa. E'en less t'get 'em all talkin'. I told 'em all three what I learnt, thanks t'Mr. Nolan.'

'Now I'm not a 'specially mean man, Rickie. Y'know that. Least I weren't no unreasonable man. But more an' more, as time got on, I lost more and more reasons to stay reasonable. Willa was th' last a 'em. So y'can say I'm a man with good reason t'have no good reason.

'But one thing Uncle Sam said was, an enemy combatant with reason and intent t'screw up the just — that always be us, Mr. Nolan, soldiers — well that combatant got t'be taken out. Each a those kids? My real target. Guess y'understand now, doncha, Rickie. Y'understand too, doncha, Nolan?'

He didn't actually expect my nod of agreement, but just in case, you understand, he got it anyway.

'I 'spect they kept screamin' down in my cellar, y'know. I live kinda far out in the woods. Leavin' a pretty girl with all them bugs and spiders down there, but what could I do? Me an' a pair a boys hadda go for a ride. That Gregg, boy is he practical at haulin' rope, I can tell y'all that. Even with his hands tied, he got t'do his hobby. That's lynchin', Rickie. Po' Kevin. Done up by one a his own kind. An' jus' like a God damned dog. But, well, couldn't be hepped.'

'Gregg, now, he begged and begged, cried and cried. We got back home and I got kinda bored with him. You'll find him, Nolan. Perks goes t'shootin' there now an' again. For laughs, I put one a them old cans on 'is head, set 'im up on one a them stumps. Told 'im don't move, but kids. None a them ever listen. Damn can fell off. Made me mad. Told him so. And me there thinkin' I don't gotta find another target. Went too quick, y'ask me. But weren't nobody there but me f'th'fun.'

What my frozen consciousness managed to lock onto was that he said I *would* find him. Future tense. Bless my degree in English. Couldn't help myself, but some relief passed through. But just about my future. I knew Perks wasn't going to walk away.

'Now doncha worry about th'girl. You'll see her. She's keepin' your boy company. Not sayin' much, I suppose, but then Ronnie probably ain't either.'

He stopped talking, saying nothing more than *Turn off here, turn off there. Park over there.* And finally, *Take the keys with you, Nolan, and get out.*

We'd left I-95 to push down a back road I doubted anybody but Cole Davis ever knew about, one that went into the Glades. Came in the back way to a place where the Park Service once had set up a long run of boardwalk meant for folks from Ohio to walk down and commune with Mother Nature without getting swamp water dirty.

He made me take lead, Perks between us, the bazooka in his hands giving me good reason to go for that walk. We all travelled more than a mile in before he said *Stop*.

'Nolan, you got that baseball?'

I turned, touched my side, nodded.

'That's good, real good. Rickie, your boy's half mile down. Why'n't y'get yerself some head start? I got business here with Mr. Nolan. Don't worry, I catch up with you soon enough. Y'might want some minutes alone with your boy. Pretty sure the girl won't mind.'

Perks did not hesitate, but neither did he pick up his pace. Twenty yards beyond us he stopped to look back. 'I said doncha worry. I ain't gonna hurt my friend here.' Perks turned and went on. Last I saw the man.

'I feel bad, sir, y'havin' t'carry that white man burden all the time. I said y'din't have to. We darkies don't need white messiahs comin' in t'hep us. But tell what, maybe y'ain't no Messiah, but y'can be savior t'part a what this is. I got a box in my trunk. In it's a letter. Couple a letters, an' some a stuff easy t' recognize. Read that top letter, an' y'll know what t'do with my baseball. Keep it safe, and you get it to its new home. Think y'got enough good in them intentions a yours t'do that for me, f'all us?'

He wanted an answer, but for the first time I had something he wanted, and I wanted to use it to get something I wanted. 'I will, but only if you'll tell me where Mrs. Perks is.'

'Connie? Where she allays been. The house, a course. She's fine, Nolan. She gonna be upset, but I think y'll find things t'talk about'll calm her down. Maybe.'

He reached inside his shirt and brought out Olivia. 'Silly gun for a growned man, but I suppose it was this or nothin', right? Here.'

He handed it over to me. I hesitated taking it. 'From here on out we part ways. I gotta make sure Rickie gets a full reward for all's been done. Oh, that girl. Made sure it went quick. Ronnie didn't put up no fight after I cut her throat. Things got easier. Sure got quieter. F'me, anyways. F'him? Gettin' tied to a poisonwood tree f'a day, smearin' all that sap, it bein' so humid. You heard a poisonwood, right?'

I had, and I shuddered to think.

'I doubt his Daddy'll find him still talkin'. But, Hell, jus' might. Speakin' a Daddy, something says that lawsuit of his's not gonna go his way, but then, Rickie Perks ain't gonna be much inna position t'care. Anyways, y'go on. Take your gun. Still loaded, see?' He fired a shot to his left. I flinched, he laughed. 'That's for Rickie. He'll think I shot ya. Wouldn't want 'im t'have hope there's cavalry comin' t'the rescue. Wouldn't be sportin'. Take it, Mr. Nolan. I don't think you'll use it.'

'Why wouldn't I?'

'Because a justice, that's why. So they be a choice. Shoot a man who never got justice to free a man who don't deserve justice, or let me walk on to get justice finally, Y'all understand an eye for an eye. When y'see me walk away, y'll know there must be end to it. Perks needed stoppin', and I didn't do it fast enough. Now everythin's facin' ruin. He's stopped, and my Willa, he's free. Besides,' he smiled a genuinely warm smile, 'Y'ain't no killer. Wiley told me. You're one a them white knights, everybody gotta get saved. Only one left t'get saved. Help Connie. Be sure about that box, and figure out who t'tell what to. Not like anybody gonna believe it. Connie, she might. People gonna believe an old nigger went off his rocker. And he did, sir, he most surely did.'

I took the gun, and watched as he headed down a boardwalk after a walking dead man.

I called June as soon as I had any signal. I thought to call Wiley, have him get to Constance Perks, but thought better of it. And no way I was calling Sheriff Beautop. She'd have to wait a few more hours.

Inside the box, under the neatly typed and enveloped letter addressed *To who it may concern,* were many of his more valuable baseball items, the framed letter from Bob Gibson, the St. Louis jersey. And the empty ball case. I put the ball among them, removed the letters and resealed the box.

I opened the typed letter. *Whoever finds this, get this box, all of it, to Kansas City where the Negro Baseball League Hall of Fame is. This ain't Negro League, but maybe they can sell it and use the money to help get the right stuff. Anyway, I'm an old black man dyin' of cancer, who ain't got much, not even his dignity. But maybe getting this stuff back to the league will be a last good thing of a not good man.*

Constance Perks was dehydrated, sore from having been made to lie in a man's bed pinned down by duct tape and rope. She'd had a terrifying time of it, but I couldn't let her not know what Coleman Davis had done.

She had grief only for her son, and, to my surprise, Coleman Davis.

I had believed that once love was given, committed, those emotions never change, unless the loved one destroys that love. Cole hadn't been the one to kill what had been between them. Another time, another place, that what continued to separate two hearts — which in all other ways were exactly the same — might not have kept them apart. Breaking off with Coleman Davis was the biggest, but not the only, regret of her life, but she believed she had for good intentions.

How well I understood that.

Davis was also right about being believed. Who could we tell, and for what purpose? Those who'd killed Willa Maes were dead, and the family who remained would have to suffer loss and confusion should they learn what their children had done.

As for Kennie Perks father, he learned his son was dead by the same method that took Willa Maes. Let him think what he would, that maybe he'd think it was a pact. Kids do that. Whitaker's boy was eventually found, thanks to an anonymous tip from a marina pay phone. The Dennison's had to wait for a typed letter telling them how Rick Perks had run off with his son's girlfriend, that maybe someday she'd come back home. Maybe that was my cruelest act, but I had no way to let them know she'd had her throat cut in the Everglades, body most likely unrecoverable.

If Mrs. Perks wanted to change that story, well, that was her responsibility. The one who knows, you understand.

As for me, and justice, what I knew was that all were dead. That had to be enough. Time passed, and I saw no good reason ever adding to the miseries of those families by letting any of them know that their children had killed a boy whose only crimes were an ability to throw a baseball better than another, and for not being the right color for yet another high school girl who wanted to like him.

Telling them that, well, that seemed just another crime.

Coleman Davis going off to die? That was no surprise to anyone, especially for Wiley and Ciminy. June and I swore to never tell our friend what we knew.

And we knew. Boy, did we.

But there was one person to tell, and Connie Perks said, *Tell it all.* Not, however, before she said some other things.

Twenty-one

Best I could do, with the pieces I had. She told me what I could not know, about her decision to leave Rick Perks, to seek out the help of someone who might help her. That someone was Coleman Davis.

'Ronnie had told me he might be in some trouble, that people might think he'd gotten involved in something bad. He never said what, or what you say Kevin did,' — *Okay, so I lied to her about some things, but she was still a mother* — 'but whatever he maybe got himself into, he wouldn't tell me. Now you say it was about that boy they say killed himself? I didn't believe Willa Maes ever killed himself, but maybe it was over that girl. I could... It's like Willa Maes was Cole Davis all over again.' She cried for awhile before asking me, 'Why must it always be hate?'

I said I did not know. She had wide, burning eyes, eyes that screamed at me. 'Ronnie just begged we leave, go away. We talked before, about leaving, together. He said some man wanted money, more money than we had, or I thought we had, and even if we paid him enough everybody knows he'd want more, and my son would never be safe from the stupid thing. I told Ronnie we weren't rich, but he said the man said Rick had more money than God. Exactly how he put it, said the man told him his father had been screwing everybody, that there was a ton of money offshore. He'd been hiding money for years. He planned to quit us and leave the country to live in another country.

'So I went to my husband and told him I knew about the money. If only he'd been faster denying it. But a wife knows, even a wife who'd dried up inside a long time ago. I demanded he give us money to get me and Ronnie away, enough to set us up. That's when you saw us in the office.

'But that night you saw us, when Rick came home, there was a huge fight. He wanted to know why I wanted out, who told me about the money. Ronnie said something smart, and Rick smashed him in the mouth. He didn't just hit him, he smashed him, like this.' She made a fist. 'I had some money, not enough to even reach Georgia, but some. I had credit cards, but I knew in a day they'd be useless. I told him I was taking Ronnie to a hotel, I'd pay for it with what I had, but he took my cards then and there. If I tried to stop him he'd have hurt me, and Ronnie would have tried to stop him, and he would have hurt Ronnie. So he drinks himself stupid enough I left. But I had nowhere to go.

'We drove some, and I thought of Cole. I thought he'd help me, he would, but who I went to wasn't Cole Davis. Not any more. I didn't know any of what you're telling me he knew then. I drank his coffee, and I woke up from the drugs he put in it, and he had taped me up and tied me in his bed. I had no way of knowing, but I knew he had my boy. Then you found me.'

I kept from her that the person responsible for what Coleman Davis knew about Ronnie had been me. Call me a coward, but it wouldn't have helped her. She wanted to know what happened after she was drugged. I figured that she had a right to know. I could only tell her what I recalled from what Cole Davis had told me on the drive south, and what I had to witness.

'Puttin' powder in her coffee weren't easy, but seein' standin' in my livin' room in plain sight was the boy who killed my Willa Maes's, I felt that drug was necessary. I only hoped it wa'n't deadly.'

I admit I couldn't look at June with what she wanted me to say. 'Cole told me that, as soon as he noticed his old love dropping off, *(oh, she said, putting her hand to her mouth)* he went into the room where he kept not just all his baseball paraphernalia but his old service pistol. He always kept it loaded, living out in the woods as he did. He called Ronnie in to see what hung on the walls, but all Ronnie got to see was the round hole in the muzzle *(No, no, please!)* that I would see later on. He said he told Ronnie, *Don't bother screaming. She's out cold.* Then Cole struck him hard against the boy's head. *(Here, June cried and cried.)* How long the boy was out, didn't know. He woke in the trunk *(Oh, not in the trunk, no! Me: Sorry)* of a big car headed south.

'As for Bonnie Lou Dennison, she came along with Cole easy. Only had to tell her that he was a friend of Ronnie's, helping him run from his father, and she jumped into the car to go to him. She complained about his radio being too loud, but there was a kid in the trunk. *(Her, moaning: the trunk, in the trunk)* They had passed the hotel he'd told her that Ronnie and Connie were staying at, forgetting he'd even mentioned a name, Bonnie Lou knew something was wrong. She really understood when his pistol moved into view.

(June: *A man with half an arm using it to drive?* Me, and I don't know why: *The girl was probably convinced that old one-armed black-skinned man was going to rape her.* Again Me, but only to myself, then, but later to June, once she had it all and could hear it: *Dumb ass kid, should have known there are worse things to fear. But then, she was Judge Dennison's little girl, or so we'd been told.)*

'He said holding a pistol on Bonnie Lou while driving was not easy. Once Cole pulled over, she almost bolted but he saw her hand go for the door latch. *Don't, girl, just don't. I'm a good shot.* He made her get out. She was very afraid, almost falling down. He opened the trunk and she fainted. (Me, again, but definitely only to myself: *Thereafter, Ronnie had nice, soft company.)*

'It's a long ride and they both were nearly too dead to walk into the Glades, but they walked. It was... (Me: *You don't want to know anymore.* June: *When you told her, did you tell her how he died? Did she ask if Coleman kill her son?* Me: *I lied to Mrs. Perks. I said I didn't know.* Later I would tell June what I had kept from Connie Perks: *Cole took them to a place he knew, and knew well. It was to a grove of poisonwood trees in the Everglades, not far from where I last saw Rick Perks, and him. You know about Poisonwood? Sap burns the skin, and if the skin is wet, and if there's a lot of sap, it burns excruciatingly painfully. The Caribe Indians would use it to torture Spaniards they'd caught.)*

'Davis said he'd kicked Ronnie Perks hard into that grove, and the kid started to scream soon as it touched him. Bonnie Lou jumped on Davis, but it was as if she was a three-year old and he tossed her off. Kid just lay on the planks to the walk, watching Ronnie scream. Davis put the gun to her head, told her to tear her blouse into strips and tie Ronnie's hands with it. If she or Ronnie refused, he'd pull the trigger. She did as he asked.'

I had to think about telling June the next part, but then she was a big girl. She'd stop me if she didn't want it said.

'Coleman said he was only sorry that Ronnie got to see such a pretty girl before he sliced the girl's throat. *(June: Oh my God. He's a monster! Me: Was.)* Cole said he'd always planned for her to go quick, and that he knew what he was doing. Him Special Forces, so I'm sure she did go quick, too, He said Ronnie started howling like, well, you can imagine.'

I could see that she well imagined. Why I said what I said next was probably to make some change to the topic, but it was stupid to say.

'Maybe that's why poisonwood is known as hog gum.' First time I ever saw June look at me that way. I didn't like it. 'Anyway, Ronnie was tied up with Bonnie Lou's blouse, so Davis felt time had come to make sure the kid had plenty more reason to cry. He sliced up the gum tree until sap ran all over the boy. Told him not to sweat, sweat makes it worse. And besides, mosquitoes love it when people sweat.'

(June: *Stop, Drew. Please.* I did, for a while. But she wanted, later on, to hear again something I felt sure I'd said.)

'Mrs. Perks, not hearing anything except my *Yes* to her question, *Did Cole shoot him,* she asked me, *Where is my boy?* I had to say to her, I don't know.

'I told her about Cole Davis getting Gregg Whitaker into his car, and using the gun, convincing him to call Kevin, to get the boy to come out and get in the car with him. When I finished lying to Mrs. Perks about the death of her son, I had to tell her that because of all that, her husband was gone, her son was gone, three other kids were gone.'

We both cried, me holding June's hands in mine. 'I sat with her an hour, letting her cry it out. She was weak from the dehydration. I got her water, a damp towel. I asked her, *What now?* That's when we talked about what we could say. I had the letter, it would be enough. She said she'd let everybody know that Cole had told her everything he planned to do, not that I had told her. I found her because I had come looking for Wiley.

Then all she said after that was, *Please, I'd like to go home.*

Twenty-two

The man behind the desk stared at me with what I had expected: disbelief. I knew I'd get that, once I got through what I had to tell about the baseball. I couldn't blame him. I wasn't sure I believed it, and as I had no proof of much of anything, I couldn't be much more help than a delivery man. I had been instructed to give the St. Louis organization the several items, give what I could to back up the ball's provenance, and that was all.

All the while he held the Willy Mays' baseball. Below his hands rested a fair number of other Coleman Davis letters, each neatly typed, each explaining how he came by the objects he had. Throughout my story I'd kept my eyes fixed on Coleman Davis's left-handed signature, thinking as I had the first time I'd read it how proud he must have felt about his intention to do the right thing. The topmost letter was meant to serve as written provenance for the ball he held.

I had ended my story, and I was out of air. 'You understand, I have nothing whatsoever to corroborate anything except what you have. All I know about how Cole Davis came by that ball is what he's says in the letter, although I can tell you he told me in person all of this, exactly as it was written. And he seemed, when he told me, a man of some honor.'

In a reverential tone, the man said, more to his museum than to me, 'Willy Mays's Basket Catch ball. Amazing. Incredible.'

'Nobody will believe it, will they, sir?'

The curator to the Negro League Baseball Hall of Fame shook his head, a deep and heavy sadness. 'But Mr. Davis was right. It does belong here. It's a part of our people's history, even if it isn't a thing associated with Negro Baseball leagues. This,' he touched the letter, 'wouldn't be provenance enough, no. But in some things proof doesn't matter. Have you ever been to Rome, Mr. Nolan?'

I hadn't, and didn't follow.

He said, 'When I was a boy, a senior in high school, I got to go to Rome, to the Vatican. There in a gold lighted case were iron chains on display. I was told they were the very chains that Saint Peter wore when he was brought to Rome to die. The actual chains.'

He smiled, seeing I still made no connection. 'See, in this country, everything about our Lord Jesus is still something of a myth, no matter how hard we believe. Saint Peter's history, just like that of Jesus's, and therefore his reality and that of our Lord, that's something we over here must take wholly on faith, as there's no evidence before our eyes. But over there, they still have the Mount where He gave His blessings, there's an actual Appian Way, you can walk it, and there were those chains in a glowing gold glass case. The actual chains of Saint Peter. It was my ocular proof, you see? Support for faith is a wonderful thing, and I was changed forever having seen them. Jesus, that day, got more real, harder to refute, or refuse.'

He could see I followed his tale, but had not arrived at the conclusion he already knew well. 'Were they, Mr. Nolan, the real Saint Peter chains? Maybe they were just old irons found when they dug the Vatican foundation. And maybe,' he said, rolling the old ball in his dark fingers, 'this is just an old foul ball somebody caught at a high school game. Chains are chains, baseballs are baseballs. But it's what we think about chains that makes things magical. It's what we think that makes life worth living. But ocular proof, you see? Helps with the magic.'

He leaned back in his chair. Surrounding him were a hundred articles of proof that something magical had somewhere happened, something that the vicissitudes of history would have made a faded, passed thing, but which had been saved from those vales of gray. Things of evidence.

'We'll find a place for this ball, and we'll say that it is purportedly the famous Basket Catch ball. But I learned one thing this museum teaches over and over. It's not what we say that returns our crippled and distorted history to us. It's what we shall choose to believe.'

I wanted to add, *Or are led to believe.* But I refrained. I knew the time to go had come. June and I both rose. 'Thank you, sir. For Coleman Davis. And for us.'

But he stopped me. 'What do you choose to believe, Mr. Nolan, about this baseball?'

'I believe...' but I couldn't say. 'Let's just say I believe I had a part in a good thing to do.'

'I'd say that was true,' he said. 'Keep on doing good things, Mr. Nolan. They matter more than all the rest.'

Halfway back, June and I stopped at a hotel for the night. It was a long fifteen hundred miles from St. Louis to our home in Key Largo.

Our home.

We were very tired, more tired than if we'd only driven from one city in Missouri to the other in Florida. We still had, both of us, the weight of all that had happened back in that sweaty, hot week in May. It was even more hot on our drive, and air conditioning in a more than forty-year old car was the four window kind. Happily the top came down.

Still, it was a beat-you-up drive, and we weren't kids any longer.

We collapsed on the motel bed, sick of road food, ready for a good steak and a couple of beers to give that steak some flotation. I felt myself drifting off, until June's fingers moved to entwine mine.

She said, quietly, 'I really do feel we've done a good thing. But I don't feel good about it.'

'Not sure that's how it's supposed to work,' I said, my eyes still closed. 'And I'm really unsure of my good intentions.'

'Does that mean you'll stop having them?'

'Who knows.'

'What are your intentions, Mr. Nolan?'

I guess these days, especially these days when my shortcomings seem to regularly get yanked into evidence, it seems hard for a man to believe in the existence of goodness, especially my goodness. But I had one intention that was at least good for me, if not exactly a good thing. Anyway, she asked, so I told her.

After a few minutes of quiet, she said, 'I accept.'

Afterword

But this I kept from June, that I may have been wrong.

All I had ever had for evidence was a rope used to kill Willa Maes, one comment from a scared boy that had been chased or beaten by his cousin and a friend, and blank, unresponsive stares from two young teenagers who had been accosted by strange men with even stranger accusations.

It could have been any rope off any boat, might even have been a suicide. What did I really know? We, Wiley and I, could only assume that Willa Maes had no ability to tie those knots. What if he'd learned in some class, perhaps a science class? And what if Kevin had indeed been chased for pressing his interests on Ronnie Perks' girl?

Put yourself in Bonnie Lou's place: a strange man, old enough for a teenaged and pretty girl to think him a pervert, comes up with a truly bizarre accusation. If you were Bonnie Lou, how would you have reacted? Engage the perv in a debate, or, as she had done, just walk away, scared?

Same with Ronnie when accosted by Frank. He'd just been batted around in an important game, a life-changing game, and one he'd lost, when a strange man, and Frank could appear really strange to a young kid, a strange man comes up and, as I had, makes a wild-assed accusation.

I'd have walked off too.

And I had nothing else. Sure, Perks was dirty, the Sheriff convinced me of that. Connie Perks had been so little informed, almost everything explaining Coleman Davis's behavior was my explanation.

And I'd told her what I did with the best intentions. We all know what road gets paved with them.

And that was the problem. I had told Coleman Davis what I had conjectured, and told him with the best intentions. Somehow I added to his self-justifications about having a lifetime of hateful feelings for a white world that had taken so much.

But what if I'd just handed a deranged and damaged man the gun he needed? If I'd said nothing, would five people still be alive?

All of this I had to keep from June. All of this I would continue keep from June. None of this could I share with another soul, because not another soul would have anything to go on but what I've said.

Coleman Davis was certainly guilty of five murders. Were those four teenagers even guilty of one?

I just don't know. I really just don't.

Running Before Thunder

preview Chapter One

Book Four in the Drew Nolan story

One

'No dead people, or you'll be next.' June had waggled a finger before her half smile, ready to disappear into a puddle jumper at the Key West Airport.

What could I say?

'Yes, dear.'

She made me swear, and I did, three fingers up and cross my heart. But, then, well, you know what they say. *The best laid schemes o' Mice an' Men gang aft agley.*

Of course three days after she left for New York my ass ganged agley onto a jet to LAX to go see a dead guy. I thought about that promise — or rather about the guilt deriving from my breaking it — as our jet wallowed into either a dismal fog or deadly smog then stalled over a soggy Los Angeles sprawl.

Sorry, June, a man's gotta do what a man's gotta do. Especially since my sister's making me do it.

Our drop into the gray soup felt appropriately poetic. Visiting the dead requires proper weather.

Truth was, I didn't have to go to LA. I didn't want to go to LA, just as much as June didn't have to go to New York, and just as much as I didn't want her to go to New York. She said she had her reasons, not that she'd tell me. What a stink that blew up. But more on that later. Let's just say

June's leaving, my being coerced into a cross-country flight to meet a dead person, and the prospect of crappy weather all conspired to sink me into a piss-poor mood.

I certainly had no pressing desire to look at yet another dead man. Anyone who knows me knows I would have preferred frivolous wasting of long afternoons on a lawn chair, drinking in the Florida sun and drinking up some Highland scotch.

Had I not gotten on that plane, had I more wisely opted for the usual lethargy derived from sun and drink, the dead guy in Los Angeles would have continued being dead, and would have eventually slipped from almost all memory without reflection. Himself would have remained unperturbed by my indifference to his updated status, arms crossed on his chest in peaceful repose, lilies fading to a smeary brown, worms itching to get at their banquet.

Such were my thoughts as we went sliding into a muck-yucky cloud.

Nope, I had no good reason to look at another dead man. But then, seemed I never needed a reason to do what I preferred not to do. For that, I usually had Annigail.

Annigail is my sister. My Big Sister. Always has been, always will be, and any man unlucky enough to be a Baby Brother understands how influencing that difference can be. But would June understand, only child that she was?

By the way, and this will become important later on, we were a Traveling Three. Besides me, on the lap of said Sis was her eighteen month-old son, Nolan van Hij, heir to the van Hij throne and fortune, emperor of all his mother's attention and kindness, the perfect progeny of a proud Papa, and a cute little shit whom I intended to kidnap someday and take fishing as soon as he could bait a fishhook.

As for Annigail's husband, Watkins van Hij — Watt — he was in Europe to advise the Queen of Holland, the Pope, or some Euro-meister what to do with the money. That's what he does. And this also will become important later on.

A few days after June's departure, sister Annigail had shown up at my little Key Largo house, the one that I — happily until recently — shared with June. The developments encouraging June's departure for New York were many, and the story is long. I will get to it eventually. But because of that circumstance, I had been moping — my usual manner for dealing with sad tidings — on my kinda beach, an old jelly jar refilled with scotch carefully balanced on my belly, attired with sunglasses, cutoffs, flip flops, on a cheapo lawn chair in some every now-and-then shade from a palm tree.

The sun had begun slipping under the yardarm when I heard a vehicle plow down my driveway, crunches and smacks upon the foliage, that required I rise and turn to see who cometh. Unsettling surprise quickly replaced placid pleasure, once I spotted a Land Rover.

The van Hij Land Rover, the second most important van Hij — sweet sister Annigail — behind the wheel.

That never happens.

Not that Annigail doesn't drive, not that she doesn't have a Land Rover, or two, not even that she was in Key Largo. She just never seeks me out for a visit. Always the other way around.

No prefatory phone call, no preordained visitation, not even an offhand warning that maybe someday, like when Hell froze over, she'd come for a visit with only me. Just bam, *I'm here!*

Big Sister wasted no time in spouting her news. I was going to a funeral. With her.

That was the *What.* I asked the *Who, Where, When* and especially the *Why* questions, but none of whatever I might want to know ever amounted to a hill of horse poop with Annigail. An impatient wave of her hand, she delivered her real reason for my going to Los Angeles.

Because I said so.

Big sisters. We gotta love them. Otherwise we'd kill them.

The dead *Who* on my dance card was one Julio Palacio, a name that rang no bells until Annigail dribbled out some family history. Julio was brother to a no-relation uncle whom she and I once addressed as *Tio Ray*. But that was when I was four.

I barely recalled Tio Ray, but nothing, zip, zero, about Julio. Said so to Sis, thinking I'd be forgiven a shallowness of memories, having been after all only four. However, Annigail does not forgive.

'You can't remember Tio? Jesus, Drew. What have you done to your brain cells?'

Everything I could, Sister. Anything I could.

So she connected the dots. Tio'd been friend to my father and mother a year or two before passing into that dim vale where most of those the Nolan Clan had befriended go to die. She reminded me, with the intent to water my guilt and make it grow, that Tio brought us silver dollars whenever he visited. That, I said, I recalled. Of course I lied, but only defensively.

I'd probably last heard of him some time well before the final year of my father's life. Since then, *nada*. As in nada thing.

Annigail also reminded me — if you can call rolling your eyes and throwing up your hands an act of remembrance — that both Tio Ray and Dead Julio had been jockeys back in the day, my parent's day. Dad had met him at the old Garden State Park in Jersey.

The Palacios were gypsy riders chasing employment all over the east coast before settling at Santa Anita Park, a racetrack near Pasadena in California, which partly explains why my butt was dropping towards the LAX airport.

By the time Ray and Julio reached California, Tio had become a respected trainer, happy with the opportunity to stop pounding his bones in multiple daily runs among thundering herds. Julio had also stopped racing, for a less noble reason — he was not good at it — going to work inside at the pari-mutuel windows.

Weight gain had stopped Tio from climbing onto twitchy thoroughbreds. Seems he fell in love not just with California, but with avocados. Those little fat bombs did him in. Training horses got him the right sort of clients, and he never looked back.

As for the Not Yet Dead Julio, he had spent the next thirty years handing over tickets covering two-dollar bets. Of course not everybody bets only two bucks. Some dropped thousands on the ponies, not something I understood. I've been known to gamble, but I would never bet on something so unpredictable as a skittish, panicky, half-ton animal with the stubborn willfulness and intellectual mastery of my not-yet-two nephew.

I know, my gambling preference is off topic, but it underscores how stranger in a strange land I was about to feel as we dropped down toward LAX. But enough about me.

A groomsman found Dead Julio in Tio Ray's stable at Santa Anita Park during the early morning hours of the very Monday that June had split for New York. Purely coincidental. He was pronounced dead of a heart attack and/or a kick in the head by a horse. The simultaneity of injuries made conclusive diagnosis difficult, but Annigail, shrugging, had just said to me *heart failure* and let it go at that.

No reason than to think the man's death as anything other than damned inconvenient. Made me break my promise to June, and it put a sincere dent in my attendance at tanning classes.

So there we were — Annigail y Yo, with her son Nolan — touching down on a mist-drizzled tarmac, rolling slowly toward the maw of an LAX concourse, where, once reached, a hundred people rose behind us to clumsily stand for the stupid wait while the door — excuse me, *hatch cover* — took forever to gasp open, just so we all, First Class and Coach, could undertake the long walk to baggage claim.

All during that trek for our bags, one question raced around my head like a racehorse on acid: *How did Julio, a horseman all his life, get himself kicked in the head by a horse?*

As far as I then knew, no one suspected anything about the circumstances of Julio Palacio's odd demise. Annigail had said everyone was happy — although that was not quite the right sentiment — to accept the coroner's ruling of a heart attack brought on by unexpected impact with an equine toenail.

As far as I then suspected, we were on a walk toward a limo that was to ferry us to the funeral of a dead man I had never met, would not look upon, nor would spend much time considering. But, then, well, as they say, *Crap happens, and it gangs agley*.

When that happens, I tend to step in it.

Habit.

I blame all that followed on a twenty-three-year old boy who, several years before, got a stupid, whimsical and somewhat naïve notion in his head about how wonderful life could be if he became a cop.

That naïve and stupid boy had been me, and I became that cop. Even made detective. Did okay, got shipped to Europe for special assignment, came home and got shot, then I quit. Bought a boat. Became a bum. Met a hot chick, got engaged, was facing maybe getting unengaged. Not a long biography.

The gem in the bio is that I had been a cop. Once the infection of detecting grips one's nature, the paradigm of detecting never departs. Suspicion continues to frame one's responses to the presence of any two facts that just won't jive.

Once a cop, you forever sweat with the compunction to ferret out an explanation which'll allow the jivation of all the facts, and that compunction can overwhelm common sense. All subsequent behaviors, no matter how far they drag you under, have a predetermined feel.

Sucks, I know.

An occupational hazard.

That compulsive disorder has turned me into a reluctant detective a number of times since I quit the force, enough to be called a pattern. Or — like I said — habit.

Reluctant, however, is the key word.

As we made our way toward baggage claim, I felt that my original expectation — that I was only to enjoy forced participation among the grieving — sounded more and more suspect. Every forward footfall that I took toward the gravesite of Julio Palacio landed like a step into deeper and deeper crap.

Kept that growing awareness to myself, though. Why interfere with Annigail's opportunity to go all weepy and sad in public?

The mid-October, unusual-for-LA weather didn't help. I had thought of California, as most East Coasters do, as The Land of Sunshine, of bodacious but flavorless oranges and busty, equally flavorless blondes in small bikinis. Nope. A low pressure twirling out from El Niño had dragged evaporated sea water onto land, clouded the skies, blued the High Sierras, dampening all joy. All near-naked blondes stayed indoors in droves. The only appropriate entertainment for such a rainy day? A funeral. And we had tickets.

A gray LA may have been appropriate for a funeral and subsequent burial, but Angelinos know bupkis about driving in rain. Actually, they know bupkis about driving period. Some guy takes a piss before jumping off the Golden Gate Bridge and LA comes to a stop. Its famous traffic was bad enough, but rain made it a horror. Drowned every instinct of how to move forward on paved roads.

I was glad not to be driving. And really glad Annigail wasn't driving.

We were, however, directing a driver on what to do, or at least Annigail was. We realized there would be no way to make the lachrymose church service, so Big Sis commanded, *Straight on to Forest Lawn, driver.*

Other than my sister and nephew, I knew not one person other than Tio Ray among those under umbrellas who had elected to hunker around the muddy open ochre hole, over which Julio lay suspended in his pretty faux-bronze and rain bespeckled casket. More people than I'd expected. Such a thick and deep — and soggy — crowd should have meant we'd hang at the back until the antique ritual had ceased, but Annigail would have none of that.

She laser-beamed her — our — way to a gray-haired man whose head drooped. Tio Ray, in real mourning. Keeping him standing upright by solid grips on his arms were two uncommonly lovely women.

The two females could not have appeared more distinctly unrelated, though. I had supposed the taller of the two, fiftyish, must have been either Tio Ray's wife or possibly his sister-in-law. She could have been, once upon a time, one of those ash blonde trophies that short dark men seek, but there was something in her face and poise — and attention to Tio Ray — that demanded she not be underestimated.

The other woman, much younger, had an Hispanic vibrancy, and the appropriate curviness that on another woman might have only exuded pure sex kitten. This one exuded the *Don't You Even Freakin' Think It* stand-offish confidence of a Radcliffe or Bryn Mawr graduate.

I couldn't help but give those curves the once over, and I was well rewarded by the adventure, but finishing at her clear-eyed and grim-jawed stare toward the casket brought me fair warning. About what, I wasn't sure.

Nothing conservative about her, yet neither loose nor wanton. Any man would say she was a lot of woman. I have no idea what most women would have said.

Of Julio, no description. June, I swear, I never met the dead man.

Of Tio Ray, however, what there was on his outside screamed what was on the inside, a man with a crumpled heart, who had aged a decade hearing that his brother had suddenly, and strangely, died. The only thing about him that said nothing was that he was really short.

Tiny.

I tried to picture him as friend to my mother and father, both of whom had been tall. Couldn't see why he in particular would have become their friend, but then Mom and Dad did like an eclectic mix at their cocktail parties. Their frequent cocktail parties.

I suspected he'd been selected as a short-term pet, someone picked up as amusement for a while before they moved on to some other fetish, but — according to my source — they had discovered an interesting, elegant, well-mannered gentleman among them. If there was a common thread tying those to my parents' friendship, it's that they were people with interesting stories, the discretionary sense to know the appropriateness of bringing one up, and the wisdom to know when the right moment arose at which to share.

My sense, listening to Annigail's stories about him, was that Mom and Dad had missed Tio Ray when he had to move on.

I guess we all have at least one friend like him, short in our time together, long in our thoughts and memories.

Not in *my* thoughts or memories, to be sure. But, undetected by me, ever, was that Tio Ray had become an idolized, idealized, long-term presence for Annigail. Inflated by her infatuation into a larger-than-life and secret hero, Tio Ray had become the first crush whose return was to be wistfully and often longed for.

She said her adoration began the first time Tio lifted her onto the back of a thoroughbred.

He was then a young man in shimmering colored silks, trim, handsome, laughing, confident and attentive. And for an eight-year-old, just her size. I wondered what she thought of her shrunk-up hero at the graveside. Something in her giddiness — appropriately hidden beneath a dour and funereal demeanor — told me that in her heart Tio Ray still wore racing silks, and would still be let to kiss her forehead.

He'd need a stool, though. Annigail got Mom's height.

Big Sis made us known to the Palacios by working herself up behind Tio Ray. She placed a gloved hand on his shoulder and leaned forward to whisper in his ear. No recognition in his quick backward glance. She whispered again.

Tio nodded but returned his attention to the self-inflated Catholic priest droning on about the Goodness of God and the Greatness of Heaven, nesses which to my mind ran counter to the very real circumstance of Julio getting untimely sunk into wet dirt in a way too expensive metal box.

The gorgeous Hispanic woman turned to see who had come up on their sorrow. Have to admit, those brown eyes, critical of our timing, still had the appropriate effect. I darn near blushed.

Being the recluse I had determinedly become, I preferred anonymity and — perhaps for having been so firmly fixed by those dark eyes — I soon drifted away from Annigail and the Palacios, retreating to the back.

Disappearing gave me a chance to look around without having to offer up faked and indulgent head nods of recognition, or offer those weird mutterings of unfelt sympathy.

Not exactly a *Wizard of Oz* reunion, but there were a lot of uncommonly short men. I'm not outrageously tall, but no way am I average. That demarcation of most common height was somewhere midway between theirs and mine.

Many were Hispanic, and several, though far from all, had the company of a requisite tall blonde. Among those women in their sizzling black mourning wear, each gave me the impression that they were more conscious of what the wet drizzle was doing to their too-high heels than to the untimely and peculiar loss of the dearly departed.

Short folks aside, a number of better than well-dressed people stood apart, in clinging quiet pairs or islands of awkward silence. Behind them hung the Fringe People, fellows without ties, a few without even jackets, more than one woman in running sweats, all of them looking like wildebeests staring blank-eyed at one of their kind having been hauled down by hyenas.

A few of the men wore hats that nobody but track rats own, snap-brimmed driving caps, plaid Homburgs and dented fedoras, two Panamas, and even one guy in a houndstooth Trilby circa 1953.

Seemed Julio could make, and keep, friends of many walks.

I spotted some who came from the obviously rich horsie set. Two of them, a man and his elbow dressing, wore countenances especially grave. His suit and her water-dappled designer dress said Big Money, but his sincere face led me to believe he at least was good people, someone worth knowing. I leaned toward the man at my right and asked, 'You know that guy?'

The replied name meant nothing to me, though it seemed to hold something magical for the man I'd asked. 'Rich guy?'

'You don't recognize him?' I got a stare down like I'd failed to identify Marilyn in her white dress and revealed panties. I took another look at the white haired, well groomed dude. Shook my head.

'Only the best damn trainer in America.'

Oh.

I quit the effort of small talk.

My disconnect from all of the people in attendance underscored how I shared none of their remorse, nor their regrets, sadnesses or confusions. What I may have shared was a slightly pissed-off attitude about having to stand much longer in a drizzle. I'd not only commiserated with the high heeled women, I'd come to the party as one.

Suddenly, unexpectedly, and most happily, the priest was done. He flung yet more water onto the coffin, said something to Tio that made him nod and sag a bit farther, and beat his retreat toward a woman holding a Taylor Made golf umbrella.

The awkwardness inherent to all burial endings begins at that point when the last flower has been dropped onto the lid but the box doesn't go down. Only thing left was to gawp and suffer fluster. Perhaps because of that, Julio's people easily gave in to a desire for cover. Folks fled, moved away from the Tio Ray family like cockroaches fleeing a snapped-on light. Everybody, that is, except Annigail. Which meant everybody but me and the oblivious to rain Nolan as well.

How she did it I don't know, but in one swift move she separated Tio Ray from his two women, pumped the pressure up in her tear ducts enough to create a western Niagara, and dropped her arms around the much smaller — and lower — man's neck.

To the dislodged women I offered a limp smile, a ducked head, a decent handshake, and a *Hiya, I'm Drew Nolan.* The elder woman introduced herself as Evelyn Palacio, Tio's wife. She gazed up at me with a placid discomfort, a growing inattention for the qualifying statements I felt necessary to make about myself. She seemed more attuned to the repeated outbursts and renewed neck hugs by Annigail upon her husband.

Happily, Nolan really wanted to get down in order to play in the freshly piled dirt. The fussing kid gave Evelyn an excuse to replace her sadness with the natural maternal pleasure of taking him from me.

Arms emptied, I had little else to do except find my own companion. Only natural that I turned to the younger woman, who really was ridiculously beautiful. She didn't seem distraught so much as broken-hearted. I also sensed a little pissed off.

Sexy.

Sure, it's creepy, but funerals make women look great. Don't know if it's the sadness or the black dresses and dark stockings, but I've not attended one funeral yet where there wasn't something sexual about the propinquity to death. Okay, creepy. But I definitely felt my blood warm up while observing — and being observed by — that young Latin woman.

Dark eyed, the liquor of melted chocolate, deep as they needed to be, cruel as I wanted them. Took all I had to drop my own Baby Blues, to break the eye-lock. Had anyone at that moment inquired about June, I would have had to answer *Who?*

Of course I asked the young woman how she was related to Julio.

'He's my uncle.'

'You're Tio Ray's daughter?' I hadn't heard he had one.

'No,' was all she said. Then she walked away.

Tio's niece, and not Julio's daughter. And obviously not a genetic relative of Anglo Evelyn. *Hmmm.*

Annigail instructed our driver to follow Tio to what I expected would be a fire hall wake or something held in a side room to a catering business. Instead we arrived at the service gates into Santa Anita Park.

The Fall racing season had begun and bad bet tickets were everywhere, fortunately the rain had ceased. Or at least at the park had become a micro-drizzle that left surfaces damp but navigable. Also fortunately. We did not have to use the public parking lot, going instead to the dirt lanes of the stable grounds, and had to walk them to where the reception was held.

Once we reclaimed Tio, he explained that the wake-slash-party for his brother was in the track's well-known Chandelier Room, compliments of a long-time friend to both Julio and Tio Ray. Later learned the benefactor was the World Class Trainer I'd observed at the graveside.

I've always considered a nice advantage having well-connected — which is to say *rich* — friends. I had a few, richest among them was Annigail's mega-loaded husband, Watt. Brings nice perks, like a fancy wake in a fancy bar, with fancy drinks and top shelf scotch. *O the latter for me.*

Once inside the Chandelier Room, I was relieved of supervising my nephew, whose head had begun lolling during the drive. Headed to the drink station.

As I waited to get a drink in my hand, I could see in the stretch of mirror that lovely niece of Tio Ray. Catching a bartender's eye, however, was a more pressing requirement, and a much less pleasurable one. I am well practiced at fetching attention, never had been a difficulty. But I must have had something Back East about me. Nothing I seemed to do worked.

In the brief stretch of time of my perplexity, Tio's niece took notice of me, of my distressed expression. Took less than a head nod toward the poor old desolate blue blood me.

Once the barkeep delivered my drink, all was well and looking propitious. Latin Beauty had headed my way, the Drink and the Beauty arriving pretty much the same time.

'Annigail said you are a policeman.'

'Drew. Andrew Nolan.'

Ramona, Palacio.'

I confess my grin at her accusation resembled exactly that, the grin of an accused. I said, 'Right. I was. Annigail insists I keep myself identified by the abandoned profession. My current one lacks dignity.'

She smiled, yeah, that kind of smile. 'And what undignified job is that? Dog catcher?'

'She'd approve of that. No, I'm a bum.'

I liked the surprised — or at least curiosity-riddled — look she gave me. Catching a theme here? Anyway, she returned, 'You don't look like a bum. Too tanned.'

'Then I shouldn't look like a cop, either.'

'You don't. So, what's a bum do on the job?'

'Fish, mostly. Charter captain, some days. Lawn chair holder downer on others. I usually let my first mate deal with the morons who rent me out to fish, which gives me time to practice being a bum.'

'Must be nice.'

'It is.' I had begun to suspect a waning of our conversation. But then, most memorably touching the corner of her mouth as if to wipe away some errant lipstick, she said, 'Shame you're not a cop.'

I didn't want to take that the wrong way. I knew a number of Badge Chasers, women who'll screw anything in a uniform. She didn't appear the type. Not like there really was a type, surprisingly enough. That gamut runs from Brownies to Grannies. But still, she seemed classier, above that kind of superficiality. I found myself wanting her *not* to be one of them. Still, my response was the one I always returned to those kinds of woman. 'You got a thing for cops?'

'No. I just could use one.'

That sure didn't help me fight the impression, weak though it was. And it didn't let me pick up on a jangly spider-sense premonition that crap was being piled in my future way.

'What could a cop do for you?'

She considered the reply for a moment, took the glass of scotch from my hand, sipped at my drink in the femme fatale fashion of *film noir* lovelies, to then say those magical, imperiling words.

'I think my uncle was murdered.'

Crap.

Why'd she have to look so good in black?